THE LAST DAWN

ALSO BY JOE GANNON

Night of the Jaguar

THE LAST DAWN

Joe Gannon

Minotaur Books

New York

THE LAST DAWN. Copyright © 2016 by Joe Gannon. All rights reserved. Printed in the United States of America. For information, address St. Martin's Press, 175 Fifth Avenue, New York, N.Y. 10010.

www.minotaurbooks.com

Designed by Omar Chapa

The Library of Congress Cataloging-in-Publication Data is available upon request.

ISBN 978-1-250-04803-5 (hardcover)
ISBN 978-1-250-04761-8 (e-book)

Our books may be purchased in bulk for promotional, educational, or business use. Please contact your local bookseller or the Macmillan Corporate and Premium Sales Department at 1-800-221-7945, extension 5442, or by e-mail at MacmillanSpecial Markets@macmillan.com.

First Edition: January 2016

10 9 8 7 6 5 4 3 2 1

For Cornel Lagrouw, Doug Tweedale, Ian Walker, and Tim Coon.
Compañeros, all, gone too soon, gone too soon.
And to the people of El Salvador, who deserve so much more.

ACKNOWLEDGMENTS

This is a work of fiction. All the events and characters have been invented by the author. But the rebel offensive of November 1989 is history, as were the murders of the six Jesuit priests and their housekeepers by the Salvadoran military, the terrible slaughter of the civil war in El Salvador, and the shameful role played by the Ronald Reagan and George H. W. Bush administrations in financing and prolonging the killings.

I'd like to thank Matt Rigney for his keen eye and insightful feedback (and occasional hand-holding). And Big Al Compagnon for his comments and time. Also, thanks to my editor, Elizabeth Lacks, at St. Martin's Press for her patience, trust, and fabulous editorial eye. And my apologies to Laura and Justine for working through that magical weekend. I am indebted to those works of nonfiction that helped jog my memory, especially Joe Frazier's *El Salvador Could Be Like That*, and Roy C. Boland's *Culture and Customs of El Salvador*. And, of course, the poetry of Roque Dalton.

Once again the deep abyss, the old customs! What shall we do, then, with our laughter, with our freedom, with our morals based on anger?

—ROQUE DALTON, "THE PRODIGAL SON"

PROLOGUE

Las Vegas Salient, Nicaraguan-Honduran border, 1986

It is time to die.

Gladys Darío smiles at the thought. Smiles through the teeth she has managed to keep these past—what? Weeks, lifetimes? She does not clock time in seconds, but in footsteps. And she has counted them all: one thousand three hundred and thirty-three as her captor has come and gone—and come again. That's how long she's been held in her dark purgatory. Sweltering by day, shivering by night. Covered in bruises and bites and sores. Chained to the floor.

But no more.

It is time to die.

She can hear them all. Can hear *everything*. She is blind in the dark. Or maybe just blind. She does not, will not, even open her eyes anymore. Stopped opening them at step four hundred and sixty-eight. *Accept the dark, refuse the light!* Her ears are her eyes. And her hands. Like a mole she can read vibrations through her hands on the rough boards of the floor. The vibrations of every life form near her. But even moles have teeth that tear—and this time she will use those teeth to make him kill her.

But wait. . . . She hears, she feels, she sees . . . something is not right. It is not the steady tread of her tormentor she feels. There are many feet moving together. Something is wrong, like all of them being called to assembly. No. *Scrambled.* There is confusion in the vibrations she reads with her hands. Many feet pound up the hill to her cell, but his feet are not among them. They are coming for her. To kill her.

Goddamn it!

This is not the covenant she made with herself. She hasn't yet gathered herself up. If they kill her now she won't have gathered herself up. She broke herself into fragments those first few days—broke herself and scattered the parts about her miserable hut like jigsaw pieces from a forgotten box in an attic—or stars in the sky. No matter what her captor did, does, will do, he could only ever do it to a part of her, even a few parts, but never the whole. That—gathering herself whole—she saves for herself. That is her bargain—she'd save her teeth, save her life for as long as she could and when she no longer could she'd gather herself whole, use her teeth to make him stab her in the brain, and then die to the sounds of *his* screams.

And she will have won, because she has never uttered a sound—you can't, not when you're broken into one thousand three hundred and thirty-three pieces.

At first she believed she might be rescued, then hoped she might be exchanged. Then she just wanted to live. But her shame at accepting the unspeakable was tempered by the vow she made that she would end it all in death—his and hers.

His and Hers. Him and Her. Him. Them. Too many men!

Goddamn all men.

Except one. But why had *he* not come?

Her captor, the Contra commander Krill—the "notorious" Contra commander Krill. What does that even mean? Notorious? *Scares the shit out of everyone* is what it means. Well, almost everyone. Krill—who'd carried her so gently, so attentively for five days through the Nicaraguan mountains to his base in Honduras one thousand three hundred and thirty-three steps ago—he had come. Came. And would keep on coming. She knows she is a great prize to Krill. Not as a prisoner of war—Gladys is, after all, a lowly lieutenant of police in Nicaragua's revolutionary government. But as an upper-class, white-skinned *ladina* from the kind of family Krill's mother and sisters and aunts would've cleaned house for? That, she knows, is her real worth. That's why Krill hasn't shared his spoils with the rest of his mercenaries. And that is why she has known a prisoner exchange was not an option. At least not before it is time to gather her pieces together and die.

Still, she has prayed for a rescue.

Insane, of course. Like all miracles are an insanity. Yet we pray fervently for them. And Gladys has prayed for hers. In her mind she's carved a small statue of Saint Ajax—patron saint of prisoners and sex slaves—and set him in a niche and prayed for salvation. Prayed as desperately as some campesino—watching his crops die of thirst and his children die of hunger—will pray to whatever old god or new saint might save them from despair and death. Yet all the while eyeing the spade he will bury them with.

So she has prayed as desperately, and as uselessly. But she has no spade, only teeth.

Silly, silly girl.

Captain Ajax Montoya, partner, mentor, friend, has not come. And now they are coming for her. He is probably just as dead as she soon will be anyways. The last time she'd seen Ajax during the firefight with Krill in Nicaragua he'd been trying to swap his life for hers. If she is here, then he is dead.

It is time to die.

They are close now, the many feet, too hurried. Could they be under attack?

The door bursts open, light stabs her eyes, even with them closed. They grab her, cut the ropes, loose the chains, and stand her up. Her legs won't hold her and she collapses.

"Fuck you, I ain't walking."

Bravado is all she has left. But they are the first words she's spoken and her voice is a croak so corrupted she barely understands herself. Then blackness once again as one of the Contras pulls a bag over her head. She is half dragged, half carried down a trail. Down. She knows she's been kept atop a small hill, above the main camp. When she'd cared about her surroundings she'd noticed a kind of parade ground below her where the Contra drilled and turned out for VIPs. They're carrying her to the parade ground. So that's it—a public execution in full view of them all.

She tries to pull all her pieces back together, be whole for her death. But the ache in her limbs, the speed with which they carry her along, leaves bits of her trailing behind like the tail of a comet. She collapses in a heap, stalling for time, but her escorts scoop her up and bear her along like a casualty from the battlefield.

Goddamn they're in a hurry.

The angle they carry her at flattens out as they reach the parade ground. The Contras stand her up.

"You must walk."

It is a woman's voice. Gladys has known there were other women in the camp, had felt their vibrations through the boards of her cell.

"Are you a prisoner?" Gladys whispers.

The woman blows through her lips. "Commando."

Commando is what the Contra call themselves because *CIA mercenary* has the virtue of precision but no dignity.

"Then you're a stupid bitch," Gladys croaks.

The woman hisses but there is no blow. Instead, something is thrust into Gladys's hands. Sunglasses? She puts them on as the hood is ripped off. Light stabs her eyes again around the edges of the darkened lenses. Gladys cups her hands around them and looks at the ground. She can count four escorts, all women. And none of them is armed. She steals glances around the parade ground—a pasture field cleared of its trees where stumps stand like pedestals awaiting sculptures. The field is empty of troops, but she feels eyes on her and looks behind, where, at the tree line up the hill, she can see scores, maybe hundreds of Contras standing silent and still. Watching.

But no firing squad.

In front of her, ten yards away, a vehicle idles in the sunshine. She recognizes it as one of those big-ass Jeep Wagoneers with smoke-blacked windows the American diplomats use in Managua. This one is yellow and white, like a golden palomino. But out here on the empty field it reminds Gladys of a hippo in a waddle—fat, almost silly, but dangerous too.

All the more dangerous as Krill stands next to it. Almost at attention, dressed in tiger-stripe fatigues, a bush hat pulled low on his head. Also unarmed.

One of her escorts pushes her. "Walk."

Gladys takes a few steadying breaths, and then a step. Her legs are wobbly, drunken. But she manages to get one foot in front of the other. Krill's eyes seem to want to burn a hole in her forehead, but she stares only at the Wagoneer's windows and makes as straight a line as she can. When she is a few feet away the windows slide down.

She stops.

Three men inside. Two in the backseat, the one next to the window is in uniform, one star on his shoulder. The driver is in civvies, light skinned, like a gringo. The third man she cannot see well. It is this man who speaks.

"Can you drive?"

A surge of electricity jolts her. She clamps her teeth and her body quakes as all those pieces she's broken into gather inside of her, enter through her coccyx, up her spinal cord, and reassemble in her brain. Reassemble her being.

That voice. That face. She *did* recognize the third man but her brain refused to acknowledge it until she was made whole. It is Ajax.

Captain Ajax Montoya.

Saint Ajax.

Holding a hand grenade.

"Gladys. Can you drive?"

When her body stops trembling she turns her head and looks Krill dead in his black eyes, which are too large for his small face. It is only because of the sunglasses that she can do so. He seems ready to explode in rage or implode in despair.

"I can drive," she croaks.

"Get in."

The gringo in the front slides over the gearshift into the passenger seat. Gladys gets behind the wheel. She finds Ajax's smiling face in the rearview mirror. He is thinner, darker, and hairier than when they'd parted. She figures he's been in the bush some weeks staking out Krill's camp. But the smile on his face is all Ajax—cocky and smug—suicidally so, given their circumstances. She sees that the grenade in his right hand has the pin out. In his left hand he has the Needle—that wicked blade!—pressed to the general's throat.

"This is General Alfredo Alvarez, commander of the much-maligned military intelligence of the even more maligned Honduran armed forces. Our friend next to you is John Joseph Cahill. His diplomatic passport says he's a cultural attaché at the U.S. embassy."

Gladys looks Cahill over—brown/brown, five-ten, one seventy-five, mid-forties, in good shape but going paunchy in the middle.

"La Cia."

"I am not CIA," Cahill objects, but with little conviction.

"'Course if you said otherwise you'd have to kill yourself." Ajax gives Gladys a wink, then he presses the Needle against the general's throat. "Remind him."

"Krill!"

Gladys watches Krill in the side-view mirror. He trembles with rage at the general's call.

"*Si, mi general.*"

"You will not impede our leaving, nor pursue us, nor interfere in any way. If we are hurt or killed because of your actions, in the morning helicopter gunships will drive your people over the border where my colleagues will make sure the Sandinista Army is waiting for you. Understood?"

Gladys watches Krill's shrunken reflection in the mirror—his diminished size the only reason she can look. She knows Krill despises the Hondurans, and the gringos, even his CIA patrons who make his war possible. He told her the story many times, usually while unbuckling his belt: the shoeless, *mestizo* peasant who left generations of poverty behind by joining the Ogre's National Guard where he'd risen to the implausibly lofty rank of *sargento*. Krill had fought the Sandinistas to the bitter end, barely escaped after the dictator and his officers had fled. Not long afterward he'd been picked up and dusted off by the gringos and their cowboy president, Ronald Reagan. Now there is no dictator, no officers. *Krill* is the name spoken and feared. He is head of a thousand troops. The elite of the Contra army. And he despises all those who've made it so.

Krill ignores the general, leans in, and smiles at Ajax.

"You."

"Me."

"You have got the biggest balls of anyone I know."

"Do as your master says, dog. Or I'll kill them both."

Krill catches Gladys's eyes in the mirror. She flinches, looks away, and curses herself for it.

"Take care of my *angelita*. I will see you both again."

Ajax sheaths the Needle. "Only if I wake you to witness your own death, *pendejo*."

Ajax raises the window on Krill. Gladys does the same, and the face of her tormentor disappears behind the tint. Out of sight. She knows he will never be out of mind. She turns to the backseat.

"Kill him, Ajax."

"Can't do it, Gladys. It was them dead or you alive. That was the deal. Make some distance from here."

Gladys puts the big Wagoneer in gear and drives off, but she doubts the distance will ever be too great.

•   •   •

She gets about five miles, the Contra camp long gone in the rearview mirror when the spasms overtake her. She slows to a stop before losing control. Ajax puts the pin back in the grenade, cuffs his hostages, and lays her down in the back of the Wagoneer. He puts the general behind the wheel and they are back on the road in no time. Soon enough she feels the hum of paved road under the wheels.

But she is still rocked by the spasms.

"I'm sorry, Ajax. Can't control it."

His rough hand strokes her face. "Don't worry, you're in shock."

"How do I look?"

He shrugs. "Skinnier than ever. But your hair's grown out. Not so butch. I kind of like it. Drink this."

He holds a vial to her lips.

"What is it?"

"Stop the shakes."

Gladys sips down the bitter elixir. It is hardly settled in her stomach when she realizes it is pushing her over the edge into unconsciousness.

"Ajax . . . what . . . what . . . ?"

"Shh." His hand rubs her forehead and settles on her cheek. "You're gonna sleep a good long while now. And when you wake up, you'll be safe."

"No . . ."

"Yes. Part of the deal."

Hours and hours later Gladys awakens, thinking at first it was all a dream and she is still chained to the floor of her cell. She finds, instead, that she is strapped to a gurney on a medevac jet, miles above the Caribbean and only an hour from Miami, where, she will find out three hours later, her family awaits her.

But she is alone. Ajax is not there.

That, too, is part of the deal.

1

El Salvador, October 1989

Maybe it was a sign of the times. Maybe it was the *end times*. Kiki didn't know. The major often spoke of it—*the end of history*—but he was a very advanced man, always thinking about the big picture. Kiki did a job at a time, partied afterward, then waited for the next one. His was a near-perfect world—he had money, pussy, and impunity. Kiki adjusted the headphones on his new Walkman and rolled the volume knob to its end. When he pressed play he could feel the wheels engage the cassette as the tape turned. Guitars and cymbals crashing in harmony, then the sirens and drums. Kiki waited until his head bobbed in rhythm, until he felt his purpose align with the music. He held his bat, El Grillo, slung low over his belly and waited for the licks he loved to finger best. It was a gift from the major, not a baseball bat, but an English cricket, *grillo*. The major insisted it was a better tool, easier on the bones, but tougher on the muscles. Kiki liked it as it made a much better guitar, the flat business side made for excellent strumming while his fingers flew over the pretend frets. Still, it bothered Kiki to no end. Nineteen eighty-nine was almost over and Mötley Crüe's *Dr. Feelgood* was stuck at #79 for album of the year.

Number seventy-nine!!

He tucked his lower lip under his teeth and wailed all the more on El Grillo. *Fucking gringos!* he shouted in his mind to be heard over the title track. *What did they know!* They're up north in all their millions, with all their millions buying who? Billy Joel? Paul McCartney? Queen! *Fucking Queen!* QUEEN?!?! Kiki felt the helplessness stir— everyone in El Salvador could buy five Mötley Crüe's and it was nothing compared to the endless rivers of indolent Americans who never stopped shopping. And their dollars decided the fate of the world. And they would give it all to Freddie Mercury.

Maybe the major was right. Maybe the Americans really were a dead end. *Like a monkey too far out on a weak branch in the Tree of Evolution, they have nowhere to go but down.* The major talked to Kiki and the others like that, sometimes. No one was ever quite sure what he meant, and no one ever cared that much to ask. Or dared. The major talked, they listened, the money flowed, the war ran on. Mötley Crüe sang "Rat-tailed Jimmy is a secondhand hood."

Kiki looked over the boy on the table—weirdly white, even for a gringo. Gangly like a stick, with the silliest orange hair Kiki had ever seen on an actual human. He grasped the cricket bat by the neck and left the guitar licks to Mick Mars.

2

Managua, Nicaragua, November 1, 1989

The catatonic and the psychopath were playing cards again.

"The queen of hearts is the greatest whore of all." The psychopath ran his grubby, chubby finger lightly over the queen's face. "Her color is the *puta*'s color," he explained for the umpteenth time. "Her heart is scarlet, her pudenda crimson. You must never let either touch you when you cleanse them. They must be placed in white rum and stored on the altar of Ometepe."

The catatonic, as was customary, said nothing. He sat perfectly still. His eyes fixed on the middle distance, palms flat, elbows locked, he held his entire body suspended an inch off his yellow plastic chair. Not a wobble in his muscles betrayed the slightest exertion. He had been so suspended, an inch above existence, for one hundred and eighty-nine days. His life was diminished to heartbeats and eye blinks. One hundred and eighty-nine beats—and blink. Tomorrow it would be one hundred and ninety.

"She is the strongest of all the succubae," the psychopath lectured, his eyes roving over the pitiful ward to fall upon their young Spanish *doctora*. "That is why she must be defused first. She is the greatest danger to us."

The psychopath knew the overworked *doctora* and her underpaid staff at the Nicaraguan Psychiatric Hospital thought it a good idea that he and the catatonic socialized together. There wasn't much else for them to do. The hospital was as bare of equipment and treatment, as unadorned in all things as its very name. It was known as Kilometro Cinco for the wobbly mileage marker on the Southern Highway, which marked its place five kilometers from central Managua.

Like so much since 1979 when the Revo had erupted into life from the loins of an unstoppable popular insurrection led by the Sandinista Front, Kilometro Cinco had begun as an admirable idea, a bold step even, a compassionate policy by the Sandinista government to actually treat the mentally ill, rather than merely house them. Or imprison them as the Ogre had done for forty years before he was overthrown. Despite the good intentions—and here the psychopath knew that when the *doctora* thought of this she would pause and sigh, as if the emotional reality was as exhausting, NO! *More exhausting* than the physical reality—the policy had withered and died from a lack of everything. *Every-fucking-thing!* He'd heard her say it before. Shout it. *Every-fucking-thing! This crazy country lacks everyfuckingthing!*

She had come, she'd told him in her succubus voice, two years ago from a state-of-the-art mental hospital in Barcelona thinking she'd do her part in *solidarity* with the scruffy Sandinista Davids in their heroic brawl with the American Goliath to the north.

Instead, she'd become just another whore to be cleansed. A black-haired, black-eyed Catalonian whore.

"Stupid, arrogant bitch!" The psychopath leaned in close and whispered it to his friend.

His friend.

The arrival of the catatonic over a year ago had been a great blessing. Proof, if more was needed, that the psychopath was chosen for greatness. That from his persecution would come redemption, salvation. He crossed one nicotine-yellowed finger over another, made an inverse sign of the cross, and intoned his secret appeal to Ometepe: *El dios de la Sangre, te amo, te adoro. Les agradezco por tu Bendiciones.God of Blood, I love, you, I adore you. I thank you for your Blessings.*

"And I have been blessed, by friends. First the young *doctora* saved me from persecution in that hellish prison. I heard her walking the hallways of the penitentiary, asking after those with signs of mental illness. Can you imagine my joy? All it took on my part was some small genital mutilation to get her attention, and what was that compared to what the other prisoners were doing to me? The chosen Son of Ometepe? Raping the rapist, violating the violator! Where was the logic in that? But would they listen? Could those dark-skinned morons fathom the difference? So the *doctora* visited me in the prison clinic and I convinced her to save me by convincing her to convince me that I wasn't a killer who raped, but a rapist who killed out of shame!"

Chemical castration had been her answer. And then a transfer to Kilometro Cinco.

Dios de la sangre, dios del odio, te amo! God of blood, god of hate, I love you!

And then his friend had arrived, the catatonic.

"Ajax Montoya. The *great* man. Hero of the revolution! It was you, a lowly captain of police, who began my persecution." And it was. Montoya had found him out, he was still not sure how, and had arrested him while he was cleansing the capital of whores as surely as the rebels had cleansed it of the Ogre's National Guard.

"It was you who paraded me in front of the press, all those photographers."

That's when they'd given him his new name: El Gordo Sangroso. The Bloody Fat Man. Always his weight, his heaviness. Since he'd been a boy they'd mocked and persecuted him.

"Even my own mother!"

The pain of the memory, even now, *No, Mami! I love you! I'm sorry. Please, Mami, I'll change!*

But then that night, the night of delivery as a teenager when Ometepe had first come to him. Ometepe had explained that it was not he, Chepe Huembes, and his massive girth that was a blight on the land, but the whores, the idolaters who worshipped the faggot Jesus. That his mother, too, was a great whore had been such a *relief*. It was not, Ometepe showed him, that she did not love him. She was a succubus, jealous of his power, greedy for his soul. And when he'd cleansed her first his pain had stopped.

Chepe lit an Alas cigarette, exhaled smoke like a memory. "What a time that was, yes, Ajax? The late seventies? The insurrection was everywhere, remember? Street battles, aerial bombardments, mayhem. No one noticed the body of one cleansed whore on the street, and no one ever thought to look for those I buried—*they'd gone off to join the Revo!*"

And then, that glorious day, July 19, 1979. The Ogre and his army fled, the Sandinistas poured into the capital, and the people poured into the streets. Everyone cheering and partying! Chepe Huembes among them. Everyone hugging. Hugging! Women hugging him amidst the delirious multitudes. He was no longer a grotesque— the Revo had freed him too!

"I became a patriot that day. I adopted the *rojinegra*"—the red and black flag of the Sandinista Front—"as my own. From that day on I vowed only to cleanse counterrevolutionaries, only the whores who'd given their poisoned pudenda to the Ogre's officers. Yes . . ." The psychopath's chest rose and fell at the memory, his pulse quickened maddeningly at the body memory. He had to control himself, the *doctora* had some power to know his thoughts when he gave in to them too much. "Yes. Chepe Huembes fell upon them like the revolutionary socialist I'd become. I carried a black banner to bind them with, and mixed it with the red of their blood. *Rojinegra!*"

He'd shouted it too loud, again. Too proud.

That was how his idolatry had angered Ometepe. A god's anger is a terrible thing—like an earthquake, the consequence of the sluggish, even listless movements of unseen plates, but when it broke it could break the world! Even now a shudder ran through Chepe like

the tremblers which habitually shook Managua. The god of blood—
rightfully! He said so even now, rightfully!—had chosen to cleanse Chepe
Huembes with a long trail of tears. Banishment from His favor.
Ometepe had put Ajax Montoya on his trail. Ometepe had given
Ajax the knowledge to hunt him down, capture and imprison him.

That had begun his true punishment, cleansing. The raping of the
rapist. But he had borne it, and borne it well, as all good sons bear
their fathers' just opprobrium. Until that sacred day, that holy moment,
when he'd heard the *doctora* coming through the cell block, asking
after inmates who showed signs of mental illness.

The black-haired, black-eyed *doctora*.

The psychopath turned over another card, the queen of clubs. "La
Negra!" The psychopath's eyes rolled ever so slightly up, he craned his
neck back ever so slightly as his chin waddle wiggled in anticipation.

For one hundred and eighty-six days the psychopath's droning had
been a comfort to the catatonic. The megalomania of the man produced
almost identical narratives day in and day out. But three days before
he had switched tenses, from the future perfect to the simple present.
And the catatonic knew the time had come. He watched the psychopath's ecstatic quivering. Those three chins shimmying. It was a thick
neck, true, housing as it did windpipe, voice box, and carotid artery.
But it made the catatonic think of glass vessels packed in pudding.

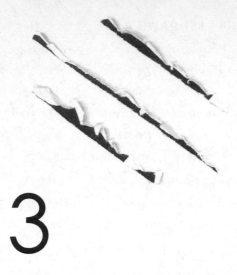

3

Gladys Darío was running for her life. She was trapped in a tunnel made of sand. An earthquake was rocking the shifting burrow, a great undulating wave raced toward her. She had to save the child. But it wouldn't run, it was too frightened, frozen with panic. The undulation sped toward her, the waves in the sand, she knew, were a great serpent rising to the surface. She had no choice, if the child wouldn't move she'd have to do it, knowing it would end badly. As the undulation reached her feet she lifted the child by its neck, felt the bones crack, and hurled it out of the way.

"Gladys!"

She awoke, looking into the eyes of her mother.

"*Mija!* You're awake now."

"Mami."

Gladys had finally moved into her own place a year before, but she still spent the weekends with her mother, if only to keep herself from realizing what she was missing in Miami.

"Was it the child? The snake?"

"I'm fine, Mami. What time is it?"

"Middle of the night, like always."

"Sorry I woke you."

"You didn't. The phone did. It's for you."

"Who is it?"

"Managua."

•   •   •

"Lieutenant Darío?"

Gladys held her breath. It'd been a long time since she answered to that.

"Who is this?"

"Horacio de la Vega. How are you, my dear Gladys?"

Sinvergüenza. The shameless old bastard. "Why are you calling, after all this time?"

"There's a mission, of course."

"What! All I want from you is to tell me where Ajax is."

"That's the mission."

Gladys's heart did a circus somersault. She had spent months trying to get Horacio—anyone!—to take her calls, tell her anything about Ajax, and all she'd gotten were busy signals and phone machines. That'd been two years ago, when she'd stopped trying, had given up hope.

"Are you there, Lieutenant?"

"I'm not. Am I? A lieutenant?"

"No, but old habits . . . you know."

"Then what do you want?"

"You will come to Managua. Briefly, I hasten to add, briefly."

"I've been trying to get back for three years, you wouldn't give me a passport."

"I? I have little control over our consulate in Miami, whatever problems you've had . . ."

"Shut the fuck up, you miserable traitor. You fucking . . ."

The line went dead.

"No! No, no, no!"

What had she done! This was the first line she'd had on Ajax since she'd woken up on the medevac. It was what kept her from sleeping, from letting go, from starting over. She reached for the packet of moist towelettes she kept by the bed. She'd just ripped it open when the phone rang again.

"Horacio?"

"You will mind how you speak to me, *chica*."

"What do you want and how do I get there?"

"The U.N. High Commissioner for Refugees has an office in Miami. You will find they will issue you temporary travel documents. Go there as soon as they open. You will then go to the TACA Airlines counter at gate eighteen for a six p.m. flight. Arrive two hours early. You will meet my guests, get their story, and accompany them to Managua."

"Who are these guests?"

There was a pause and meditative grunt from the other end. "They are the ghosts of Christmas past."

4

Chepe Huembes's eyes fluttered closed, his body shuddered as he felt Ometepe's will move through him. He opened his eyes—gray eyes, eyes the color of Lake Managua, a body of water so polluted it was known as the toilet of the world—and watched the *doctora* talk to an aide. Chepe smiled and patted the catatonic's hand.

"She will be the first to be cleansed. And you will assist me at the altar of Ometepe."

Chepe traced a finger over a scar on the back of Montoya's hand. A perfectly round scar, puckered as burns will pucker as they heal. He'd used a cigarette on Montoya a few times—he'd had to be sure the catatonia wasn't a trick. When they'd first brought Montoya in, all bundled up in a straitjacket, Chepe was terrified—his nemesis! Sherlock to his Moriarty, Kryptonite to his Superman!—and had hidden himself away. But that night, after the *doctora* had left, *the specialist* had come. As he always had: only after she was gone.

Chepe had listened and learned the *doctora*'s trade as best he could. From the muffled grunts, that first night, the sounds of a body wracked by painful spasms, he'd reckoned the specialist had given Montoya insulin to shock his body into surrender. Every night for two months after that the specialist had come with his needle, injecting what *he* thought was Thorazine, but what Chepe knew was the spirit of Ometepe. The spirit of the god of blood, the god of hate, in order to destroy Montoya's very soul.

Chepe ran his finger over the puckered scar again. It had been a mistake, burning Montoya on the hand, the *doctora* had seen it and almost broken up the friendship. Chepe had learned to hide the burns, and he had, until he'd been satisfied the specialist had completed his task—*No! Ometepe's will.* After weeks of Thorazine injections Montoya showed all the signs of catatonia. The specialist stopped coming then, but Montoya's waking coma continued.

Now Chepe was ready. Twice a month the *doctora* stayed overnight at the hospital, tonight was one of those nights, but it was also the night all the overnight staff would be women, whores. Chepe would cleanse them all.

He turned over another card—the king of diamonds.

"The king of diamonds represents ambition, power, discipline, trustworthiness, and control. He is a fatherly figure who likes to take care of others."

The psychopath laid his hand on the catatonic's hand, felt the power of Ometepe moving through them both, two rivers of fate, joined at last. "Tonight I will cleanse her, and you, Captain Montoya, will watch. Because I know that somewhere deep inside there is still a watcher who watches."

And in the catatonic's vacant brown eyes Ometepe *lit the terrible closeness of a star.*

"The terrible closeness of a star." It was a good line, from "The Myth of the Jaguar," one of Nicaragua's best-known poems by one of its best-known poets. It was one of Ajax's favorites. As he watched El Gordo Sangroso waddle off to his therapy session with the *doctora,* he knew that after eighteen months of playing catatonic opossum, it was time to let the jaguar out.

5

Gladys stood in the doorway of the 747 at Sandino International Airport, closed her eyes, and took a deep breath. She wanted the smells of her *patria* to light up parts of her brain like welcome-home fireworks. It'd been three years since she'd been back, and she wanted to recognize the scent of home—differentiate its smell from Miami, which had become her forced refuge.

But all she got was a snoot full of jet fumes and a gentle push from the stewardess—"Please proceed to the immigration terminal."

Gladys descended the stairs in a cauldron of feelings as hot and sticky as the Managua night. She was excited, but also worried, even a little frightened. When her feet touched the tarmac she felt no desire to kneel and kiss the ground. Instead, she scanned the arrival area for an unwelcome welcoming committee—either uniformed or in plainclothes.

There was no one she could spot, friend or foe. Which was good, she guessed, but it pissed her off nevertheless.

She'd tried to return four times in three years, but never made it past the ticket counter.

After she'd awoken in the hospital in Miami—and had realized, horrified, that Ajax was still in Honduras, Gladys had burned holes in the telephone trying to get someone, anyone, to hit the panic switch.

But all she'd gotten were busy signals and answering machines. No one, it had seemed, had been at home in all of Managua.

Then her sister had brought the newspapers. Her rescue had been *everywhere*. After seeing her safely away on the medevac, Ajax, like a magician pulling a balloon rabbit out of a hat made of pins, had conjured up a press conference right there on the tarmac, amidst the battalion of soldiers. Surrounded by local reporters, and still holding the Needle and the hand grenade, he'd explained he'd kidnapped a Honduran general and an "American consular official" in order to save his partner from Krill.

And then, like that magician taking a final bow, he had serenely surrendered. The wire services had been there and the story landed on front pages around the world. Screaming headlines calling him a *Don Quixote, Sir Galahad,* or a *love-crazed terrorist* had been surrounded by photos of what appeared to be a hirsute college professor calmly lecturing to his students.

Saint Ajax, she'd marveled. He really did have the biggest balls in the world!

But would he keep them?

The headlines had explained why no one was home in Managua—who would want to admit knowing Ajax or Gladys? The headlines also had explained why Ajax had not been taken immediately into the bushes and shot—like the naked emperor, the Hondurans refused to admit they were hosting a CIA mercenary army in their country. But the presence of the general and the CIA station chief were like two giant genital warts, not even the Hondurans could ignore that. Still, Gladys knew, it didn't mean he couldn't be killed.

She'd barely changed from her hospital gown before she was at the Miami airport. But instead of getting on a plane she'd fallen into a vortex of catch-22s. As she'd arrived without passport or papers she couldn't get on a plane. The Nicaraguan consulate in Miami had refused to issue her a new one. The manner in which the consular officer had carefully called her señorita instead of compañera, had shown her she was in deep shit back home. The Americans also refused to help unless she'd claim asylum as a political refugee fleeing persecution—which she would never do.

Eventually she'd gotten through to Horacio de la Vega, Ajax's oldest friend, and his ex-wife Gioconda Targa—both well-connected big shots in the Revo. They'd confirmed Gladys's worst fear—that Ajax had not only been slung into a Honduran hellhole of a prison, but he'd already been stabbed once and was a dead man as soon as he was discharged from the prison hospital. Gladys had gotten them to agree to have cash smuggled into him. More importantly, Horacio had reached out to a Honduran underground group the Revo had contacts with. They had dozens of comrades in the prison and had drawn a line around Ajax.

And then, nothing.

Her letters all had been returned. Her frequent packages, she assumed, consumed by prison guards. Her own government had not wanted Gladys back, and the Americans were interested only in a gotcha-moment of forcing a lieutenant of the Sandinista police to declare she was a political refugee who feared persecution.

Fucking gringos! Fuck them before she'd do that. Maybe the Sandinista Front was no longer loyal to her, but she was loyal to the Revo.

She stepped aside on the tarmac and waited for her companions to pass her and then followed a few paces behind them. They'd decided in Miami to arrive as strangers to each other, in case one of them ran into trouble at immigration. Her companions had almost identical heads of red hair, almost comically carrot-colored, so that following them Gladys felt she was a jumbo jet being guided by ground crew with those big, orange flashlights. *The ghosts of Christmas past,* Horacio had called them. Indeed, Gladys had thought when she'd finally met them at the airport. A damned bloody Christmas, too, with more ghosts than old Scrooge could've counted on ten ugly toes. The "mission" Horacio had briefed her on seemed ludicrous. But as the first phase was Managua and Ajax Montoya, she'd agreed in a heartbeat.

Inside, the dingy airport was delightfully cool. Not the perfectly temperature-controlled environment of a Miami mall where every square foot of air was precisely 70 degrees, Gladys thought, but an imperfectly chilled place where overworked, underpowered air-conditioning chased but never vanquished the unrelenting heat.

As she queued in the immigration line she realized that was what she'd most missed about her country. The perfect imperfection of it. Gas shortages, blackouts, brownouts, water rationing, empty super-market shelves, too few resources chasing too much need so that each day began not with the question, *What do I need?* but rather, *What is there today?*

In Miami there was everything, literally, *every-fucking-thing.* Yet the gringos never seemed to stop looking for more. Even her mother and sisters, especially them! Their lives revolved around malls like moons around a dead planet. *Bless them,* she thought, and their uncompli-cated infatuation with shopping. They'd taken her in with no ques-tions asked when she'd arrived on that medevac. They'd left her alone for a month in a darkened bedroom while Gladys slept and mourned and wept and slept some more.

And when the day came her mother couldn't bear it anymore—couldn't bear the silence, the brooding, the waiting for death—she and Gladys's sisters had dragged her out shopping. *Retail therapy* they'd called it. They'd spent three days at spas, hairdressers, and malls, forc-ing Gladys in and out of so many dressing rooms that one day she found herself giggling along with her sisters when their mother stepped before a mirror in a halter top that left nothing to the imagination.

"What are you *putas* laughing at," her mother had demanded in a Nicaraguan vernacular so crude the Cuban attendant hadn't under-stood. The sisters had fallen out of their chairs in hilarity. Of course, Gladys ended up on the floor weeping uncontrollably, but she had fi-nally opened the door of Krill's cage.

Retail therapy, only in America.

"Passport."

Shit, Gladys cursed herself, as she handed over her passport to the weary-looking uniformed officer behind the glass. In her distraction she'd lost sight of her redheaded companions. She spotted them just on the other side of immigration—so they'd made it through. They seemed to linger idly for a moment while they cast their eyes around looking for her. And they couldn't find her because they were looking in the wrong line. Gladys was in the wrong line.

"You can't read Spanish anymore?" The officer was pointing at the sign which said NICARAGUAN NATIONALS while holding Gladys's newly minted travel document.

"Sorry," Gladys said. *Fuck!* is what she thought.

"You're a *Nica*?"

"Born here, yes."

"But you live in Miami?"

"Yes."

"This travel document is brand new?"

"Yes."

Gladys saw the officer's hand go under the counter.

"You're coming home for a visit?"

"Yes."

"You like Miami?"

"Look, compañero, whoever you just called will be here shortly, no? So stop making small talk."

The officer flicked her papers back to her like it was a crumb fallen from his mouth. "Get in the line for foreigners."

Gladys reached for her documents, but the hairy hand of someone who chewed their fingernails slipped in and pulled it away from her. The officer was dressed in army fatigues, not immigration—male, five-nine, brown/brown, about twenty-five, which was young for the major's insignia on his shoulder.

"This way, compañera."

"About time." Gladys couldn't help it.

"You've been waiting long?"

"Three years."

"This way, *compa*."

The major, to her surprise, took her directly to a door Gladys knew led to the VIP lounge.

Yeah, she thought, it *was* about time.

6

From behind, Margaret Mary and James "Big Jim" Peck, with their matching red-orange hair, going grayer in him than her, looked more like brother and sister than husband and wife. Horacio de la Vega Cárdenas had watched them from the moment they got off the plane. He'd watched them through the big window as they milled around outside on the tarmac, like just a couple more *Sandalistas* come to soak up the Revo's vibe. He'd watched them shuffling through customs, all smiles and *Gracias!* He watched them now, through the two-way glass, sitting comfortably in the VIP lounge casually looking around, watching everything but not seeing the one thing they wanted to watch: Gladys Darío—their guardian angel.

Poor Gladys, he thought. He'd come to admire her as a real asset in the little time they'd worked together before her kidnapping. Or, rather, she'd worked for him. But she was going to be very angry soon. The Sandinista government, which he'd served his entire life, was going to be very embarrassed soon. And the Pecks, those poor people. He'd met them briefly three years ago when they'd come to fetch home the body of their murdered daughter. Amelia. Horacio had not known her, really, but Ajax had been in love with her, and her death weighed heavily on Ajax's soul, Horacio knew. The Pecks, too, were going to be grievously disappointed at the failure of their mission.

Almost everyone Horacio had gathered for this drama would be thwarted. So things were going well for him.

He was an old man with a limp and a cane, and a hard lump where his heart used to be. But he slept well and was still, mostly, master of all he surveyed. He waited for the major to deliver Gladys to the VIP lounge before he emerged from behind the two-way mirror.

"Mr. and Mrs. Peck." Horacio put his hand over his heart. "I am Horacio de la Vega. I knew Amelia. I am a friend of Ajax Montoya. And of Gladys."

He turned to Gladys. Her face, as usual, was not hard to read. She wanted to show anger, disappointment, even aloofness. But the hurt, the deep wound, was there for him to see. He switched to Spanish.

"We were friends, weren't we, Gladys?"

"That's what you call it? I didn't see you at Krill's camp. Only Ajax."

"That's because I told him where to find you."

"And afterward? He was jailed and you wouldn't even take my calls."

"Because I was busy paying off the Hondurans to keep him alive."

"But you left him in prison!"

"For a decent interval. Then I arranged his return. He's in Nicaragua," Horacio gestured to the Pecks, "as you know."

"I couldn't get back! My own country refused me entry!"

There it was, Horacio thought. She was a child spurned by her parents, and it wounded. Horacio reached for her hand, and squeezed.

"That is because in the middle of a peace process that can end three *wars,* which have killed *hundreds of thousands,* you and he *kidnapped* a Honduran general and the CIA station chief—both of whom, oddly enough, were peaceniks. So you might ask why I helped at all."

He was by now making like a python with her hand. Gladys struggled to free herself, and eventually he let her.

"Stop crying like a lost child, Gladys. Mommy and Daddy had more important things to attend to." He turned to the Pecks and switched to English. "And you are all here now because I spoke to Senator Teal and he agreed to help."

The Pecks, especially Big Jim, seemed relieved the family drama had given way to recognition that they were even in the room and had their own drama.

"Mr. De la Vega." Big Jim held out a steelworker's mitt that six years of retirement had done nothing to soften. He might have crushed Horacio's hand, but he could tell Big Jim had practiced how not to mangle mere mortals.

"Please, señor, Nicaragua has few virtues. One of them is our glorious casualness. You will call me Horacio, and I will call you Big Jim, as you are known. And you are Margaret Mary?"

Margaret Peck said nothing. She held out her hand and in her grip Horacio could feel strength and hope. Poor woman, he thought, she would need both.

"You have been so kind to arrange this visit, Horacio."

Margaret led him gracefully to the sofa where a table was already laid out with coffee and *pan dulce*.

"Your daughter was a kind and sympathetic person," he said. "I was devastated to hear your son is . . . missing."

The pause where he substituted "missing" for "also dead" had a visceral effect on the gringo couple. Big Jim bit the inside of his lip. Margaret turned her face as if slapped.

"No one will help us." Margaret buried her face in her husband's boulder-like shoulder, which twitched as he, too, fought for control.

"What can you tell me?" Horacio asked.

"Sons of bitches say there's nothing they can do!" Big Jim unleashed his not inconsiderable anger, the better to bring his feelings to heel.

"Jim!"

"It's alright, Margaret." Horacio patted her hand. "Our casualness allows for copious cursing. Big Jim, which sons of bitches do you mean?"

"The government of El Salvador."

"They are notorious sons of bitches."

"But the American embassy?"

"Forgive me, but down here they are also notorious sons of bitches."

Margaret almost laughed, but it became twisted, like a repressed sneeze. It unleashed her tears.

"It's alright, my dear. I am here to help you." He gave Gladys a *make a report, Lieutenant* look.

"James Peck, known as Jimmy, age twenty-four, been in El Salvador about nineteen months. Went missing about three weeks ago, October eighteenth, to be exact. Few witnesses to the abduction. 'Men with guns' was all they had to offer. The government and American embassy say he's either run off with the guerrillas or has been killed by them. The FMLN says he was murdered by death squads—which would mean the government."

"Which would mean the government," Horacio agreed. "The FMLN and the FSLN are very close, do you know the history?"

"The Farabundo Martí National Liberation Front and the Sandinista Front for National Liberation," Big Jim recited like a schoolboy making a report. "Farabundo Martí and Sandino were friends, allies. Martí was Sandino's secretary here in Nicaragua when he was fighting the U.S. Marines . . ."

"Forgive me, Big Jim, but that was when Sandino was *trouncing* your Marines from one side of the country to the other. I don't mean to be rude but it is a point of national pride here. But please . . ." He gestured at Big Jim like a teacher who's already assigned an A+ but wants to hear the rest.

"Then Martí went home to El Salvador and tried to organize his own rebellion and was killed in the, the Big, the Big *Manzana* . . ."

"*Matanza*," Horacio corrected. "*Manzana* is apple, the Big Apple is New York. *Matanza* is massacre, the Great Massacre is El Salvador."

Big Jim kept reciting as if it was important to him to be able to account for it all. "Then Sandino was killed by the first Somoza and years later the rebels here became the Sandinista Front and the rebels there became the Farabundo Martí Front."

"Exactly correct, Big Jim. Thank you. You are much better informed than most visitors who come here, even our supporters."

Big Jim looked to his wife. "I read the books Jimmy suggested. After he got down here his letters were so full of, full of stuff I didn't know what he was talking about, I . . . I . . ."

Horacio reached out and took his hand. "You wanted to share his life."

Big Jim smiled. "When he was a kid I'd take him to all the movies. I had to know what a light saber was, the Force, a wookie. When he got older, he didn't want to be seen at the cinema with his old man, so I used to go alone so I could keep up."

"'Luke, I am your father,'" Margaret Mary intoned.

Mother and father guffawed at the private joke so loudly it drew the attention of the other passengers.

"He almost shit himself when I laid that line on him." Big Jim's face was suffused with an inner light at the memory. "He looked at me like, like . . ."

"Like you were his hero," Horacio finished it for him.

Big Jim didn't reply, but, rerunning the memory in his mind, he unconsciously nodded his head in agreement.

"But then, he got into politics . . ."

"*Star Wars* became ideological wars," Horacio concluded.

"I guess."

"And he wound up in Central America. He worked for your government?"

"Oh no!" Margaret Mary smiled. "He hates America down here. He thought Ronald Reagan was the devil himself."

"A man after my own heart." Horacio smiled with such gallantry that no one could be offended.

Big Jim shrugged his shoulders as if to say, *Don't know where he gets it from.* "He was a bit of a firebrand."

The VIP lounge seemed to go dead still at the simple past tense.

"Is. Is! IS!" Big Jim's massive shoulders—upon which, Horacio knew, the man's son had ridden many times—rocked with emotion.

"He works for the Democratic National Committee." Gladys stepped in to finish the story and provide Big Jim's pride with some cover as he failed to hide his tears. "Gathering human rights reports for the certification."

"Ah. The semiannual farce by which the United States 'certifies' that the most murderous regime in the hemisphere is 'making progress' on human rights."

"He didn't do that, though," Gladys added. "The embassy does that. He works for some liberal American congressmen looking for counterfactual reports to challenge the certification with."

Horacio noted Gladys's use of "American" instead of "gringo." Three years in Miami was changing her.

"So he might have been viewed by the Salvadoran government as an enemy?"

"Enemy!" Big Jim exploded. "He's a fucking American citizen! Without us those sons of bitches would end up just like . . ."

"Jim!" Margaret took her husband's hand in her own iron grip.

Horacio smiled. "Just like Nicaragua, Big Jim?"

"I didn't mean . . ."

"It's quite alright, I assure you. Your government sees us as a communist nation, an enemy, and they thought they were paying to keep El Salvador from following us into the ranks of the *Evil Empire*." Horacio did his best to make that last sound like he was narrating a documentary about the perils of STDs. "But if you were to ask your average, say, Salvadoran death squad assassin who his enemies were, I can assure he would list them as"—Horacio ticked them off on his fingers—"their homegrown *terroristas,* meaning our Marxist brothers in arms; the Communist International, meaning the Soviet Union and Cuba; terrorist sympathizers, meaning the international press corps;

and communist fellow travelers, meaning the Democratic Party and its leaders in Washington."

"But they are part of *our* government," Big Jim protested, "my son was working for a part of the U.S. government!"

"Not in El Salvador he wasn't."

Big Jim blinked big eyes. Horacio only just then noticed they were the same green as his daughter's had been. Their son had inherited his blue eyes from his mother. As for the freckles spotting their skin like iodine raindrops, they seemed the dominant gene of their clan.

"I don't understand." Big Jim sighed.

"El Salvador is a nation in a full-blown psychosis, not a civil war. It is a very small place, much smaller than Nicaragua. As big as your Massachusetts, I have read. In ten years over seventy thousand have been murdered. For perspective's sake that would be some three million dead in your America. I wonder if you can imagine such carnage?"

Horacio gave them a moment to try, but he could see such numbers could not be grasped by these *Middle Americans* with their social studies' view of the world and their nation's role in it.

"We have heard that before," Margaret Mary said. "Jimmy often mentioned it."

"On the phone?" Horacio leaned forward too quickly—hoped Gladys hadn't noticed. "He spoke to you that way on the phone?"

"No. He seemed more, I don't know, circumspect on the phone? But his letters were full of diatribes against the government, the death squads . . ." Her voice trailed off as her mind turned, like a camera lens zooming the faraway up close. She began to see her son in the country he had chosen to live in, and maybe die in.

"When was the last time you spoke to him?"

"A few weeks ago, October twelfth. He said he was going to . . ." Margaret Mary's voice trailed off.

"Gazpacho?" Big Jim said.

"*Guazapa*," Horacio corrected. "It's a volcano, not that far from the capital San Salvador. A major base for our rebel brethren."

"But he was abducted from his home," she said.

"He lived in a hotel?"

"No. He called the hotels 'whorehouses full of journalists and day trippers.' He had an apartment."

"Pity. There'd have been more witnesses had he stayed in an actual whorehouse."

Horacio looked up from the anguished gringos to Gladys. She'd heard all this before, on the flight down. He wanted to read her opinion about this impossible mission. But Gladys read his mind and veiled her face. Still, he knew what she wanted.

Satisfied he knew her mind, Horacio studied his own hands. *Gnarled* was the word, a cliché but accurate. The arthritis eating his knuckles had been sown from all those years in the wet mountains— when *he'd* been the ragged-ass rebel. Or at least that's what he told himself. Otherwise, what? Karma? He didn't believe in karma any more than he did the Risen Carpenter. But the first debilitating pain— hands frozen like stone, but feeling on fire—had struck not long after Ajax had disappeared into that Honduran prison. The pain was constant, but he'd been taking treatments for it in Mexico City. Bee stings, of all things. What a sight! Fingers and joints covered in delicate honey bees stabbing him with their minuscule darts. But it brought some relief, and it gave him good cover for the other tasks he had in Mexico—and elsewhere. The long wars of Central America were winding down. Certainly the Contra war in his own country was, but wars were as messy, and as dangerous, at their demise as at their inception. And the shadow world in which Horacio had established his fiefdom was still as full of schemes and plots as any modern-day Machiavelli could conjure.

He leaned into the Pecks, placed his knotted hands on theirs.

"My friends, I can assure you that the Farabundos of FMLN did not kill your son. But that doesn't mean he is alive. Now, what do *you* want to happen?"

Big Jim cleared his throat. "We want our boy back."

"Or at least his body," his wife wailed.

"No, Margaret."

"But if he's dead, Jim!"

Horacio saw the fire in her blue eyes.

"We want his body, Horacio. I want his body, please! Wouldn't they do just that, let us have the body?"

Gladys stepped forward and touched Margaret Mary's back. The mother instantly sat up and ceased her blubbering. Now Horacio knew how close they'd become.

"You know what they want," Gladys said. "They want Ajax and me to go in undercover, find their son, and get him out. Can you do that? Can you spring Ajax from prison?"

Horacio sat up. "He's not in prison."

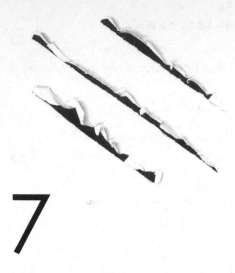

7

"You shit-eating sons-of-bitches are the worst, most ungrateful . . ." Gladys had run out of curses on the drive from the airport. Horacio, she knew, had let her drive his Jeep Cherokee to give her something to do besides cursing. ". . . shit-eating sons-of-bitches in the goddamn world!"

She pulled Horacio's Jeep to a stop in front of Kilometro Cinco, which was unremarkable during the day; at night, like now, it looked abandoned. The electricity must be out in this barrio. "A fucking nuthouse?"

"*Cállate*, Gladys!" Horacio switched to Spanish to give them some privacy. "Shut up! How dare you? This is the best psychiatric hospital we have. It is not a prison, nor a 'nuthouse.'"

Gladys climbed out of the Jeep, making sure to accidentally lay on the horn as she did. *Shut up?* She wasn't going to be quiet.

"Ajax Montoya! He's a goddamn hero and you've got him penned up like some goddamn Soviet dissident!"

The Soviet Union had been the Revo's best friend for ten years, if you counted barrels of oil or lightbulbs. But, like the Americans, their friendship came with suffocating hugs meant to shape a thing more like them, and less like itself.

"Gladys, please." Horacio seemed actually embarrassed by her outburst.

"Ajax! Ajax Montoya!" Gladys was ready to raise the dead—but also to give him a heads-up.

A black-haired woman, Spanish, Gladys guessed, came hurrying outside swinging a Coleman lantern like a train conductor.

"This is not a hospital if you need emergency help," she said.

Gladys was satisfied her racket had been misinterpreted.

"It's an emergency, and you're the right hospital, *compa*."

"*Doctora*."

Margaret Mary Peck's heart sank as slowly as Ajax Montoya walked. She had known from the tone of Gladys's furious conversation in Spanish that something had gone awry, but she was unprepared for the sight of the man—upon whom all of her remaining hope had rested. But his robotic shuffle, his focused but empty eyes had been the end of her faith that she would see her son again.

When Ajax had sat opposite her, his rigid arms holding his entire weight off the chair, not a tremor of strain in his muscles, the final light she'd left burning in the window was snuffed out.

Gladys, she noticed, had gone as silent and as still as Ajax, but when she'd tried to blink away her tears, they instead rolled down her cheeks. Horacio had declined even to come into the hospital. The Spanish doctor, Ana, her name was, had looked over whatever papers Horacio showed her outside and had sent for Ajax and even reviewed his file with them: his arrival, attempted escapes, assaults on staff, and a long course of Thorazine to "neutralize" his aggression.

There was no need for words, no need to explain anything. It was clear to both her and Big Jim that Horacio had known their mission was doomed before they'd even arrived. It wasn't them Horacio had brought here so Ajax might rescue their only remaining child, but Gladys, so she might rescue what remained of Ajax. The doctor had gone off to find some paperwork for Gladys to sign, and the silence left in her wake was unbearable to Margaret—for in it there was nothing to do but contemplate the grassy plot next to their murdered daughter that would now be taken up by their disappeared son.

So Margaret did what she'd planned to do.

"Captain Montoya, I have a letter from Amelia."

No movement, no flicker as she unfolded the blue airmail stationery from Managua's Intercontinental Hotel—Amelia had sent it via the local post so Big Jim could collect the canceled stamp with Sandino's picture. The American embargo against all things Nicaraguan had kept the letter bouncing a circuitous route via Panama and Mexico. It had taken nine weeks to arrive—almost two months after they'd buried her it had arrived like a ghost.

"'Dear Mom. The stationery says The Intercontinental, but I am in the Hotel Ideal in Matagalpa, which is funny as the hotel is anything but ideal! I leave tomorrow to pick up the Nicas Tony and I will bring home to Cleveland. What fun I am having! But don't let on to anyone that I am anything other than a Republican warrior battling *the Evil Empire.*'"

Margaret paused to smile. "That was a kind of code word she used, 'Evil Empire.' She didn't think of you all as evil, but it was the buzzword of the day, so we used it too. . . ." She realized no one was listening. Her husband was staring out a darkened window. Gladys was staring open-mouthed at Ajax, who was staring, it seemed, at nothing at all.

But there was nothing else to do until the doctor got back.

"'You remember the policeman I mentioned, the one who ruined Tony's press conference?'"

Now Margaret managed an actual smile. Amelia had been very proud of that moment, all the publicity she'd gotten for slapping Ajax after a prisoner he was escorting through the airport had escaped and turned her boss Senator Teal's press conference into chaos. "Do you remember that, Ajax? She slapped you, and said she was so embarrassed by it, but she had me collect every newspaper clip about it. It made her kind of a hero back home, at least to the Republicans."

But there was nothing in Ajax's eyes but an empty vista.

She read on. "'Well, he's here in Matagalpa. Ajax Montoya. When Tony first heard the name he thought they'd named him after a toilet cleaner! He's going to escort me and Father Jerome along with the American journalist I met in Managua. I wouldn't tell him, but I am glad to have his company. He is as abrasive as the cleanser, but there is something strangely, even sadly heroic about him too. When he's not an arrogant gringo-hater there is in his eyes the years and trouble of getting to Troy and home again. And despite my U.S. passport and letters, I am a little nervous about heading into the "wilds" of Nicaragua's mountains. They have swallowed more expeditions over the centuries than the Gobi Desert, but this cop seems to know his stuff. He is as bigheaded as any frat-boy jock at Ohio State, but there is a calm, a steadiness at his core that gives me confidence. I wish Jimmy could meet him, he'd find his ideal *socialist man* behind those brown eyes.'"

Margaret paused. Maybe the letter was not such a good idea. Ajax registered not a flicker of anything, and Margaret felt she'd just read a roll of the honored dead. They were all dead, weren't they? Certainly Amelia, Father Jerome, and the journalist Matthew Connelly had all been gunned down. And that poor Nicaraguan family, wiped out. Now Jimmy was as gone as their daughter, as gone as Ajax's mind.

The Spanish doctor returned with a thin file folder from which she drew a single piece of paper. She seemed a little embarrassed, not sure whom to address.

"You understand he will need constant care? This," she gestured to the empty shell slowly swaying over his chair, arms locked, muscles rigid like steel cords, "this condition does not just go away."

"You're talking to me." Gladys sat forward, took the paper the doctor had brought. "This is the release form?"

"Yes. But how will you get him out of the country, he has no papers."

"That dried-up piece of shit outside too cowardly to even come in will take care of that." She signed the paper several times, initialed it as well. "What about his belongings?"

"Well, he actually has no belongings. Not even the clothes he's wearing. But . . ." The doctor looked over her shoulder as if expecting someone. "I thought there'd be at least one person to say good-bye." She passed the folder to Gladys. "Take this, for whoever's care he comes under."

Gladys took up the folder like a pallbearer would a casket. She put a hand on Ajax's arm, his muscles like bowstrings. "Ajax? Ajax, it's Gladys. I'm going to take you HOME WITH ME!" Her voice rose almost to a shout.

"It's okay." The doctor took his other arm. "He's very pliable. Ajax, stand up."

The catatonic stood.

"Ajax, walk."

And the catatonic walked out of Kilometro Cinco. But the psychopath did not come to say good-bye.

8

Chepe Huembes had fled to the spartan room as soon as the visitors had arrived. He'd fallen to his knees and prayed. *Bless me, Ometepe, for I have sinned, it has been fourteen months since You last chastised me and these must be my sins, because why else would You send these creatures to interrupt Your servant?*

He'd been ready, was still ready, to cleanse the *doctora* and the other whores working an overnight, but now the god of hate, the god of blood had sent these . . . these . . . interlopers! . . . to turn Chepe's course against him. Those two otherworldly, white-skinned, redheaded gringos? *My god,* Chepe had shivered, *what a frightening sight they were.* And that old man, Chepe was sure he'd remembered him, some face from an old newspaper. And then that fucking dark-haired *lesbiana* whore—he knew her from the airport three years ago when he was dragged back from Costa Rica to be paraded, all over again, as El Gordo Sangroso. A queen of clubs that one. She was a friend of Montoya's, and now here she is yelling for him? Was she going to take the only friend Chepe had?

He'd turned toward the altar he had made to Ometepe. It was only in his mind, true; they would never allow him the actual holy relics he needed for a proper altar to his god, but he turned toward it nevertheless and prayed as he had not prayed since he was a child.

"God of hatred, god of blood, please, please, please let me make this offering to you, let me lay these cleansed whores at your feet.

Please, please, please, god of all things, do not let them take my friend, not the one living trophy you have bestowed on me. . . ."

Chepe had heard a sound, a muffled shuffle behind him. He knew it could not be his roommates, they would not dare enter without his permission. He'd turned, and to his delight there stood his friend, the catatonic. He must have felt Chepe's alarm at the invasion of their friendship, why else would he have come to the altar of the god of blood?

"Come, come, my friend." He'd grabbed Ajax's arm and pulled him to his knees. "Pray with me. Pray!"

Chepe had helped Ajax make the inverted cross, under his corpulent fingers the catatonic's limbs seemed more pliable, as if he, too, sensed the urgency of their plight. Chepe grasped his own hands and bent at the waist, rocking back and forth and praying as if for the last time. "God of blood, god of hate. God of blood, god of hate. God of blood, god of hate . . ."

El Gordo Sangroso had been so engrossed in prayer he did not recognize that it was Ajax's arm that went over his shoulders as if to comfort him. That it was Ajax's arm that hugged his neck as if to reassure him. By the time the catatonic's muscles had coiled around Chepe Huembes's neck it was too late.

"Wait . . ."

Suffocation was, and should be, a slow process, like drowning. Not like in a movie where it was over in seconds. Suffocation takes minutes of conscientious effort—the air supply must be choked off long after unconsciousness falls. But Ajax's arm was long enough to clamp shut the carotid artery as well as crush the larynx. All those months balancing his weight on his hands had made his arms like steel bands. Killing the blood to Chepe's brain and the air to his lungs had quickened the process, true. But when Ajax got to his feet, Chepe had dangled like a sack of maize. It was a simple enough thing for Ajax to use his free hand, the one with the puckered scar, to snap the neck of the Son of Ometepe.

9

Gladys looked at her watch: 9:45 p.m. She'd not been in the country for more than four hours as she walked Ajax up the stairs to the TACA jet out of Costa Rica that would have them in Miami just after midnight—the witching hour.

The ride back out to the airport had been a lot quieter than the ride in. Gladys had held Ajax's hand in the dark as Horacio sped through the streets. Horacio had not said a word upon seeing his somnambulant protégé led to the car like a scarecrow. She'd refused to weep or bitch or do anything other than execute the small details of getting Ajax out of the country that had betrayed them both.

Now they were seated in the 727. Held until last and then escorted aboard quickly and quietly to their first-class seats. Horacio had disappeared without a word. *Cowardly motherfucker.* Gladys could not now believe how in thrall she had once been to that treacherous old man.

The Pecks were almost as quiet as Ajax as they fastened their seat belts—it was clear their mission had failed and there was little to do but bury an empty casket for their undoubtedly dead son next to the plot of their murdered daughter.

A stewardess helped Gladys get Ajax strapped in. She was a tall *ladina*, probably Guatemalan, Gladys thought, with her Indian cheekbones and jet-black hair but pale, white skin.

"Can I get you anything? Either of you," she asked.

"Just the hell out of here." Gladys hadn't meant to say it out loud.

She certainly hadn't meant it as a jinx. But no sooner had she said it than there was a commotion outside the closed door of the aircraft. A scrum of flight crew and then the captain peered out the tiny window. The captain looked back at his passengers before giving the order to open up.

Uniformed men entered. Six cops, led by a bantam cock of a man with a colonel's insignia. The cock had a brief word with the captain, and before they made a move Gladys knew they'd come for Ajax. But why? They strode the few steps and stopped right at her row. The cock slapped Ajax across the face, like he was waking a drunk.

"What the fuck! Leave him alone! Can't you see he's catatonic?"

Gladys was out of her seat on the second try, having forgotten her seat belt the first time. But she had the colonel's slapping hand painfully bent back. The others swarmed over her and forced her down.

"He's under arrest." The cock shook Ajax as if from a drunken stupor. "You're under arrest. Wake up!"

Gladys caught sight of the Pecks three rows behind. Those poor people, she thought. They looked adrift somewhere between horror and astonishment. The man on whom they'd placed their last best hopes to return their only remaining child was incapable of speech or thought, but could be arrested for leaving the country?

The cock continued to try and shake, rattle, and roll Ajax out of his waking blackout. Gladys was about to have another go at him when Horacio stepped on the plane. Carrying a satchel.

Hijo de puta, she thought. *Who the fuck is this guy?* No one had ever fully explained Horacio's role to her—*exactly* what his portfolio was in the Revo. Yes, she knew he'd been a *comandante guerrillero* in the days before the Revo triumphed, although he'd been wounded and lifted out to Cuba before '79, when Ajax had taken over his old command. She'd known he'd recruited Ajax to the Sandinistas when he'd been a teenager still living in Los Angeles. Hell, he'd even recruited Gladys out of the police academy where she'd graduated top of her class. He'd partnered her with Ajax three years ago, and before she knew it, nor understood why, she was reporting on him back to Horacio for reasons he'd not explained. It just seemed that everyone she'd known did Horacio's bidding without question.

She'd done the same and had not questioned him even as the bodies piled up.

Then he had abandoned her to Krill and the Contras, let Ajax rot in prison and gotten him transferred to a nuthouse where he'd lost both mind and soul. Now Horacio was clearly letting her take Ajax out of Nicaragua with no papers and probably no approval other than his own.

She had no idea what the cops wanted or why, but here was Horacio again, alone, frail-looking, carrying only his cane and a satchel, getting on the plane and stopping the cock in his tracks.

She watched their whispered conversation. The cock's obvious objections and Horacio's calm reassurance that all was well. There was no shouting, no ordering. Just Horacio's comradely pat on the shoulder and the cock and his posse trooped off the plane. Horacio barely glanced back at Gladys, did not look at Ajax at all, and left the plane after a quick and quiet word with the captain. The door was closed and in a minute Gladys felt the quickening as it lifted itself into the air.

She watched through her own reflection out the window until the moonlit land below gave way to the sea, certain that she'd never see her homeland or Horacio again. Miami was less than two hours away.

That's when she noticed the satchel at Ajax's feet.

Son-of-a-bitch.

Gladys waited until the flight crew came through with drinks and food and the cabin lights had been dimmed before she dared slide the satchel over, slip it under the blanket she'd pulled over herself, and have a look.

Money.

Stacks of *yanqui* hundreds and fifties. A number popped into her head: $125,000. She was certain of it.

That's how much cash had been left over from the last case she'd worked with Ajax. The murder of a coffee grower named Enrique

Cuadra had led to the downfall of Vladimir Malhora, the former head of the Revo's DGSE, the General Directorate of State Security. A first-class *come mierdo, hijo de puta*, the J. Edgar Hoover of Nicaragua, Malhora had had at least eight people killed to cover up his larceny from years earlier when he and Ajax had both worked the DGSE chasing down the Ogre's old National Guard and the CIA's new Contra rebels.

Malhora had stolen it from an inept CIA mole, and she and Ajax had used it to make sure Malhora *disappeared* forever. The cash at her feet had to be that. She gingerly picked through it, making a quick count but not wanting to touch it, recalling the appalling amount of blood spilled over it, including Amelia Peck's.

She got near the bottom of the satchel, sure of the count, when she saw it.

It.

The Needle.

Son-of-a-bitch!

The Needle was a wicked knife Ajax had carried since his early days in the mountains with the Sandinistas. It was long and thin like a knitting needle, but the upper half was forged into a diamond shape so that four razor-sharp edges presented to whatever flesh it was pressed into. It was a specialty blade, and Ajax had been a specialist with it. So good had he gotten at sneaking up on the Ogre's Guardsmen and slitting their throats that he'd earned the nom de guerre Terrorifico. Spooky, in English—although The Terrifier would also be correct.

It was a blood-soaked and haunted tool, and she knew Ajax had used it to kill his way out of Krill's camp, leaving a dozen corpses behind. The last time Gladys had seen it Ajax had the business end pressed up against the Honduran general's jugular in order to save her ass.

Now Horacio had dropped it at her feet along with enough money to take care of the empty shell Ajax had become.

"Son-of-a-bitch," she said.

"That an adjective or a noun," the catatonic asked.

10

Captain Ajax Montoya smiled, and his smiling muscles ached merrily from lack of use, just like the Tin Man's joints must've ached after he'd been freshly oiled. A joyous pain. Ajax put a finger to his lips.

"Shh."

Then he used the finger to close Gladys's gob-smacked mouth.

"No fucking way," she whispered.

"Catatonic opossum."

"No fucking way."

"You must've suspected."

"No fucking way!"

"Then why'd you make so much noise when you got to the hospital?"

"I was pissed off!"

"Shh." Ajax nodded to the first-class cabin. Gladys had a peek behind her. The Pecks and the other passengers seemed unaware that Lazarus was in their midst and rising like a motherfucker.

"You gotta explain, Ajax."

"I was getting by okay in the penitentiary outside Tegu," the Honduran capital of Tegucigalpa, "when one day . . ."

"Wait, 'getting by okay'?"

"Yeah. Turns out being in prison is not all that different from fighting an insurgency. Like the Frente back in the day, we fought each other as much as the National Guard, then we got unified. It was helping the guys see it was the Guards who were the common enemy . . ."

"What, you *persuaded* them?"

"That, and a bankroll? Did you smuggle in that money to me?"

"No."

Ajax saw her face fall.

"I tried, Ajax. Tried to get . . ."

"That's not what I meant, Gladys. Someone did. Five grand. American. Maybe it was Gio."

Gioconda Targa, Ajax's extremely ex-wife and the Revo's most glamorous vice foreign minister.

"Why her?"

"Don't know, seemed like a woman for some reason. Anyway, I was using that money to get by pretty well. Loans, drugs, women."

Gladys's mouth dropped open again. Again, Ajax shut it for her.

"It was prison, Gladys, it was either that or be everyone's piñata."

"But Horacio said he'd bought you protection."

"He did. But protection is to longevity what a life insurance policy is to a healthy lifestyle."

Her mouth began to drop open again.

"Quite the drawbridge you got going there, Gladys."

"So you mean . . ."

"That a life insurance policy ain't nearly as important as healthy living."

"So you became a *criminal*?"

Good ol' Gladys. She'd always been a true believer. First in the Revo, then in Horacio, and then in Ajax. How she had held on to her black-and-white morality after what she'd been through was a mystery he'd get around to solving. But first he'd enjoy the look on her face, like someone too old to believe in Father Christmas, yet unable to resist the allure of the fairy tale he was spinning. She didn't believe, but really, really wanted to.

"A regular kingpin actually. Controlling stake in the three C's: conjugal visits, cigarettes, and coke."

"Not the soda."

The drawbridge quivered, but when he reached for it she slapped his hand away.

Cocaine. That'd be tough for Gladys to accept, he knew. The last case they'd worked ended up being, in retrospect, about Malhora's larceny. But it had begun as a murder to cover up a cocaine smuggling ring Malhora had been running as a black-bag operation against Uncle Sam. America's then cowboy president, Ronald Reagan, had mercenaries like Krill to unleash a shit storm of misery and death on Nicaragua in order to bleed the Revo to death, which in truth he had—the gringo cocksucker. Malhora had conceived of cocaine as a "poor man's weapon of mass destruction" and concocted an absurd scheme to wage a kind of chemical warfare in America's inner cities with the cheap white powder.

"I know, Gladys, but in prison if you don't provide a commodity, you become one."

"Okay. So . . ."

"So one day about every guard in the joint shows up at my cell door and gave me minutes to pack my shit and go. An hour later I'm on a plane to I don't know where but it seems Managua. A private plane too. Two pilots, one stewardess, and me. She brings me a cup of coffee like I've never had, like some elixir of the gods, which reminds me . . ." Ajax pushed the call button. "Order me a Coke with lots of ice and *limón*."

He went catatonic until the stewardess returned with a setup and upended the can into a frosted glass. He listened joyfully as the cola fizzed over the lip and slid down to make a perfectly round ring on the cocktail napkin.

Gladys peeked around the cabin. "Clear."

Ajax slid his hand around the glass, felt the icy coolness in his palm. It was almost erotic. He actually giggled.

"I haven't felt cold in a while."

"You want something in that?"

He shook his head.

Ajax took a long, slow drink and swallowed with difficulty. But the sensation down his throat was heavenly. "So I am on the plane out of Tegu, drinking that delectable cup of coffee, but before I can get a refill whatever she put in the first one had me out cold. I woke up in an ambulance in a straitjacket pulling into Kilometro Cinco."

He emptied the can refilling his glass. The effervescence made him giggle again; it seemed so *silly*.

"I thought it was an invitation to walk out, but the first time I tried to escape . . ."

Ajax set the glass down. There was slight tremor in his hand. He saw Gladys see it, and didn't try to hide it.

"What'd they do to you?"

"The first time, whatever they gave me sent my body into a shock, convulsions, like every muscle and tendon seized and cramped, locked down." Ajax looked at his hand and bent the joints into a twisted arthritic claw.

"That cute Spanish doctor?"

"No. Male. Five-ten. Late fifties. Soviet Bloc from the look of him, maybe East German. He didn't talk much, but once or twice a week he shot me up with some shit." Ajax shook his head and blew out his lips. "I started to see myself moving further away from me, like," he pointed to the plane's aisle, "like I was standing at the cockpit but seeing myself at the ass end of the plane. Telescoping into the distance."

He rubbed a finger over the puckered scar on the back of his hand. "El Gordo burned me with a cigarette and I could see it happen to me, way down there, but not feel it . . ."

He turned and looked at Gladys.

"Gladys, I wasn't in that shit hole outside Tegu five minutes before someone tried to put a blade in me. But that needle . . ." He shook his head.

"You were frightened."

He looked Gladys in the eye—she seemed to want him, to need him to confirm he was afraid.

"Anyway, they wanted me quiet, compliant—I gave them catatonic. After a while it stopped."

"I could fucking kill Horacio."

"Yeah. I'm sure he explained to you Kilometro Cinco was a kindness of some kind?"

"He tried to. But then, if Horacio had the go-ahead to let you go, why did those cops try to take you off the plane?"

Ajax had another long pull on the soda and let it slide orgasmically down his throat.

"I'm sure the cops came 'cause they found Chepe."

Gladys caught the drawbridge lowering and restored it to closed.

"Yes, *that* Chepe Huembes," he clarified.

"El Gordo Sangroso was in Kilometro Cinco? With you?"

Gladys had been with Ajax at the airport three years ago when the Costa Ricans had returned Nicaragua's only serial killer to their custody. The fat fuck had tried to escape during Senator Teal's press conference and the ensuing melee had landed Ajax in deep shit and on the front page, again.

But she also recalled it was how he and Amelia Peck had met.

"Wait," she said. "'Found Chepe'?"

Ajax took another long drink, drained the glass, sucked out the lime, and chewed it.

"Ajax?"

"All three hundred pounds of suet-colored suet of it."

Gladys peered around the cabin, front and back, again.

"You . . . ?"

"Gladys, you liked that Spanish doctor?"

"She's gorgeous."

"Now she stays that way."

"You mean . . . ?"

"He thought he was some Aztec priest, was gonna make me his altar boy."

"You *killed* him?"

Gladys sat back in her seat. She looked at him, then shook her head.

"You get soft and squishy on me?" he said.

"No." She shook her head. "But . . . I thought *I* was coming to save *you*."

"I don't need saving." He smiled. "But you did *rescue* me."

Ajax turned in his seat, kept half his face hidden but one eye free to observe the Pecks three rows back.

Margaret Mary had a blanket over her, her head tucked into Big Jim's shoulder. But she didn't sleep. She just stared into her lap. Big Jim had ill-fitting earphones stuck on his grizzly sized head, his eyes staring at but not seeing the private viewing screen hanging in mid-aisle. The wife held her husband's hand and slowly ran her thumb the length of it, from wrist to knuckle. It seemed an old habit, Ajax thought. So old she might've made a rut on his hand, like some old groove in a rock.

After a while he turned away.

"So what do you think," he asked.

"About you needing saving?"

Gladys was breaking his balls, which was a good sign.

"About the mission." He nodded behind them. "Young Peck. El Salvador."

"You going?"

"Thought that was why you brought my crazy ass out."

Gladys set the satchel on the floor between her feet and slid it under the seat in front of her. "It is why I brought your crazy ass out."

She didn't mean it the same way he did, but Ajax sensed commitment in her voice. He peeked around his seat one more time. But it wasn't the Pecks that made him whip back around. The seat behind Margaret Mary had been empty, the only empty seat in first class.

It wasn't empty anymore.

Ajax reached under Gladys's feet, yanked out the satchel, and opened it.

"I was going to tell you after we landed," Gladys explained.

Ajax studied the stacks.

"Malhora's money?"

"What I figured, the one-twenty-five left over."

Ajax shook the satchel, spotted the Needle on the bottom.

"Ah." He didn't want to unsheathe the blade, so he ran his finger along the handle. "That would explain it."

"Explain what?" Gladys asked.

Ajax smiled. "Good luck getting this through customs."

Gladys frowned. "Should we ditch it?"

Ajax smiled. He looked back over his shoulder. In the seat behind the Pecks that had been empty a familiar face stared blankly: The boy with the long eyelashes. The ghost of the boy with the long eyelashes, if Ajax would name him fully, sat in the empty seat, a little slumped, like a tired traveler with a thousand-yard stare.

Ajax turned back to Gladys.

"It's okay, no worries."

"You sure?"

Ajax checked again. The ghost was still there.

"Yeah."

11

Miami, November 1989

Gladys left her guest and pounded up the stairs to her apartment in North Miami Beach. Some of her neighbors stood outside, hands to their ears against the booming music crashing out her windows like heavy horse cavalry pounding down on an undefended town. She flew through the door. *What the fuck is he doing?* Everything seemed undisturbed, except for her stereo in the living room that vibrated so hard the speakers shimmied across the hardwood floors. She cleared each room, the kitchen, the spare bedroom she'd given him, even her own bedroom. Then she saw the bathroom door closed. She ran to it, but stopped, her hand almost on the knob. An unbidden image crossed her mind—a blood-splattered bathroom, the Needle in the tub with him, his lifeless body half submerged. Why had she left him alone? Her hand shook. Krill had told her more than once the story of Ajax's escape from Krill's camp. He'd regaled her with the story of Ajax slithering amongst Krill's sleeping troops like the Angel of Death, cutting throats to escape, until, Krill always insisted, blood flowed downhill like a fresh stream out of the Earth's heart.

She'd feared for Ajax's safety, his sanity, since she'd brought him home two days before. Now, now what? She pulled her hand back, readied her nerves, and kicked the bathroom door in.

The sight was worse than she'd feared.

"Gladys, what the fuck are you *doing*!"

"What the fuck are *you* doing?"

"I'm having a bath!"

Jesus Christ, he was.

Ajax sat in her tub, soap bubbles up to his chin, surrounded by electronics as if he was planning the six best ways to kill yourself while bathing. He had her Walkman in one hand, the earphones stuck on his head, her little sixteen-inch TV perched on the edge, a clock radio balanced on the TV, and her hair dryer in his other hand.

Her hair dryer?

"Get out!"

He was screaming over the music, which she'd not turned down. Gladys quickly unplugged every goddamn thing and then killed the stereo. Silence restored, she waved apologetically at her neighbors through the windows and drew the curtains. She stomped back to the bathroom. "What are you doing?"

"What's it look like?"

"A bubble bath?"

"Get the fuck out!"

"Any of this shit falls into the water you're dead, right?" She lifted the TV and clock radio out of the danger zone. "The laws of physics escape you during your confinement?" She picked up the hair dryer. "This in particular will kill you in a fucking heartbeat."

Ajax modestly gathered some bubbles around his chest. "It's called priva-fucking-cy."

"What were you doing with the hair dryer while you're still in the goddamn tub, anyways?"

"Can I finish?"

Gladys should've been mortified to be in his naked presence, but somehow her assumption he'd done himself harm made her feel disloyal, and she still wasn't sure all was well. She collected her electronics, and as she did, she noticed the soapy spires rising up out of the tub like pyramids.

"You making soap sculptures with my hair dryer?"

"Get out!"

"Teal's here."

"What?"

"Senator Teal. He's in the courtyard."

Gladys fled as he rose from the tub.

She found the two pencil marks on top of the fridge, which marked where the TV had to sit. She returned the clock radio to her bedside table and set it at a 45-degree angle, set the volume to 4.5 and made sure the alarm was still set to 6:55. Then she gave them both a good wiping down. When her world was restored enough to reestablish her elusive calm, she fetched Teal from the courtyard.

The last time Ajax had seen Senator Anthony Teal was outside a cathedral in Nicaragua where he'd gone to collect Amelia Peck's bullet-ridden body. Back then he'd been the kind of gringo Ajax despised: rich, powerful, and clueless. Three years ago he'd treated Ajax's country like a game of Monopoly. The man before him still had his frat-boy good looks, but there was a touch of salt in the pepper that made him seem a more serious player.

"Senator Teal."

"Captain Montoya."

"Just Ajax."

Teal blanched. Ajax assumed he knew the history.

"I hope I didn't have anything, I mean . . . well . . ."

As articulate as ever, Ajax thought. "How can we help, Senator?"

"The Pecks called when they got back. They said, well, I'd hoped, we'd hoped, but . . ."

"They told you I was a useless shell."

"Yes. I'm glad you're not!" Teal threw up his hands. "But . . ."

"You called Gladys anyways."

"Yes."

"Why?"

"I'd heard, no, I mean, I'd hoped . . . hoped." Teal dropped his head. "I owe the Pecks so much. Amelia, too, she . . ."

Got me reelected. Ajax kept that one to himself.

"You want us to go find their son."

"Yes! Please! I mean, I know you don't owe me anything. But, still, you . . . she . . ." Teal shook his head in surrender, defeated by the complexity of it all.

Ajax checked in with Gladys—the slightest of nods and she was in.

"We have to move fast, Senator. Do you know what this will take? Passports, cover story, money? You have that kind of pull?"

"I do. I mean I can. There's a guy . . . well, that sounds . . . but he'll contact you in two days. He'll arrange all that. Has arranged it."

Ajax looked Teal over. He seemed out of his depth, out of his element—a second-term Republican senator playing snakes and ladders with someone like Ajax. It didn't add up. Still, guilt was a harsh overseer, Ajax could witness that.

"Senator, you keep the Pecks misinformed of my condition. The chances of finding their boy alive are slim. And if he's dead there'll be no body. You keep them believing it's hopeless, they won't be disappointed."

"Yes! I can, I will. Thank you." Teal almost leaped to his feet and, it seemed to Ajax, was relieved to have it done with. He shook their hands, lingered, Ajax felt, a bit too long.

"You know, Captain, uh, Ajax, it's still, you know . . . our countries . . . I mean even with Eastern Europe, our countries, your country . . . well actually *our* countries, umm, I don't want you to think I don't . . ."

"Our countries are technically still at war and we should not contact you directly. When we get back we will inform the Pecks, they'll let you know."

"Yes! Thank you. Thank you." He shook their hands again, the politician's reflex—when in doubt, press the flesh. He looked around

Gladys's apartment like there might be a baby for him to kiss. "Well, thanks again. God bless Ameri . . . I mean, God bless you both."

Senator Teal left, taking, it struck Ajax, far too much care closing the door. He and Gladys stood in silence a moment.

"You drove him here, Gladys?"

"Yep."

"How long you think he'll stand outside before he realizes he doesn't have a ride?"

"Maybe all day."

"That man might be president someday."

"God bless America."

Ajax laughed. "Get him to the airport."

Horacio de la Vega Cárdenas gripped the day's *Miami Herald* and used it for camouflage, its front page frenzied with news from Europe where old borders and old orders were coming undone faster than belt buckles in a whorehouse. He'd watched Tony Teal settle into the VIP lounge at Miami International and order a double single-malt on the rocks. He needed Teal just off-kilter so he waited until the senator had that first long sip, and had exhaled in satisfaction before he approached.

"My operatives are on board?"

Teal almost baptized himself in Glenlivet. "Why are . . . we . . . I can't be seen with you."

"You're not being seen with me, Senator. You're having a rather early drink in the VIP lounge, and an old man has sat down next to you to read the paper. Calm yourself. Time is important here, are my operatives on board?"

Teal looked around the lounge. "They're not coming with me."

Horacio took a long, quiet breath and said a silent, secular prayer for patience. "Not on board the flight, Senator, on board with *the plan*?"

"Yes. Yes. They'll go."

"Good. And the rest? Their papers? Passports?"

"Two days, it was the fastest I could, you know, get them."

"That will do. Now, if all goes to plan we won't meet again."

Horacio folded the paper, he thought to toss it—the *Herald* had been no friend to the Revo for all these years—but reconsidered. Capital *H* history was happening in the old Soviet Bloc, maybe he should keep it for his files.

"Wait!" Teal set his scotch down with a splash. "I need a body for this to work, at least that. You promised."

"And you have promised six votes on the Contra Relocation Bill."

"You'll have them!"

"And you will have young Peck—or at least his body. If anyone can accomplish this it is them. It's why I chose them."

Teal took a long pull on the scotch, sucked an ice cube into this mouth, and cracked it, searching, Horacio knew, for resolve.

"Senator, it is not easy for us to trust, but you reached out to me. Time is of the essence so unless you want the Pecks' only remaining child also to be devoured by the cannibal of collateral damage, then trust we must. And the risk is mine: I must act now but this Contra vote might not be for weeks. Correct?"

Teal's eye darted around the lounge, which was whisper quiet and smelled of citrus. He nodded. "Alive would help."

"But in any event, his body."

Teal took another drink, and swallowed rapidly.

12

Ajax slid the long tool between the two white flanks and into the sweet goop buried inside. The flanks yielded to his by-now expert technique. Once all the way inside, he slowly twirled his tool until it was covered, drew it out with excruciating patience, and used his mouth to clean off the dripping ooze.

It was his second banana split in a row, yet no less satisfying for it.

He and Gladys had been waiting for an hour on the mezzanine in Miami's South Beach mall for their contact to show. Ajax was killing three birds with one stone: air-conditioning, ice cream, and immersion in an America he'd not seen for twenty years.

"You make that look . . ." Gladys didn't finish.

Ajax slowly drew the spoon out of his mouth. "Delicious?"

"I was gonna say repulsive."

"Oh come on, Gladys! This is doctor's orders."

Ajax swept his hand over the mall—the pride of South Beach, which was the pride of Miami, or so he'd been told. They'd been two days in the city and Ajax allowed himself a moment of giddiness at the casual excess of America.

Gladys, he'd noticed, was less giddy. The more they were around each other the more awkward she became.

"Actually you suggested it to the doctor," she noted.

Ajax had had a full physical that morning. The doctor pronounced him fit if a bit malnourished. Gladys had asked what to do, and the doctor had asked Ajax: he'd said three things and now here he was, at a Ben and Jerry's getting them all. He was delirious. Families of Anglos and Cubans idly patrolled the floors, their kids crying or smiling as the fleeting truth of their lives dictated. Teenagers flirted and gossiped, and monitored their reflections in the shop windows. And the shops! Ajax could almost literally not believe, not factor or fathom the seemingly infinite shit for sale. And every single thing, the walls and floors, every item arrayed in endless displays, even the air itself was perfectly cooled—temperature and humidity flawlessly controlled. A catchy salsa tune by Gloria Estefan, the Cuban-American pop singer, quietly enlivened the place, while reruns of *Miami Vice* filled an entire window of the electronics store across from the ice cream parlor.

Ajax found it glorious.

As lasciviously as possible, he spooned another heap of banana, chocolate-mint ice cream, and hot fudge into his happy mouth.

Gladys shook her head disapprovingly, but not really.

"Well at least this trip isn't a total waste."

Ajax smiled. She hadn't spotted him.

Reynaldo Garcia was their contact for all things Cuban in Miami, which was saying a lot. The Cubans had arrived by their thousands thirty years previous when Fidel Castro and his band of raggedy-ass guerrillas had driven out their dictator. They had come for the refuge but stayed for the lifestyle. It was rumored the white Anglos viewed them much the way the original Seminoles had the Spanish—with much late-night gnashing of teeth that they'd not killed them all on the beach when they had the chance.

Ajax smiled.

Gladys frowned, she knew that look. "Where?"

"Next level up, white guayabera, Panama hat with a black band, and an unlit cigar."

Gladys discreetly reconnoitered the gallery above them. "Don't see him."

"He's walking the floor, when he gets to that pillar to your right, he'll stop and eyeball us. I make him as our man, he seems pretty cagey."

"Well, strictly speaking it's treason for him to help us, at least among the *gusanos*."

Gusano was Spanish for worm, it was how the Cuban government referred to anyone who'd fled to Miami, as if only such a low form of life would abandon subsistence living in revolutionary Cuba for, well, Ajax thought, for ice cream and shopping malls.

"He better have what we need." Gladys ripped open a Handi Wipe from the ice cream store and gave her fingers a thorough cleaning. It was the third time that day Ajax had watched her do so.

"They say he's the man."

They were an oddly powerful group of people to be surrounding a couple as ordinary as Margaret Mary and Big Jim Peck. But Teal had proved he had the pull. Ajax, Gladys, and the Pecks had been met at the airport by unmanned "officials" and hurried through customs— Gladys sweating the whole way with the satchel full of money and the Needle. No one had even checked. Ajax wasn't sure why Teal was so keen on helping the Pecks, unless it truly *was* guilt over the death of Amelia.

Amelia Peck.

Ajax bore her death heavily. He could understand why Teal did as well. Amelia had been on a straight PR mission in Nicaragua during Teal's first visit as a freshman senator and disciple of the Great Cowboy Ronald Reagan. Amelia's job had been to find a family of Nicaraguans that Teal would "take out" of the country to reunite with family already in her home state of Ohio. It was pure propaganda for the newspapers back home—get the new guy a little bloodied down south with the tropical commies. Show the folks back home he was serious about keeping them safe from the impoverished Marxist children of farmers and fruit sellers.

But Amelia had only started out that way. She'd gone into a

war zone for PR, but she had stayed for Ajax. Stayed that one fatal extra day.

Fucking fool!

Fortune's fool.

He and Amelia had tried to hew a stolen season out of their accidental meeting. And like other star-crossed lovers it had ended in death all around.

"There he is." Gladys spotted their contact.

Reynaldo Garcia was a classic example of a Cuban caught in time. He was in his late fifties, silver-haired, clean-shaven, wearing a well-pressed white guayabera, tan slacks, and coffee-brown loafers, carrying an unlit Montecristo in a tortoiseshell cigar holder. He could've been in a Havana café in 1959, as well as a Miami mall in 1989.

Reynaldo sat down with them, smiled a real charmer's smile.

"We'll speak in English here," he said, shaking hands with each of them. "Your Nicaraguan Spanish is very, well, let's say very identifiable and rumors are out that some Sandinistas have arrived in Miami."

"And how do rumors get out in this town?" Ajax asked.

"We Cubans run Miami." He turned his palms up. "We've had the local muscle for some time, but your revolution, Captain Montoya, the horror of another communist nation menacing the land of the free and the home of the brave gave us national power for the first time these past ten years. Our people dominate the best jobs, too, so your little party arriving at the airport late at night, no papers but a lot of VIPs, needed five minutes before our eyes and ears passed on the word."

Gladys and Ajax exchanged a look. Not for the first time Ajax was wishing Horacio had passed him his chrome-plated .357 Colt Python rather than the Needle. Not that *they* could cover him in a shootout, it was rather that Ajax felt naked since his arrival—he wore no weapons, no uniform, nor any disguise, and that, oddly, was taking some getting used to. Miami was like a very hip nudist colony—he liked it, but being bare-assed around civilians would take time to adjust to.

"Do not fear." Reynaldo patted their hands. "We Cubans are too middle-aged now to do any real violence other than with words, and usually at dinner after a bottle of good Cuban rum."

"You can still get that?"

"Oh yes! Montecristos." He held up his cigar. "Havana Club rum, smuggling the old pleasures in is about as clandestine as most of us get these days."

"Really?" Ajax slipped another spoonful of cold orgasm into his mouth. "I thought you Cubans spent most of your time prepping to parachute into Havana."

Reynaldo smiled, shook his head, and lit his cigar, slowly rolling the end in a flame. "Miami is like Paris after the Bolshevik Revolution. Full of white Russians with money and a deep ache for revenge, but no idea whatsoever what's going on back in Moscow. They were too in love with Paris, like we are with Miami, to ever actually go home again, except to visit and sniff at how déclassé home has become. The white Russians bled the Americans for funding for every harebrained scheme they concocted for fifty years. In the war against communism you could sell to the gringos anything you can imagine and for any price you had the balls to ask for."

"And so you run Miami and have the American dog by the tail," Ajax said.

Reynaldo smiled. He rolled the cigar in his fingers, as if reading a scroll. "It's a fickle thing, getting what you wish for. We thought you Sandinistas would relaunch the war we lost at the Bay of Pigs. We couldn't lose twice, could we?"

"You sound nostalgic."

Reynaldo spread his hands wide. "It seems rather than relaunch the Cold War, your revolution was the last battle of that war."

"Was it?"

"Oh yes, look at the Soviet Union, you read the papers."

"Not recently." Ajax smiled.

"So I've heard. The Berlin Wall is gone, can you imagine? *The* icon of the Cold War is gone. People pulled it down with their *bare hands*. And no one shot them. Breaching the wall was supposed to set off World War III, nuclear apocalypse. Instead? Fireworks! Dancing in the streets. Communism is collapsing under its own load—no mushroom clouds, just an old man in the corner wetting his pants."

"Is that why you're helping us?"

Gladys seemed impatient with Reynaldo's eulogy. The Cuban smiled ruefully and re-lit his intractable cigar.

"One must prepare for the post-communist world and you two have friends, it seems, who cannot be ignored."

"But if communism is collapsing," Gladys challenged, "doesn't that mean the war in El Salvador has an end date?"

Reynaldo laughed, heartily and loudly, then abruptly stopped. "No. Look, I know these Salvadorans, the hardliners, the death squad Charlies who come to Miami for R and R to wash off the blood. They think Miami is what they'll get if they kill all the communists. If they think the clock is ticking *down* on their war, they will only ratchet *up* the killing before the glory days are over. Trust me. El Salvador is still the hottest of hot wars, and you two are going into the inferno. And you might not be the only Nicaraguans pitching up in El Salvador these days."

Ajax saw the twinkle in his eyes. Reynaldo just adored hoarding intelligence. "Meaning what?"

"Your government . . ."

"Not really mine, but go ahead."

"The Sandinista government concluded a truce with the Contras not that long ago. Word is some of them, the Contras of course, were getting fat and bored and decided to freelance around the region. El Salvador, for example."

"You wouldn't think they'd be needed," Ajax said.

"What? Freelancers? The Contras may not have made an effective war in your country, but some of them are effective . . ." Reynaldo paused, and in that pause Ajax knew he knew about Gladys and Krill.

A security guard nearby—a Haitian, if Ajax guessed right—ambled over to the table.

"Sorry, sir, but there is no smoking in the mall, you have to put it out or I have to ask you to leave."

"Of course, I'm terribly sorry." Reynaldo stuck the cigar into the leftovers of Ajax's banana split.

"I wasn't finished with that."

"Thank you, sir." The security guard picked up Ajax's ruined dessert and slipped a manila envelope from his jacket and left it on the table as he went.

"A friend of mine," Reynaldo explained and slid the envelope to Ajax. "Inside are your passports, letters of introduction, and your cover stories—you are two right-wing Havana-born *gusanos* with lots of money to spread around among the *victims of communist terrorism* in El Salvador. Of course, as you are not actually going to donate the money, I don't actually have to give it to you."

"And the Salvadorans would buy that story?" Gladys asked.

"Buy it? They threw themselves at it! El Salvador is like the plain girl at a school dance—she desperately hopes a boy from the football team will cast a glance her way. And America, you know, is the handsome quarterback. But El Salvador is the plainest of the plain, downright homely—crooked-toothed and unibrowed." He spread his hands to take them in. "If the water boy asks her to dance, she will feel like Cinderella."

"You do like to talk." Gladys wasn't asking.

"Gladys, the ruling clique in El Salvador has no friends anywhere in the *world* other than the American government, and, well, I think we all know what a mixed blessing that can be."

Ajax smiled. Not for the first time he found himself united with what should be a political enemy agreeing on the mixed blessing of being America's pet. It seemed no matter the ideology, all Latin Americans had the same lament as their credo: *So far from God, so near to the United States.*

Reynaldo reached into the envelope. "Your flight leaves in the morning. Your passports are only good for travel to El Salvador. If they are used in any other port they will be canceled within forty-eight hours. But that is also your escape plan. If you need to flee by any, let us say, unofficial route, you will have two days to get back to the U.S. After that you are stateless. In El Salvador I have arranged one friendly contact for you—the code name is Mata Sofá."

Ajax laughed. "Couch killer?"

"I'm sure there is an amusing story behind the name," Reynaldo said, but to Ajax he didn't look amused. "They will make contact with you using that name. Also, in the American embassy a political officer named Michaelson is aware of your mission, the official cover only, should you need a contact there."

Gladys reached for the envelope, but Reynaldo slapped his hand down on it.

"There are also, as of early this morning, three photographs that have just come into my possession that might make your trip unnecessary."

"Then why didn't you start out with that information?" Gladys seemed anxious, or angry. She forced the envelope from Reynaldo's hand.

"I was paid for what else is in this envelope. The photographs I include for free, out of friendship."

"Friendship? Between us?"

Now Ajax could hear the true believer in Gladys—no matter how badly the Sandinista government had treated them both, Gladys was still with the Revo, and this right-wing Cuban *hijo de puta* was still her enemy.

Reynaldo stood up, placed his hand over his heart. "Gladys, the old world order is gone." He turned both palms up, like weighing something on a scale. "Balancing between left and right, the Soviets, the Americans, all gone." He hid one hand behind his back like a magician at a children's party. "And what happens when the United

States no longer has to bid for the loyalty of its friends? No longer has a bogeyman to shake at you? No longer has a rival for its power and dictates?" He brought his hand from behind his back—in it was a fresh Montecristo. "We Latin Americans will soon be looking to each other. Time for us to be friends, or the Goliath to the north will devour us all."

Gladys ripped open the manila envelope and spilled the contents onto the table.

"Oh shit!"

She blanched at the three eight-by-eleven color photographs of a brutally mangled body, dead many times over from the looks of it. One was a close-up of a pulped face, unrecognizable. Another, a full-length body shot revealing severe lacerations on the buttocks and legs, the victim's thumbs tied behind his back. The final photo was full frontal. The corpse was not much tortured on the front, except for a sickening swelling around the genitals.

The body was of a young, white Anglo with orange-red hair.

Young Peck.

He had not died well.

"Goddamn it!" Gladys looked away.

Ajax, however, could not take his eyes off the gruesome images. That pale white skin, the same as Amelia's. That same red hair so orange Ajax had called her Jugo for *jugo de naranja*—orange juice. Looking at the photos took Ajax back to that terrible moment in the church in Matagalpa when he'd said good-bye to Amelia's bullet-riddled body.

There had been six of them, the three Nicas she was taking out, a journalist named Connelly that Ajax had partnered with, and a priest named Father Jerome. They had all been at a coffee *finca* in one of the worst war zones in northern Nicaragua. The farm had belonged to the man whose murder Ajax had been investigating. It'd been too dangerous then, as it would be even now, for Ajax to travel alone to, so he had pretended to be the journalist's driver and fixer as a disguise.

At the time three years ago, everyone had wanted to insist the victim was murdered by the Contras. Ajax hadn't bought it so he and Connelly had trooped off into the bush to find the local Contra commander and eliminate them as a suspect.

That's when he'd met Krill.

Ajax had thought he'd figured out the whole mystery and rushed off back to Managua to bust Malhora, and in doing so left Amelia and the rest at the *finca*.

The next time he saw them all was in the nave of the cathedral in Matagalpa, ripped from *corona a culo* with bullets. He'd cut a lock of that orange hair of hers and carried it until the Hondurans tossed him naked into his first jail cell.

For three years he'd chased away the *why?* of his fate in prison, in the madhouse, with that image of Amelia's body. He knew what his penance was for. There even had been times at night, in his dreams, when he'd relived their stolen season: her voice, her laugh, that mad hair. The pale skin, the freckles speckled over her body like chocolate flakes on strawberry-vanilla ice cream.

Those freckles.

"So." Reynaldo held out his hands. "Maybe your mission is not so pressing."

Suddenly Ajax found this Cuban very interesting.

"Dead or alive," Gladys said.

"Who?"

"We bring him home, dead or alive. That's the mission."

"Very well, my friends." Reynaldo stood. "Good luck." He shook Ajax's hand. "God bless." He offered a hand to Gladys who, to Ajax's eyes, only pretended to study the morgue photos so closely she did not notice. Reynaldo strolled away and Ajax saw the Haitian security guard follow at a discreet distance. For some reason Reynaldo made him think of Horacio de la Vega.

"What do we tell the Pecks?" Gladys was turning the photos face-down.

"Nothing." Ajax turned the photos back over, but did not take his eyes off Reynaldo's back. "That's not young Peck."

"What?"

"Look at the photos, Gladys. Don't see the gruesome death, see the body. You met Amelia?"

"Yeah."

"And her parents."

"So?"

"They share that dominant Celtic gene: red hair, pale skin, blue or green eyes, and freckles. Amelia was covered in them."

Gladys checked the photos again. She finally saw. "Freckles?"

"No freckles."

"No freckles."

"No freckles, no Peck. It's not him."

"But . . ."

"And no buts. Come on!"

13

Ajax had sent Gladys sprinting for her car while he took a spot out front to watch for Reynaldo's car. It had taken her a couple minutes to pull up. In that time, Ajax had felt the change come over him. His step had quickened, his senses sharpened, like some great telescope coming into focus after years of disuse. A slow broil of anger warmed his guts. He had a mission. He was coming back to life.

When they saw Reynaldo drive past, they pulled out behind him. Their two cars said a lot, Ajax thought. Gladys was driving a Yugo—a Yugoslavian compact and one of the most ridiculous cars ever made. It reminded Ajax of his old Lada back in Managua. The Lada was the Soviet Union's answer to the "people's car"—an affordable model for every member of the proud proletariat. It was also a complete piece of shit, which was of little import in a country where customer service was run by the KGB.

Reynaldo, however, drove a Chevy Impala, almost as old as Gladys was.

"Don't lose him."

"I know how to tail someone. You think your Cuban's dirty?"

"He's not my Cuban, and we don't know his game."

"The passports looked legit."

"Exactly. His job is to get us there, and he lays these photos on us and a reason *not* to go?"

"Maybe it is young Peck."

"Maybe."

"Now you say 'maybe.'"

"No, you said it. I know it's not him. So why does this Cuban drop another dead body on us?"

"Another? You said 'another.'"

"If young Peck's been taken by the death squads, he's dead."

"Then why are we going?"

"It's the mission. Watch him now."

Reynaldo's car left the expressway and headed into the heart of Miami. They rode in silence a while. Ajax was trying to get comfortable in the Yugo's cramped bucket seat. "Jesus, Gladys, you just can't let go, can you?"

"Me? Me!" She exploded. "I can't let go? Look at yourself! Three years in hell and first thing you think you can go back and fight old battles? I'm sorry, Ajax, but she's dead. Amelia is dead. The people with her are dead. The men who killed her are dead. Look at the fucking photos! Peck is dead. There's no reason for you to put yourself in danger. But no, Ajax Montoya knows different because of the Case of the Missing Freckles. Who can't let go, Ajax!"

There was a long pause as oxygen came back into the cramped space.

"I was talking about your car."

"My what!"

"The Yugo, Gladys. It's like the Ladas back in Managua. You come to the capital of capitalism and buy a fucking socialist Yugo is what I was talking about."

Ajax actually counted to six before Gladys's eyes cleared and she understood.

"My car?"

"Yeah. Get yourself a Mustang."

"Fuck Fords."

They followed Reynaldo, but the signs pointing to Calle Ocho told Ajax they were headed to Little Havana. Ajax watched the homes and mini-malls go by his window, the restaurants and small businesses, the soaring palm trees lining the streets and the palmetto bushes squatting in every yard. It wasn't hot in Miami in November, just like in Managua, so Ajax rolled the window down. Air gusted into the car. The breeze, Ajax realized, might have begun in the actual Havana, only ninety miles away.

Inside the bubble of her car, Ajax had the feeling all of Miami was under glass, the terrarium of some giant kid who enjoyed watching the neat comings and goings of his pets. He knew there had to be another Miami, or other Miamis, darker, dirtier, poorer. But he'd not seen them yet. Gladys turned west onto Calle Ocho, Little Havana, where you might not ever hear English spoken. They'd cruised it a few times since their arrival, but as they were trying to keep a low profile in case any blowback followed them from Managua, they'd not dared more than just cruising.

Cruised it.

Ajax had forgotten how much time Americans spent in their cars, or rather how much driving itself was thought to be a social end, rather than a means of transport. He'd certainly spent his early teens cruising L.A.—the drive from his family's North Hollywood home to the skanky streets of *the* Hollywood was often the only action he and his friends saw.

Still, Little Havana enchanted him. It was like a small Latin American theme park at Disney World—as if all the best bits of the continent had been swept clean and put on display: Cuban coffee houses with crowded tables and domino boards, hole-in-the-wall Dominican restaurants, Argentine *parrilladas* brimming with beef and Mendoza wines. But all Disneyfied, scrubbed clean of the homeland's blood, sweat, and tears. No potholes or broken sewer lines, no crumpled sidewalks, corrupt military police, nor the flotsam of third-world poverty hovering everywhere like memento mori.

Suddenly, Gladys made an illegal U-turn and parked a half block past an upscale Cuban café in the heart of Little Havana, the sidewalk in front crowded with small tables. She adjusted her rear-view mirror to catch the sidewalk customers.

"There he is."

Ajax adjusted his own mirror to watch.

Reynaldo pulled over in front of the café. A squat man detached himself from a chair and greeted Reynaldo as he hit the sidewalk. Reynaldo gave him the keys and the guy drove the car off.

"Valet parking?" he asked.

"Not likely."

"Then he's got another meeting set up."

Ajax nodded out the window. "You knew the real Havana, didn't you? I mean the Cuban one. I mean, you know . . ."

"Sure. The police academy was near the Malecón. Class of eighty-five." She shifted in her seat to face him. "So, you ever meet the *comandante?*"

"Fidel? Sure. Back in the seventies, before the triumph. All the factions showed up. He laid on quite the feast and we all lined up like kids in a locker room while Babe Ruth shook our hands. When I got introduced, Fidel goes, 'Ah, the gringo.'"

"No way!"

"Right there in front of everybody. It was funny Gladys, 'cause I'd forgotten all that . . . growing up in L.A."

"What'd you say?"

"Nothing. Horacio put his arm around me and said, 'Not this one, *Comandante,* we reclaimed him from exile.'"

"So it was cool?"

"Thought it was 'til this colonel from State Security slid up on me and asked for a word."

"Goddamn. You and State Security. They interrogate you?"

"He took me into a side room off the banquet hall where these two dough-colored KGB agents were hip deep in mojitos and cigars."

"No shit? They thought you were a spy?"

"Not really." Ajax saw Gladys clocking the action behind them at the café, so he readjusted the Yugo's itty-bitty side mirror to take in a better view. Doing so, he let a warm breeze fill the car. "They were vetting us, the Cubans and Russians, for later use. Which really was a good sign. If they didn't think we would win they wouldn't've bothered to vet us. I was an American-born compañero, I suppose we would've done the same. Anyway, one of the KGB was an old World War Two vet, Anatoly Shermanov." Ajax smiled at the memory. "His family had been kulaks, rich peasants purged by Stalin. They recruited him out of a Siberian labor camp, sent him to Stalingrad. We got to swapping war stories, his specialty had been cutting Nazi throats."

Gladys recoiled a little. "So you had that in common."

"If you wanna call it that." He turned to her. "He gave me the Needle."

"No!"

"Yeah. Took me back up to his room. Showed it to me. Said he never was without it." Ajax shook his head. "Funny, but he held it and told one story after another about creeping up on Germans while they were sleeping or shitting, sipping tea. And all the while he poured us one shot of Havana Club after another. After a while, I got the feeling it was him talking but the Needle telling the stories."

He looked to catch her reaction, not so much because he'd said too much, but because he hoped she might understand.

"Bloody goddamn thing that blade."

"That it is," he said.

She adjusted her rearview mirror, pointed. "There's his meeting. Guy in the white jacket, sleeves pushed up."

Ajax found him in the mirror. Early thirties, five-six, black/brown, muscled, tanned, with a jangle of gold around his neck, and a tangle of shining curls. He was talking on one of those new cellular phones that were about as small as a coffeepot with an antenna as long as a riding crop.

"Oily-looking *puto,* ain't he?"

"Jheri Curl."

"Who?"

"His hair, it's called Jheri Curl. Black dudes use it mostly, but some Cubans, too, if they got kinky hair."

"He looks like that guy from *Miami Vice*."

"Which one?"

"Your man there."

"Which character?"

"Oh. The white guy's jacket and the black guy's hair. Who is he?"

"The white guy? Don Johnson."

"Not the show, the café guy."

Gladys drew binoculars not much bigger than opera glasses from a bag on the backseat. She slumped down and peeped the oily Don Johnson.

"*Puta!*" Gladys said it in the Nicaraguan fashion, drawing out the *U*s so it came out *Puuuuuta!* "I know that guy." She peeped him again through the glass. "He's a coyote. Human smuggler."

"I know what a coyote is, Gladys. How do you know him?"

"I've been working with this church group." She shrugged like it was a small thing. "Sanctuary movement. Refugees come in, mostly Salvadorans and Guatemalans. They make landfall, the churches take them in—sanctuary. I help reunite them with families. Mostly long-haul driving, but if they don't know where their family is I find them, treat it like missing persons work."

Ajax smiled. "Gladys Darío, you're a private dick!"

She shot him a look that could sharpen a knife.

"A detective. Missing persons work, you're a P.I."

"Yeah." She studied the coyote and Reynaldo through the glass. "Except for the part where I don't get paid."

"I always figured Mommy and Daddy had money. Let me have a look."

She handed over the binoculars. Ajax spied their prey.

"Actually, Papi's been dead a while, but yeah, Mami's set. And she wants to meet you."

"Really? Heard all about me, has she?"

"No. Well, yes. But like so many others she's taken an intense dislike to you without really knowing you."

Ajax chuckled. "Me? Why?"

"She says you're my bad-luck charm."

He put the binos down and studied her face, but she had no comment on her mother's pronouncement. "So what's with *tio coyote*?"

Gladys turned. "Two things. I been looking for him 'cause I got three families in Houston, New Orleans, and Miami looking for loved ones who signed on with him but never made it ashore."

"How so?"

She smiled. "You think Miami's all malls and ice cream, but it's mostly drugs, riots, and refugees. Guatemalans and Salvadorans use coyotes, they can't get asylum 'cause America backs their government. Nicas, like the Cubans, get in for free 'cause the gringos oppose the government. Coyotes like him meet the refugees who get as far as Jamaica, the Bahamas, maybe Haiti. They take cash to transport them here in cigarette boats, just like the narcos use."

"What's the second thing?"

She smiled. "He's Salvadoran."

Ajax felt his inner cop stir, a smile spread across his face like the Cheshire cat's, if the Cheshire cat ate dogs for breakfast. "What's his story?"

"Supposedly he's been here a while, got here in seventy-nine or eighty . . ."

"So just as the shit hit the fan back home."

"Yep. Word is he was ARENA, death squads."

Ajax grunted. "He don't look hard to me."

"No?"

"No way. Look at him, Gladys." He put the binos down. "Sitting outside so everyone can see him on his big fat phone. Sun gleaming off of his chains and his Jheri Curls. Any heavy lifting, he doesn't do himself. Errand boy for people like Reynaldo there."

As he said his name Reynaldo stood, shook hands with the coyote, and walked to the curb. A moment later another car pulled up and whisked him away.

Ajax suddenly felt the need to push the crazy button. "Let's go brace the fucker."

"No!"

Her grip on his arm had more iron than he'd expected—he wasn't the only one who'd stayed fit.

"He's not dangerous, Gladys."

"It's not about *him*."

Now he looked her over. "This about El Gordo?"

"Yes! No! Ajax, you're in hell for three years—prison, the nuthouse, playing catatonic for over a year. By a fucking miracle you get sprung and on the way out—you kill the guy!"

"El Gordo was a dead man whether you came to get me or not. It was him or the doctor and every other woman in that place."

"Fine. Good. Then look at yourself. You've been free for two days and now it's 'Let's go brace the fucker.' This isn't Nicaragua, the Wild West, you aren't a hero here and no one will cover you for your shit!"

"My *shit*?"

"Your shit. You know if I had been your C.O. back in Managua I would've taken your gun and badge long before—"

"Before what? Before you met me?"

The look on her face was uncertain.

"What do you want to know, Gladys?"

She looked him over, Ajax could hear it: *Can I trust you?* "It's not about if I want to go with you to find Peck."

"Young Peck."

"Young Peck. It's that you can't do this job without me and I need to know where your head's at." But her eyes went back to the mirror and her oleaginous coyote. "I wanna know if he's taking refugees' money and then stiffing them offshore, or if he's dumping them in the ocean."

Ajax looked in the mirror.

"Him? He's no killer."

"Famous last words."

"Let's find out." And he was out the door and down the street, affecting a shuffle somewhere between drunk and crazy.

"*Oye, 'mano!* Man, look at you, brother. Don Johnson in real life!"

The coyote, like any normal person, ignored Ajax, assuming he could not possibly be talking to him.

"Hey, man! Is that one of them *teléfonos celulares*, right? Bouncing off of spaceships and shit, right? Can I make a call, I can pay you?"

Ajax took out a few crumpled bills, flashed it like a pimp roll. But the coyote now knew he was in crazy's crosshairs.

"*Ve te, loco.*" Get lost, crazy. He pretended he had to make a call.

"No, serious man, *de veras*, I got people in the Bahamas, paid some fuck-face coyote to bring them ashore, I ain't found 'em, *primo*. Help me out, cuz."

The coyote, Ajax was certain, thought he was being jacked, and looked around for Ajax's accomplice, but he didn't make Gladys as the backup. He did, however, clock that all eyes were on him, and Ajax knew his macho pride was about to make a mistake. The coyote dropped the cellular phone into what seemed a holster big enough for Ajax's old .357, tossed some bills on the table, then made what he must've thought was a fast move on Ajax.

Ajax grabbed the wrist of the hand reaching for him, twisted the arm straight out and a little back, rabbit punched him in the kidneys, sat him down in the chair, lifted his phone, pulled out the antenna, and whipped the coyote across the cheek with it.

"AHHHHHH!!!" The coyote screamed as a crimson welt raised up like invisible ink revealed. To Ajax's amazement he made to take a swing, so Ajax whipped him on the other cheek.

"Ajax!"

"It's alright, Gladys. I got this."

"Behind you!"

Shit. Ajax knew the coyote was not a boss, but he'd forgotten that even underlings can have minions, and three of them were rushing Ajax from inside the café. The minion closest to Ajax, a terrier of a man, took that one second to eyeball his boss, cradling his stinging cheeks. It was all Ajax needed to recover. He fake-stumbled back one step and when the terrier went for him, whipped him across the face too. When the terrier reached for the wound Ajax let him have it on the other cheek, then kicked him in the nutbag. But there was no time to admire his handiwork as the second minion hurled a chair at Ajax's head. So Ajax threw the phone and nailed him in the forehead.

Ajax was just about to admire all his handiwork when a scream slit the air.

The third minion had Gladys in a bear hug.

"Let go! Let go! Letgoletgoletgo!!!!!!"

Ajax had seen Gladys in action before. She had an unconscionable deference for authority, but if you got her beyond that, in a tight spot she had some sand and usually took no shit from any man.

But this was hysterics.

Gladys writhed like an eel in the minion's grip. Her arms and legs flailed like a child in a grotesque temper tantrum, or an epileptic in the grandest of grand mals.

Everyone, including the minion holding her, recoiled at the outburst. The minion released her as soon as Ajax made a step in his direction. Gladys fled into the café. The coyote was still cradling his whipped face, so Ajax patted him down, yanked a fat wallet from his pocket, and rifled through it for his driver's license.

"'David Gutierrez.' Look at me. Look!"

The coyote lowered his hands, peered almost tremulously over his fingers, all fight gone, as was the case with most bullies. Ajax reached into the dark, stinking outhouse in which he had hidden the dark stinking shit of the last three years and took one quick whiff before he swiftly shut it again.

"Do you know who piggy is?"

"What?"

"DO YOU KNOW WHO PIGGY IS?"

Ajax could see and smell the fear now, as he wanted and needed to.

"You're my little piggy. You charge people their life savings to get them into Miami. From now on, piggy, you either bring them here or stop taking their money. Otherwise you're gonna wake up one night," Ajax read the license, "at eleven forty Sixteenth Street, apartment three, and find me standing over you holding a stick sharpened at both ends. *Comprendes*, piggy?"

The coyote held up both hands, a look of awe making his eyes huge. "Yeah, yeah. *Comprendo*."

"Good. Now sit down." Ajax eyeballed the minions who, as their boss had backed down, did likewise. Ajax righted the overturned chairs, retrieved the cell phone, and gave it back.

"Reynaldo," Ajax said.

"What?" The coyote seemed genuinely confused like Ajax had spoken Latin.

"Reynaldo Garcia, he was just here. You know him and so do I. He gave me some photos a little while ago, gruesome shit. I think you gave them to him and he gave them to me."

The coyote's eyes roved around in their sockets trying to adjust to the sea change in the conversation. As he did, a Miami prowl car cruised by, the two cops maybe having sensed some trouble. Ajax gave them a smile and a wave. The coyote eyed them.

"Go ahead, *puto*. We'll tell them about your missing cargo."

The coyote turned away and the cops rolled on. Ajax was certain that Gladys was right about him.

"The pictures, the dead body. Where'd you get them from?"

The coyote made a show of rolling his shoulders, all nonchalant, but Ajax knew he was just making sure no one could overhear.

"I got a fax."

Ajax nodded like he was inspecting him for honesty, but really he had to think for a moment to recall what a fax was—he remembered his ex-wife had one, those papers rolling out of the phone. He guessed you could send a photo over it.

"From who?"

He shrugged. "Friends. Reynaldo told me to check around, some redheaded gringo. I got those photos this morning. Passed them along as asked."

"From who?"

"Look, man, I don't know. The people who hook me up with . . . my clients. I don't know where they got it from, I haven't been in El Salvador for ten years. Reynaldo asks, I pass it along, they pass it back. A fax is what I got, I gave it to him."

Ajax gave him the dead-eye stare. It was a trick he'd picked up in the old days in the mountains interrogating captured enemies: you look them in the eye while thinking of someone you'd killed. It never failed. The coyote swallowed.

"You heard what I said about them refugees."

"Hey I . . ." The coyote reconsidered. "Yes. I heard."

Inside the café a waiter nodded to the restroom when he saw Ajax scanning for Gladys. He heard her sobbing through the closed door. He tried the knob and opened the door a crack when he found it open. Inside Gladys had her shirt off, wearing only a black bra. She'd ripped open the paper towel and soap dispensers, filled the sink with them, and was frantically scrubbing herself. She was covered in soap from fingernails to shoulders whispering, "Get off me, get off me, get off me."

Ajax quietly shut the door. What had been soiled by Krill could not be cleansed with soap and water.

14

Gladys worried about the manatees. She sat on the deck of her mother's home in Coral Gables watching the boat traffic in the late-afternoon light and wiping down her hands with a moist towelette. She tore the little package three-quarters open, removed the towelette, and used her right hand to clean her left. First the fingers, always from tip to base, then the cuticles, under the fingernails, and then the palm and finally the back of her hand. Then she always refolded the towelette as best she could and stuffed it back into its package and then folded the package into as small a square as possible. Then the right. Sometimes once was enough. Sometimes not. She didn't always have time on the fly to do it this way, but here, on her mother's deck, there was always time to try and cleanse herself.

When she'd first arrived to her family's house, or rather, when she'd first ventured out of her darkened room, her mother had told Gladys about the manatees in the channels. Gladys had thought she was making it up: a walrus crossed with a cow and a bit of puppy thrown in! But then one evening, one just like this, Gladys had been sitting on the deck, rubbing herself down with a moist towelette (about the first one, how many ago had *that* been?) when a whiskered head had bobbed out of the water chewing on a stalk of something. It was the most ridiculous living thing she'd ever seen and she'd giggled at the sight. *Giggled!* Then a passing yacht had sent the creature back underwater. As it'd slipped away Gladys had seen the three long scars down its flank, caused, her mother had explained, by boat propellers.

She'd never told anyone about the scarred beast, but she might tell Ajax, if he'd stop staring at the back of her head and sit down.

"You tryin' to burn a hole in my head?"

"Didn't want to interrupt the revelry." He sat down and eyeballed the towelettes. "Mind?"

"Help yourself."

He did and she watched him wipe down his hands and face, his forearms, then his chest and armpits.

"*Puta!* Mami's got a shower inside, you know."

"Sorry. It's how we did it in prison. 'Course the towelettes weren't so moist."

He finished his sponge bath and looked around for some place to toss it. Finding none he folded it up and put it in his pocket. "I'm sorry about today. It was your case. I shouldn't've interfered."

"It's alright. Truth is I didn't mind much seeing you flog that coyote with his own phone."

They sat in silence as the sun slid down—going, going, gone.

"We don't have to go, Gladys. Hell, we got American passports, we could go anywhere."

"Fuck you Ajax-fuck-you-Montoya. Like you're fucking thinking about not fucking going? Fuck you."

Ajax took the towelette out, unfolded it, and wiped his forehead down.

"Okay. I'm going, you don't have to."

"Why?"

"It's a one-man job . . ."

"No! Why are you going? Huh? How much time did you have with her? Three weeks?"

She didn't know why but it infuriated her, his devotion to this dead gringa he barely knew.

"More like three days."

"So?"

It was, Ajax had to admit, a good question, *So what?* How to explain? All his adult life, since he'd joined the Sandinistas at nineteen, had been duty, obligation, and patriotism. *Guerrillero. Comandante guerrillero.* Then Captain Montoya, then major, colonel, and back to captain. Shit, even his marriage to Gioconda had been part of the Revo—the dashing guerrilla and the glamorous compañera.

Amelia Peck had been the one event in his life that had not sprung from duty. The one thing that had surprised him—astonished him. It was time to admit that.

"I need this case, Gladys. You've got a life here." Ajax waved at the waterway. "Family, even a career as a private dick."

"Gross."

"You know what I mean."

"You could have a life here too. You got family in L.A., you're an American citizen, right? You were born here. Things have changed since Reagan. The Bush people aren't so fanatical; look what Teal was able to do. It might take some time but you can get *your* passport back."

"Me?" Ajax laughed. "I never had an American passport. There's no paper on me here. My parents were mostly illegal when I was born. No birth certificate, driver's license, no passport. Maybe some high school transcripts in North Hollywood."

"So, you're a man without a country."

"I got a country, Gladys. So do you. That country has fucked us about, but that bothers you more than me because you've never served in a war." He paused. "Or been married."

She was about to demand he make that link when a motion offshore drew her eye. A little alien face with long whiskers popped out of the water and looked around like a tourist getting his bearings.

She whispered, "Look!"

"What is it?"

"Manatee."

"Oddball-looking thing, like a walrus crossed with a cow and a bit of puppy thrown in."

Gladys's mouth dropped open. "How did you . . ." She caught the mischievous smirk on his face.

"Your sister told me. She says most of them have scars from getting run over by boats."

"Most of them, some worse than others."

"Why don't they just move where there's no boats to hurt them?"

"This is their . . ." She caught herself before it slipped. But there it was.

The gorgeously silly creature bobbed on the surface, seemed to have found its bearings, then dived away. They watched the spot where it had submerged. Both of them alert now to how the liquid membrane of the water concealed all sorts of comings and goings from miles away. Gladys knew the manatee would not be back that night. Nor would it leave its home, despite the dangers.

"So young Peck's not dead," she said.

"Seems so."

"So it's a missing persons case."

"That it is."

Gladys tore open another moist towelette and gave her hands a thorough going-over.

"Think we can pull it off?"

"Fifty-fifty."

"Finding young Peck or getting out alive?"

"Fifty-fifty the former, sixty-forty the latter."

"I'd give us better odds than that."

"Really?"

"Yeah." She stood up. She really was ready to go. "We're a good team."

"Said the traumatized obsessive-compulsive to the homicidal catatonic."

She held out another moist towelette and for a moment Ajax took one end while she held on to the other. She studied his face in the vanishing light—night coming on like a line of skirmishers leading an army of stars onto the battlefield. That face, *Saint Ajax*. He wouldn't not go, and so she couldn't not go.

Ajax packed a few things into a suitcase. He'd been careful not to buy a brand-new kit. The suitcase was borrowed from Gladys's sister. He'd bought used clothes on Calle Ocho, using Reynaldo Garcia Gavilan as a model, *estilo cubano*—guayabera shirts, cotton slacks, loafers, and a Panama hat that he really thought looked fetching on his head. He'd been working a few minutes on peeling back the suitcase lining. He didn't need much space to hide the Needle and the concealment would not stand up to professional scrutiny, but he would not go without the blade, and if they really were VIPs they should sail right through customs in San Salvador.

Gladys's mother had given him the spare room. She'd hardly spoken a word to him since he'd arrived, thinking him, he was sure, as bad an omen as could be imagined. Or maybe she blamed him for what had happened to her daughter.

It was a nice house. Done up with a tasteful mix of Central American and Spanish design. Panamanian rattan chairs, old-forest mahogany from decades ago, Mayan-style pottery from Honduras, and beautifully framed prints by Spanish old masters. On the wall over his bed was a print of a Goya, *The Third of May 1808*, from the Napoleonic Wars. The massacre in Madrid. A clutch of Spanish men, civilians but maybe anti-French guerrillas, stand in a slaughterhouse of corpses. Opposite them a firing squad of faceless French dragoons, muskets leveled, about to shoot. The central figure, clad in white, arms raised, not so much in surrender, it seemed to Ajax, but rebuke or resistance. The last act of a doomed man? Or maybe he was stepping forward to speak for himself and the others, who cower behind him.

Ajax, too, had once believed that it was better to die on your feet than to live on your knees. He'd killed a lot of men, and sent even more to their death, believing that. But looking at the Goya he found nothing heroic in the pose. He wasn't sure why.

He finished packing, drew the curtains on Coral Gables with its manatees and malls, stripped to his skivvies, and slid between the sheets, which filled him with as erotic a feeling as that first banana split had.

Ajax awoke in the dark. Naked. Cold. The sheets off. The Needle in his hand, as naked out of its sheath as he was. The curtains were open and moonlight flooded the room.

And he knew he was not alone.

"So you've finally come."

He didn't have to look, to strain in the pale light to make out who stood at the end of his bed. There was no doubt the boy with the long eyelashes was standing there. Ajax hadn't seen him since the airplane, but he knew he'd come, or maybe feared he wouldn't. But he'd had the feeling when he'd slid the blade out to oil it that the boy would visit, or materialize or whatever ghosts do. He'd rubbed the Needle's long, elegant blade like a lamp and his genie appeared. But this genie was a specter of nightmare—the ghost of a young boy, a soldier, who in death still bore the horrid gash across his neck where Ajax had slit his throat and bled him out ten years before. The front of his fatigues, saturated in blood, appeared as wet with the gore of death as the night Ajax had murdered him.

And Ajax had always thought of it as murder.

Well, in truth, no, he hadn't. He hadn't thought about the boy much at all for years, what with the Ogre's downfall, the Revo's triumph, and that cocksucker Reagan unleashing the Contras on Nicaragua like a pestilence. But of all the killing Ajax had done, God help him, there was only the boy with the long eyelashes whose death had filled him with shame the moment he'd slipped the Needle into his jugular and sliced out.

That had all changed three years ago when Ajax had gotten sober and initially confused his haunting with insanity. The ghost had materialized slowly over a few weeks, appearing first as a formless entity outside Ajax's window, but by degrees he (it?) had taken shape. Until that night in Krill's camp after he and the journalist Matthew Connelly had deliberately been taken prisoner while solving the murder of a coffee grower. Krill had planned an elaborate and gruesome death for Ajax, but the ghost, whom Ajax had assumed had come for revenge, instead came to his rescue. In a trick Ajax still did not want to think too long on, the ghost had appeared in Krill's camp in the dead of night and actually passed the Needle to Ajax. *Put it in my hand!* It still made no sense, but one moment Ajax was tied to a tree and doomed to an auto-da-fé worthy of Torquemada, and the next he held the Needle and had become the Angel of Death. He'd left a dozen butchered corpses behind in Krill's camp.

And the boy had stayed with him until he'd gone into Honduras to get Gladys. Then, nothing, until that night on the plane from Managua.

The boy stood at the foot of the bed, his gaze, it seemed to Ajax, lingering on the painting. Ajax threw back the sheet and dropped his feet heavily to the floor. The cool tile sent a tingle up his legs so he walked to the window, his eyes scanning the night, sweeping left to right and back again. For what? For whatever was there.

"Crazy, right? That's what you think? Crazy?"

Finding no danger outside, Ajax turned to the boy.

"Three years. Was it?" He shook his head. "I can't find them, can't feel them. It's like, it's like chess pieces when the players walk away. Does the earth turn? Or is it just play or not play?"

Ajax retrieved his bag, dropped it on the bed, and slipped into his trousers.

"All that time, it was like sucking water out of a needle. All those months listening to El Gordo talk. And then three days ago—three fucking days ago!—he starts talking murder." Ajax turned to the Goya print and threw his arms out like the figure in white. "Three days ago! And then the next second," he snapped his fingers, "they show up. Horacio, Gladys. Her parents, bearing her letter. Her voice."

Her voice.

He dropped his hands to his sides. "And no more time. Touch the pieces, the game resumes. It's yesterday, in the cathedral. I cut her hair, put some in my pocket." He slipped his hands into his pockets, expecting the orange relic to be there. He looked at the boy's face and for the first time Ajax considered the ghost as a presence, an existence.

"Is that what it's like for you? You wait to be touched, summoned?"

The boy just stared at the Goya print. What did he see? Was it a warning to Ajax? Did the ghost foresee Ajax standing before that firing squad? The boy seemed transfixed by the print, then he got it: "That's you, isn't it? The man in white? I thought it might be me."

Then footsteps in the hallway. A knock.

"Ajax? You ready?"

15

El Salvador, November 2, 1989

El Salvador from above, like all of the Central American land bridge, is an immense green steppe in the rainy season. But as with so much about the country, it is all packed into a too-small place. It is blessed with more rivers, lakes, and water than much of the region, but cursed with more active volcanoes than most places on earth.

Ajax reviewed all this in his mind as his charter plane began its decent into Ilopango Airport outside San Salvador. For luck, or nervousness, he fingered his new American passport and reviewed his cover story. For the sake of ease, or maybe superstition, he'd taken the name Martin Garcia—the same pseudonym he'd used in Nicaragua when traveling with Connelly and Amelia. Gladys had taken Gladys Batista—her phony surname the same as the last dictator of Cuba.

Amigos de America was the front group created by Reynaldo Gavilan back in Miami and Ajax carried paperwork and brochures—repurposed from the plethora of anti-Castro groups in Miami—to further cement the cover story. At almost the last minute Reynaldo, insisting on maximizing their safety, had chartered a smallish Gulfstream jet and filled the belly with "donations for the victims of communist aggression" to be distributed upon arrival.

Ajax had made sure he watched the cargo get loaded. There were barrels of what looked like vitamins, crates of assorted other odds and ends—cold remedies, aspirin, hydrogen peroxide, mouthwash, tooth-paste, some of which were already opened and only half full. The sad look of whatever people had grabbed out of their medicine cabinets and tossed in a donation box. Then there were other crates of toys for the children. He'd opened a few at random and was struck by one in particular: a "Mr. T Water War Toy." It looked like a plastic bust of a black man and the instructions said if you filled him with water and hit him in the face with a wet sponge he would spit water back at you. All you needed was a garden hose and sponges.

Ajax had no idea who Mr. T might be, but he made a mental note to count how many garden hoses he came across in the barrios and refugee camps.

But he didn't begrudge Reynaldo his skinflint ways. He and they knew it was a front. But he did worry his hosts might sniff the miserly nature of the donation.

Ajax studied Gladys who was studying the landscape from her window seat.

"Looks just like home, doesn't it?"

"Everything looks the same from up here." She turned from the window and shut the shade.

"All good?"

"I'm fine, Ajax, good. Just trying to remember about the Spanish."

The accents among Latin Americans were as pronounced, as iden-tifiable, as the English of a New Yorker or a Texan in the States. Cubans were famous for rapid-fire Spanish. Nicaraguans spoke it slower and tended to eat their *S*'s, so that a phrase like, *Asi es, pues*—so it goes—became *Asi e' pue*. They would have to mind that difference.

The captain's voice came over the intercom telling them to buckle up for landing.

Maximiliano Hernández Martínez III had what in El Salvador passed for a blueblood pedigree: his grandfather had been *the* General Max-imiliano Hernandez Martinez, a notorious nut job, a voodoo practitioner, alchemist, and occultist who—regularly during his bloody reign in the 1930s—would strangle the capital in miles of colored lights to fight off the smallpox that just as regularly would kill hundreds in the multicolored glow, leaving San Salvador looking like a plague tent in Santa's Village. It was the general who had launched La Matanza in 1932, the greatest single slaughter of human life in the Americas since Cortez had wiped out the Aztecs. The general's army had exterminated almost the entire Indian population of El Salvador in a matter of months, and only using machetes and bolt-action rifles to do it. When asked by a foreigner about the slaughter, the general, a great believer in reincarnation, had said, "It is a greater crime to kill an ant than a man, for when a man dies he becomes reincarnated, while an ant dies forever."

If you translated it into Latin, Ajax thought, it'd make as good a motto as any for today's El Salvador as well.

But the general was still a hero in his homeland, the same way, Ajax thought as he eyeballed the grandson, Himmler would've been a half-century later had the Nazis won.

And Himmler's grandson might dress as ridiculously as the dandified mosaic of a man waiting for him and Gladys at Ilopango Airport. They'd agreed in Miami that one of the biggest dangers in the mission was being spotted by a journalist on a commercial flight, so they'd chartered this small Gulfstream, courtesy of Senator Teal.

The plane taxied to a stop on the military side of the international airport where Little Max, as Ajax now named him, waited with a small entourage and three Jeep Cherokees with smoke-blacked windows.

"Jesus Christ, would you look at that!" Gladys leaned over Ajax to get a look out the small window. "That him?"

"Gotta be."

He understood her incredulity. Little Max wore his clothes and styles like a map of all the places he had been, but also as proof that he was not some yokel but a sophisticated jet-setter, just like a yokel might line their walls with all the swag they'd bought in airports around the world, but without ever having left the terminals.

Little Max wore a white sport coat just like that cop from the TV show in Miami, only Max's was made of a fine leather, probably European Ajax guessed, and that clung to him in the heat so that Max sweated rivulets down his face behind big sunglasses which screamed Beverly Hills. His hair was done in the perm style Ajax had noticed in Miami, but his pants had a narrow, skinny cut that made Ajax think of Italy for some reason. His shiny shoes—reflecting the tropical sun back into his face so that he really did need those shades— were made by some actual human hands somewhere—London?

Each bit of wardrobe was like a stamp in his passport. Ajax guessed Little Max had been schooled in the States and then topped off at some finishing school in Europe, probably civilizing Switzerland, before coming home exactly as uncivilized as he had left it.

"What the fuck does he think he looks like?" Gladys almost giggled.

"You can take the Himmlers out of Bavaria but you can't take Bavaria out of Himmler."

"What?"

"He only looks like a clown, Gladys. I'd be more encouraged if he actually was more sophisticated."

Their Gulfstream came to a soft stop. The pretty stewardess who'd kept them comfortable and Ajax in cold Cokes unfastened the door and lowered it down to unveil the stairs.

"Be careful with these types, Gladys. He's come to meet some bigshot Miami Cubans, which makes us *cubanos-gringos,* and he's putting on his best to show us he does not feel inferior to us, which shows *us* just how inferior he does feel. Follow?"

"Yes."

"But if we embarrass him, show him just how unsophisticated he is? These types will slaughter you to prove they're as good as you. Follow?"

"He's flamboyant, but also flammable."

They stepped off the plane.

"Welcome my friends, welcome to El Salvador!"

Little Max greeted them with an excess of bonhomie that Ajax would later diagnosis as borderline psychosis. He seized Ajax's hand in a manly crush and engulfed him in a bear hug that left Ajax impregnated with the man's cologne, which was as subtle as his attire. He gave an elaborate bow to Gladys, then planted a kiss on her cheek, which Ajax knew would have her rubbing it down with towelettes at the first opportunity, but on the tarmac she took it in stride.

"We are honored to the depths of our soul to have such guests visit us. How was your flight?"

"Short," Ajax said.

"Ah yes, only two hours from Miami, but as you will see, you have been time traveling as well. My country is two centuries behind yours. Let my men get your things."

And it was his "men" who most interested Ajax. Little Max had an entourage of twelve, bodyguards he was sure, in three Jeep Cherokees and a covered pickup truck. The bodyguards were dressed more sanely than Little Max, but each had a bulge where a sidearm was concealed, and Ajax could see the muzzles of automatic rifles peeking over the dashboards of their Jeeps.

Those Jeep Cherokees with smoked windows were the vehicle of choice for El Salvador's notorious death squads—and were as sure a sign of your demise as the Reaper himself knocking at your door.

Two of the men relieved them of their luggage and led them to Little Max's Jeep. Max got in the front and Ajax and Gladys in the back. From the heft of the door when he shut it, Ajax could tell the Jeep was armored.

"My men will unload your generous gifts and see them safely to the camps." Max smiled.

Ajax was sure he meant refugee camps, or hoped he did.

Little Max kept up a polite patter as they and a second Jeep pulled away. The third Jeep and pickup rolled toward the Gulfstream to unload it. Ajax couldn't see what was in the pickup, but he had the feeling it wasn't empty.

They drove from the military side of the airport, with its rows of American helicopters, gunships, and a handful of newish-looking jets, if Ajax guessed right, all heavily patrolled by soldiers and dogs, to a gate so loaded with iron spikes and sandbagged machine-gun nests it might've been the Gates of Hell. He also noted a large cargo plane with Air America painted on the side. He tapped Gladys's knee so she saw it too.

At the approach of their little convoy the guards snapped to attention and saluted. Max dismissed them with a wave and they rolled through without stopping and were soon doing better than eighty down the highway to the capital. Fast-moving targets are harder to hit.

"We don't have to go through immigration?" Gladys seemed to ask more out of curiosity than concern.

Max turned and smiled. "Allow me to say that I am immigration. These are all you'll need."

He handed them ID cards identifying them as members of ORDEN. Ajax felt Gladys's eyes briefly flick to him and back. He understood. ORDEN, Spanish for *order*, was the original political party all the death squads had united under ten years ago, lorded over by a genuine Prince of Darkness—Roberto D'Aubuisson. But ORDEN had become so blood-spattered, so synonymous with murderous terror, that to actually stand candidates for political office they'd had to change their name to ARENA, Spanish for *sand*.

It wasn't a perfect analogy, Ajax knew, but if ARENA was like the Nazi party, which included as many regular folk as it did psychos, ORDEN was like the SS—only psychos allowed.

It was a testament to how tight their cover was that Little Max thought they would be flattered by the gesture.

"You show these to anyone, with your passports, and you will see what honored guests you are."

Ajax took his and expressed his gratitude, but he was alarmed to see the IDs already had their photos on them. Gladys noticed, too, and gently banged his leg with hers.

"So, you've never been to El Salvador before, eh?"

"No, never had the pleasure." Ajax slipped the ID into his passport.

"Well, why should you have?" Little Max waved, dismissing the entire country just as he had done the airport guards. "If I couldn't get to Miami three or four times a year, I'd blow my brains out." He produced a .44 revolver and pointed it at his head.

"You have a visa for the States?" Ajax meant it as a pop quiz for Little Max.

"Oh no, I have a green card."

And there it was. A flash of pride at having that most coveted of objects—the American green card. It was a function of the highly confused Central American psyche. In a certain class of people one's loyalty to one's own country was tempered with a desire to ditch the poverty and the violence of your *patria*, no matter how high your status, for a green card that guaranteed you entry to America, no matter how low your status there would be.

The Contras in Nicaragua were the same way, or at least the leadership in Miami and Honduras were. Play the gringos' game however they wanted it in exchange for unimpeded access to El Norte. And if the gringos' best-laid plans went south? You just had to up stakes and go north. But how loyal could you be to a cause from which you had a first-class ticket out? The foot soldiers didn't have such a pass. People like Krill, they had to stay and die—either in battle or in the revenge killings after defeat. Their leaders were all guaranteed a seat on the last plane out.

The Jeep slammed to a stop, the driver violently applying the brakes. Ajax saw a roadblock ahead. A bus was pulled over and a platoon of soldiers seemed to be inspecting IDs. Several of them aimed their M16s at the Jeep. There must have been fifty people crammed on the aging bus, its roof packed with their meager possessions. The passengers now lined the road, families huddled together, others standing in groups of three or four, all of them seeming to not want to stand alone. Some were country folk bringing goods to the city—canvas bags on the roof held dry goods, bags of corn, at least a dozen cages with chickens and a few of ducks. One family must've been pig farmers as each member held a piglet or two.

The soldiers wore basic green fatigues with baseball caps. Not regular army, Ajax thought, maybe National Guard. They were fanned out around the bus, about half of them covered the passengers, the rest faced away from the bus, toward the dense foliage that grew down the hills to the roadside. By ones and twos the soldiers checked identification, asked questions, then sent them back on the bus. None of the civilians made eye contact with the soldiers.

Little Max made a gesture to his driver who inched forward. An officer approached as Max lowered the bulletproof window. He flashed an ID that made the officer snap to attention and wave them on.

Little Max grunted and turned to his guests, a little embarrassed by the sight.

"The communists try to infiltrate using our public transportation, weapons, explosives, operatives."

He rolled the window back up. As the Jeep made its way slowly around the scene they came to the punch line: in front of the bus, lining the roadside, a half-dozen souls knelt on the ground, their foreheads touching the pavement, thumbs tied behind their backs, as if awaiting a beheading.

But it was an unmistakable calling card—for all the killing done in Central America, only the Salvadorans had perfected this method of controlling people—a thin but sturdy cord tying the thumbs together behind the back was as secure as steel handcuffs. But it was not used merely to subdue a single suspect, but an entire nation. Thumbs tied behind the back was Terror's calling card as surely as the guillotine had once been. If one member of your family turned up dead with thumbs tied, it meant your entire family was covered in dust.

Three men and three women were trussed like turkeys. From the looks on the faces of a gaggle of children, Ajax knew some of them were parents, some traveled solo. But he knew they were all bound for the boneyard.

They drove on in silence for a while. Ajax could not help but scan the terrain. It was a lot like home, he thought. Verdant forests growing down the slopes of the hills right to the roadside. Perfect for ambushes. The many streams running down the slopes were strewn with trash, but the roads were in much better condition than home. Billboards lined the highway advertising far more merchandise and services than Nicaragua had seen in years. Shit, Managua hadn't even seen a billboard in ten years! Let alone the supermarkets, car dealerships, and beer these advertised. El Salvador was the bloodiest place in the hemisphere, he thought, but compared to Nicaragua's grinding poverty it was a virtual cornucopia of consumer goods.

It was a hell of a choice: blood or Budweiser.

"So," Max broke into Ajax's thoughts, "what is your agenda?"

Ajax felt Gladys stiffen imperceptibly at his side, but she jumped right in. "We'd like to see some of the victims of FMLN violence, distribute the gifts we brought, do some fact finding, maybe even a little tourism. I hear you have some wonderful artisans here."

"Oh yes, our Indians are fairly famous in Central America for their little crafts, pottery, primitive paintings," Max said as if talking about an idiot savant cousin.

But Ajax knew *our Indians* were mostly famous for being slaughtered so regularly over the years they'd abandoned their culture, even their language, as a survival tactic. None would even *admit* to being indigenous anymore.

"We need to resume our tourism," Max said. "You know we have wonderful beaches here. El Salvador used to be part of the hippy trail, did you know? Some of the best surfing in the region, surfers and hippies used to come here in droves in the early seventies." He turned to the backseat and gave them a conspiratorial wink. "I used to hang out with them, smoke pot, drink beer. It was wonderful!"

"You'll have to take us!" Gladys, Ajax was relieved, seemed to really be getting into character.

"Oh," Little Max gave a dismissive wave, seeming to chase away the memory, "no one goes there anymore."

And Ajax knew why. When the latest round of slaughter had begun in the mid-seventies the death squads used the main surfer beach, Playa del Rey, as a dumping ground. Once the surfers had to dodge decomposing bodies with their thumbs tied behind their backs, they had decamped.

They sped along the *carratera* for a while, but when they came to a roundabout with signs pointing to the city center, they did not turn. Ajax's stomach did a little backflip.

"Max? What hotel are we at?"

Max turned on them, grinning like that Cheshire pussy, only Max's incisors were a bit more pronounced.

"Oh you're not going to a hotel."

Ajax and Gladys successfully failed to register their mutual alarm at this.

"I thought we were going to the Camino Real." Gladys's voice did not waver.

"*Por favor!* My friends, the Real is full of *journalists*." He said it like he was talking about venereal disease. "They're *all* terrorist sympathizers. And what with their scandalous gossip about us and their whore mongering the Real is no place for such friends as you."

"Then?"

"You're staying with me!"

"Of course we are."

"But I have one other surprise for you."

Ajax watched Gladys slip a moist towelette out of her bag. Ajax placed an affectionate hand on Max's shoulder.

"That sounds great, Max. But we've got to stop by the embassy first. We've brought some personal items from Miami, family things, you know. Just take a minute."

16

In San Salvador, Ajax noticed, poverty, like shit, seemed to roll downhill.

They'd entered the capital from the southeast and gunned the Jeep along rutted roads through several poor barrios where the certainty of the country was on display in the bullet-pocked walls and deadly graffiti—deadly in that the penalty for spray-painting rebel slogans was death. As soon as they neared the center of the city all the streets inclined up: the houses, streets, stores, and people all becoming better-off, tidier, neater, cleaner as they rose, Ajax thought, out of the poverty if not the shit.

The embassy of the United States of America in San Salvador was much like the mission itself: a fortresslike, eyeless, blockheaded-looking thing smack in the middle of town with a constant "Fuck you, who cares?" snarl of traffic snaking around the cordon of blocks barricaded to everyone but the Americans and their exclusive guest list.

The only upside Ajax could see was that the security ring created a kind of concrete park that had been taken over by vendors, some of whom, he knew, had to be spies.

The cordon seemed impregnable, but all Max had to do was roll down his window and he was waved through. Still, Ajax thought, the detour had put Max off his game, deflated his manic bonhomie. When he made no move to follow them in, Ajax and Gladys went to the gate. There were two—one clearly for the consular offices where dozens of

Salvadorans waited in the sun for a chance at a visa. The other led directly into the main building. They milled around outside the gate, the sounds of the Stars and Stripes flapping overhead in a heavy breeze.

"What're you thinking here, Ajax?"

"His not taking us to a hotel kind of threw me."

"Me too! He's gonna take us to his house?"

"Yeah. Let's get seen by someone first, eh? What'd Reynaldo say? Michaelson? Political officer?"

"He'll vet our cover."

"True, but if there's been a leak, let's find out now."

The inside of the embassy was a perfect 70 degrees and quiet as a church, owing to the bombproof glass. One wall of the main lobby was dominated by a mini-exhibition of Jasper Johns's paintings of the American flag. Another wall had a big COMMUNITY NEWS bulletin board. Ajax figured the suits and ties had to be embassy employees. The few Marine guards wore sidearms but there was no obvious sign that the embassy was a prime target in the dirtiest war in the Americas. The Marine at the main gate had not given them a second look once they'd produced their passports. But the vehicles entering, he'd noticed, were searched thoroughly. Car bombs were the worry here.

Skip Michaelson was absurdly young to be an office manager, Ajax thought, let alone a political officer at the second-largest American diplomatic mission in the hemisphere. Maybe they wanted them that way—young, unmarried, and unmarred by too much experience in the field. But the large closet-like office seemed to signal his status.

Ajax found him and his diplo-speak easy to read.

"Gladys Batista and Martin Garcia." Michaelson read off their passports. "Welcome to El Salvador."

Your passports are brand new is what Ajax heard.

"Thank you. Reynaldo suggested we check in when we arrived."

"Reynaldo. Yes. A good friend, I often see him in Miami."

Another Cuban busybody trying to complicate my job.

He returned their passports.

"I can't tell you how glad I am to see you."

What the fuck are you doing in this war-torn shit hole?

"People don't realize from reading the news that El Salvador's number one problem is handling the internally displaced. It is a humanitarian issue."

We got the army to stop trying to murder everyone, but they won't stop burning down their villages.

"So your gifts will be doubly appreciated."

Band-Aids for bullet holes, great idea.

"But you have some assistance here, I hope?"

"Yes," Gladys jumped in. "Maximillian Hernández is sponsoring us."

Michaelson smiled but folded his arms over his chest, a defensive gesture Ajax knew from his cop days. "Oh, Max! I know Max, everybody does. He's quite a card."

He's quite a psychopath.

"He's from a very old and venerable family here."

A long line of psychopaths.

"We like to register visitors; what hotel are you at?"

"We're staying with Max . . ." Ajax let the statement trail off.

"Oh great! I've been to Max's, he throws great parties."

Lock your bedroom doors.

Michaelson checked his watch and opened his wallet. "So, your mission is unofficial, but if there is anything I can do, take my card and be sure to give me a call in a day or two, let me know how it's going."

Do not get killed on my watch. Please!

They shook hands. Ajax studied Michaelson's face. There was no sign he knew other than he let on.

Michaelson led them back to the lobby. "You are good Samaritans and your mission will be welcomed by the people."

Distribute your toys and go home.

"And if I may . . . Be sure to carry your passports at all times. And, if it comes up, with people you don't know . . . maybe don't mention you are Cuban."

Everybody hates you.

Ajax and Gladys stood in the lobby a moment. Gladys let out a sigh.

"I feel better."

"Me too."

"Max's?"

"Yeah, let me see if they've got a map of the city first. We need to get oriented."

Ajax found a vivacious Salvadoran woman behind a desk while Gladys wandered over to the community board. She had only a tourist map, six years out of date, but Ajax used it to track their journey in from the airport. San Salvador was about fifteen miles from the coast—if things went south, that'd be their best bet. He memorized the names of towns and routes down to the coast, and studied the map until he felt his dead reckoning on the run could get them there.

Then the hairs on the back of his neck stood up, or bristled like a hand had passed over them. Ajax turned to find Gladys staring a hole into his head. He checked the lobby, could find no immediate threat, then treaded as nonchalantly to her as he could.

"What?"

She mouthed the word, *Peck.*

Ajax scanned, found nothing. *Where?*

She nodded to the bulletin board behind her and stepped aside.

And there he was.

Or not.

Affixed to the board was a full-color poster.

MISSING SINCE OCTOBER 31. LIAM DONALD-SON. AMERICAN CITIZEN. DOB 9/22/68. 6'1" 185 LBS. LAST SEEN AT HOTEL ESPERANZA.

There were several phone numbers, American and Salvadoran. And in the middle a clear head shot of a lanky, rather thoughtful-looking young man with almost comical red/orange hair and pasty white skin.

But not a freckle to be seen.

The shot was a medium close-up, Ajax thought, a college graduation. The boy was clearly in some kind of blue gown, and Ajax could detect over his shoulder an ivy-covered building. The eyes looked straight into the camera, an easy smile curled the lips and crinkled the blue eyes. The face in this photo was as clear and open as the face in the other photo had been pulped and dead. He pushed aside the image of that latter face before his mind could supply the sound track to the excruciating death Liam Donaldson had suffered.

"Copy down those phone numbers, Gladys, but, you know, don't appear to be. Then go ask that pretty Salvadoran if she's got an American phone book. Find out where the two-one-nine area code goes to."

Ajax studied the face, knew that face—that type. He'd seen it often enough over the years in Nicaragua: the earnest American tourist with unlined face who wishes to embrace the world, the other, and fully expected their earnestness to be returned. It was a safe enough bet in Nicaragua, the Sandinista revolution *loved* tourists. And the worst you could expect back was a picked pocket and loosened bowels. Ajax did a quick scan of his tourist map—all the major hotels were listed and marked.

Gladys returned. "Two-one-nine is Indiana. What're you thinking?"

"I think the odds on young Peck being alive just went up."

"This is the guy in Reynaldo's photos?"

"Gotta be. No freckles. Look at the picture, he's graduating college. There's no Hotel Esperanza on the tourist map, so he's traveling cheap, saving money while backpacking through Central America."

"Backpacking? *Puta madre.*"

"Don't get me started on the naïveté of gringos."

"Why didn't you ask Michaelson about Peck?"

"He's too low level. And be glad we didn't."

"Why?"

"Two gringos looking like that go missing almost on top of each other? Coincidence is too small a mule to pack that."

"So?"

"So let's not keep Max waiting."

17

The rest of their ride was fairly quiet. Max seemed a little piqued, as if he'd been ditched by his friends. The only communicating had come when Gladys had dug a pen and paper out of her purse and scratched, "If not coincidence, what?" Ajax had made a sympathetic but otherwise helpless gesture with his hands. Their hope for a short ride and the privacy of their hotel rooms had been dashed and there was nothing to it but to play their roles.

The driver had made a right turn and they'd been going up a fairly steep hill for several minutes, the homes, streets, and sidewalk traffic becoming increasingly upscale as they rose toward barrio Escalon, the tony part of town where Little Max kept his lair. But they'd passed through Escalon and were nearing the edge of the city, high up the hill. The houses here were few and the driver finally slowed in front of a long white wall encasing what must be a very fine house, if the iron gates and gun towers were anything to go by.

At some unseen signal, or just Max's presence, the iron gate rolled back and the Jeep rolled in. The area beyond the gate was crowded with vehicles, mostly armored Jeeps, but a few Beemers and Mercedeses. More than a score of drivers and bodyguards milled around.

"Surrrrrrrrrprise!!!" Little Max was newly ecstatic. "Anyone who is anyone is here for a little reception we planned for our VIPs."

"A party?" Gladys did not do well hiding her disappointment.

"A reception. A small affair."

Ajax guessed there'd be almost a hundred people inside, figuring two to four per vehicle.

"Max, you shouldn't have." Gladys meant it to the very depths of her soul.

"Everyone who is anyone is here to meet you."

In a Central American country not in the grip of psychotic civil war that would've meant the local celebs—TV reporters, talk-show hosts, intellectuals, a few bearded poets, and alcoholic writers. In El Salvador, Ajax knew, it meant bloody-minded colonels and generals, the death squad Charlies, as Reynaldo had called them back in Miami.

The scene reminded Ajax of a film he'd watched playing on the one television back at Kilometro Cinco. A Mafioso movie where all the big gangsters arrive for a wedding.

"Thank you, Max, this is wonderful." He knocked Gladys's knee with his own.

"Yes, thank you."

Max's house was meant to be lavish, with marble floors and Grecian columns. But as the three of them entered to smiles, too-firm hand-shakes from the men, and air kisses from the women, Ajax noticed the house was more bombproof than palatial: more money had been invested in walls and bulletproof glass than actual marble. Max escorted them through the entryway into a large *sala* that looked as if it had been decorated from a catalogue—lots of white furniture with big white paper ball sculptures and white vases with white-tipped pussy willows. *Where the fuck does he get pussy willows from in El Salvador?* Max led them through tall glass doors to a lawn with a pool and a to-piary sculpted, it seemed, by a nearsighted child with a DIY kit. There was a dancing bear with the snout of a cow, a ballerina whose arms seemed longer than her legs, and a frog that looked like it was mating with an enormous flowerpot.

Somewhere an unseen DJ spun a song by Gloria Estefan and the Miami Sound Machine.

Little Max dispensed with the lesser introductions and led them to several tables nearest the pool, where the dons sat. The button men were scattered farther back along the high rear wall topped with razor wire. There were two squat guard towers at either end of the wall, manned, Ajax noticed, by gunmen in civilian dress.

"Caballeros!" Max called out. "Let me introduce our new friends from Miami. This is Martin Garcia and Gladys Batista."

None of them stood, it was clear they felt they had more pressing business than meeting these two fucking *cubanos-gringos* from Miami.

"This is Colonel Benivides, head of our Treasury Police. The oldest uniformed service in our country." Max said the latter like it was the greatest of compliments. Ajax knew the Treasury Police, Policia de Hacienda in Spanish, was the worst of a bad and bloody lot. They had begun as just that, a private militia raised on the massive coffee haciendas that dominated most of the fertile land in a very fertile country. The PH—*pay achay* in Spanish—had begun as private gunmen used to maintain the literally feudal conditions on the big haciendas, and to slaughter at will anyone who sought to bring the miserable campesinos into the nineteenth century, let alone the twentieth. Somewhere along the way someone had put them in uniform and organized them at the national level: the better to maximize their violence. Like adjusting a magnifying glass to focus the sun's rays into a single beam to train on a line of ants.

Ajax held out his hand. "*Mi coronel.*"

Benivides had barely looked up, but when Ajax used the proper form of military address, the colonel stood and offered his hand.

"*Bienvenidos.* You were military?"

"No, *mi coronel,* but my father served in Cuba, before the communist takeover."

"Then he was on the losing side."

"He was, but he gave his life for that loss."

That had the desired effect. These officers clearly had no use for these Cubans, but they respected men who died in combat, and their offspring. They all stood and shook hands with Ajax.

"Gladys is related to President Batista, who that pig Castro drove out."

This, too, impressed the officers.

"He was my grandfather's brother."

She, too, was rewarded with a greeting somewhat warmer than arctic.

"So," Benivides said, "you have come to give presents to our people?"

Crooked smiles broke out on the faces of the others. He'd addressed Ajax but Gladys took a half step forward.

"Relief supplies for the refugees of communist terrorism."

"There are no refugees, the communists kill them." That from another of the officers, which drew smiles from the rest.

"She means," Max stepped in, determined to get everyone back on script, "the displaced people in the *refugee camps*."

A palette of blank stares.

"Of course," Benivides finally said. "The refugee camps."

"Come, my friends," he took Gladys and Ajax by the elbow, "let me introduce you around."

He steered them away, Ajax thought, toward others who might get the story straight. Because if they did see any "refugees" they would be those poor bastards whose villages had been emptied to make free fire zones in the countryside.

"Maximiliano!" Benivides called out. "You unloaded their supplies?"

"Of course, Colonel."

"And that's all done?"

"Of course."

"Their plane returned safely?"

"We'll know soon enough."

"And El Mayor?"

Max held up his hands like a maître d' promising a guest his table would soon be ready. "He's coming, he's coming."

As Max walked them from one table to another, Ajax wondered who the head of the PH would deferentially call El Mayor—the major—but that gangster movie came back to him. *Il capo di tutti capi.*

After an interminable round of introductions, Max had finally been taken by the elbow and escorted off by an oleaginous-looking underling. Ajax and Gladys finally had a moment more or less alone. They stood before an enormous oil painting, a portrait of Little Max's psychotic grandfather, the *generalissimo* and architect of La Matanza. The portrait might've been painted by the semi-skilled older brother of the child who chopped the topiary—it was not that badly done. They studied the portrait respectfully. It gave Ajax time to scout the rest of the guests.

Now that Ajax thought of it, the same family who did the decorating might have dressed the guests, whose fashion sense ran from the common to the outlandish. Their tailors were either limited to reruns of *Miami Vice* or fashion magazines pilfered from dentists' offices. Oddly, considering the homicidal makeup of the crowd, Ajax felt a twinge of something, some feeling—regret? A lament of some kind—as he surveyed the scene. These people were important in their own country. And yet when they came together for a celebration, what did they have? The salsa music was from Miami or Colombia, the country and western from Mexico, the fashion leeched from whatever gringo vein was available. But nothing of their own, he noted. Anything organic, indigenous, had long ago been abandoned as Indian and so too racially impure, or peasant and so too culturally humble, or too artistically subversive. All that was left was this mishmash of self-loathing and imperial mimicry.

"Jesus Christ, I'm a nervous fucking wreck," Gladys whispered.

"It's cool, we're cool. You did good, Gladys, you're doing good. We're doing good."

"I feel like Daniel in the lion's den."

Ajax had a discreet look around. "More like the hyenas' den."

"What's the difference?"

"Lions kill and then devour. Hyenas start eating before the prey is dead."

"Thanks, *Martin,* that settles my nerves." She squinted at the painting. "Jesus, would you look at that!"

"What?"

"The back of his hand."

The painting showed the *generalissimo* in uniform, half his weight in gold medals on his chest. One hand rested on the saber at his side, the other on a book with a title in Latin. Now Ajax saw it, on the back of each hand was a small, faint circle, just slightly darker than the flesh.

"The stigmata."

Gladys snorted. "The butcher of El Salvador as *el salvador.*"

"Give thanks and praise for it. Works in our favor."

"How?"

"No one, Gladys, is easier to fool than the already self-deluded."

"Okay."

Ajax was already back reconnoitering the guests. "What do you see with them?" He directed her gaze to the far side of the pool where twenty or so men and women sat at tables at the farthest reaches of the party, like barracuda scrumming at the edge of a school of tiger sharks.

Gladys scanned them. "Bodyguards, lieutenants, midlevel minions. Wives, girlfriends. Couple of professional girlfriends."

"Good. Now, pick one of the men, any one, count how long it takes for him to touch his nose."

Gladys did. After a moment she almost giggled, it seemed some kind of party game was on, as one after another, over a minute at most, the men would touch their noses and sniff.

"I see it."

"What is it? Sniffles? Summer colds?"

"Shit. *Cocaína?*"

"Got to be. See the guy in the black shirt and skinny tie? Watch him, watch him!"

Gladys clocked him as Ajax narrated. "Hand under the napkin, napkin to the nose. *Achoo!* Out he blows. Big sniff back in."

"*A la gran puta.*"

"High as monkeys in the canopy."

They watched as Monkey Man made another pass with the napkin. As he did his "girlfriend" made a reach for it and he deftly struck her in the face with his elbow—right on the nose. It was, Ajax saw, a practiced move by a veteran batterer.

"I'd like to kneecap that fucker."

"Take it easy, Gladys." But he was glad of her anger. She'd done well so far, held strong, and he'd not seen her use a Handi Wipe since they'd landed. Controlling that compulsion said a lot for her. "You're not armed."

"Wait, I'm not? Meaning you are?"

"Never leave home without it."

"What if they find the Needle on you?"

"You kidding? In this crowd? I could sit and talk shop with these fuckers for hours about it. Probably get offers to buy it. Look, look . . ."

Ajax nudged her gaze back to Monkey Man. He'd given his napkin to the girlfriend who was using it to staunch a tiny stream of blood leaking from her nose. She rose and left the table.

"Follow the girl."

"What?"

"To the bathroom, she's gotta be going there. Talk to her."

She got it. "Okay."

Ajax spent the next ten minutes making a slow circuit around the party, meeting and greeting, air kissing, and exchanging pleasantries about nothing. Few of the guests seemed to know who he was or why he was there, considering he was the alleged guest of honor. Every few minutes he'd check the table of officers, who just as frequently checked their watches. Someone was late.

He made his way vaguely back to the garish portrait. Strangely, Ajax felt disappointed. He and Gladys had concocted a sack of stories about Miami and how anxious the Cuban community was to make common cause with their Salvadoran cousins.

"You must be the Cuban."

Ajax started, as if someone had read his secret thoughts. He turned to find himself caught in the gaze of a remarkably attractive woman. She was tall for a Salvadoran, with the black hair and eyes of Indian blood but the pale skin of Europe. But her nose and cheeks gave her face a Semitic look. The parts seemed to belong to different countries, but her looks incongruously came together, the way Central America would if all the borders came down. She seemed amused, and also, somehow, familiar.

Sphinx, Ajax thought, for some reason.

"I didn't mean to ambush you," she said in flawless English.

"No, that's, that's quite alright. I'm . . ."

"Martin Garcia, from Miami, bearing gifts for the dispossessed of the earth."

"Why, yes."

"And Gladys Batista is . . ."

"Somewhere around here."

"I am Jasmine Maximiliana Lourdes Montenegro de Hernandez. Also known as Max's cousin."

That's why she looked familiar.

"A pleasure to meet you. So you are granddaughter to . . ."

"The *generalissimo,* yes," she gestured to the portrait, and held up her hands, "but no stigmata."

Ajax could not help but smile, it was the first light moment he'd had since touching down at the airport. He felt himself breathe for the first time.

"You and Max are close?"

"Well, we grew up together. I spent most of my time at his house when we were children. His father was"—she leaned in conspiratorially—"much more liberal than mine. Not politically of course. But Uncle Max always said everyone, and by *everyone* he meant our class, should learn to read and write, ride and shoot. It was a lot more fun at his house."

"And did you? I mean, ride and shoot?"

"Oh yes! Uncle Max was an old cavalry man who never accepted the mechanization of his trade. Do you know he rode a horse into the Soccer War?"

Ajax laughed. The Soccer War was certainly the most absurd of Central America's many conflicts. It was a brief but bloody crusade between Honduras and El Salvador in the late sixties, sparked by the disputed outcome of a soccer match. El Salvador lost the game, but won the war.

"He didn't survive. The horse, I mean. Uncle Max died in his bed."

"Are you any good, a shot?"

She cast another conspirator's glance about the room. "Cousin Max long ago stopped competing with me on the pistol range. Now he has," she gestured around the room, "others to do his shooting."

It was an odd point to make and an awkward silence settled on them, broken by a girlish giggle which made Ajax smile a real smile.

"Once, I haven't told this in ages, but the first time I fired a pistol I'd snuck into Uncle Max's office. He had this old revolver, a very heavy one from the American Civil War, it had six bullets but also fired a small shotgun shell . . ."

"A Le Mat."

"Yes, you know it."

"My father taught history."

"Well the damn thing was so heavy I had to use two hands, and I was just playing, you know, cowboys, Powpowpow! And it went off! BOOM! But I swear I never even touched the trigger!"

She giggled that girlish giggle and Ajax found himself chuckling along, out of more than politeness.

"Well, the servants went screaming out the doors, throwing themselves to the ground, they thought the Indians had risen again! But Uncle Max came charging in, you know, charge to the sounds of the gun!"

"He must've been very angry."

"I think more scared. He was so relieved to see I'd only shot the furniture and not myself. And let me tell you it was very nice furniture, Max's mother"—she gestured at the décor—"was a much better decorator than her son is."

"No spankings?" *That* came out differently than he'd meant it.

She smiled—the sphinx in her smiling too.

"No. He just very gently took the pistol from my hands, surveyed the damage to his divan, patted me on the head, and said . . ."

She paused, the sphinx look again, inviting him to solve her riddle. And suddenly Ajax understood—and the air went out of him for a moment. "Mata Sofá."

"Mata Sofá," she whispered.

"Couch killer."

"Couch killer."

Their contact.

He wasn't sure how long he'd stood there, dumbfounded, maybe only a moment. But long enough for her to lean in close and touch her finger to his chin. "Martin, your mouth is hanging slightly open."

She shut it for him alright.

"Where is Miss Batista?" she said, louder, back in the mood of the party. "Point her out before our guest of honor gets here."

"I thought that was us?"

"Oh it is, Martin, but all these people would not linger this long just for two *cubanos-gringos*, if you'll pardon my candor."

Just then Ajax spotted Gladys coming out of the toilet with the battered girlfriend, who, he noticed, slipped something into Gladys's hand before giving her a brief embrace. Ajax could've sworn she'd pinched Gladys's nipple. "There's Gladys. I'll introduce you." Ajax took her elbow.

"She's pretty. But no. You tell her. I'll meet her tomorrow, I'm staying here too. Max keeps a room for me. I'll insert myself into your itinerary. We'll distribute your *relief supplies* and get the other matter taken care of as well."

"You certain? Max seemed pretty determined to escort us."

"Max, frankly, has bloodier fish to fry than you two. He doesn't like to mix with common people, particularly refugees. He'll mostly want to take you around to the nightclubs and show you off. I'll arrange for the days to be ours, you'll have to endure the nights with him."

"Did you know him?" Ajax leaned in close enough to smell the perfume in her hair, which made him think of a dry, clean place, like a desert. *Sphinx.* "Peck, James Peck?"

For the first time her eyes cut left and right—cautious, careful. "Know him? *Everybody* knew him. But which one? James Peck? Jimmy? Jaime? Santiago? I knew him. So did Max."

That struck Ajax as odd. The lefty firebrand and a doughy death squad Charlie like Max? Outside, there was a clamoring, the big iron gate rolling back, people began to get up, move toward the foyer. Someone shouted, "*Viene el jefe!*"

"That's my exit. I can't stand the man, frankly. He slobbers over my hand thinking he's a chevalier."

"Who?"

"El Mayor, of course." She pecked him on the cheek. "Ciao."

Now Ajax understood. The Mafia movie came back. All these people had not been waiting for him and Gladys, they'd been waiting for the godfather to finish dispensing favors and come out to the party. The real guest of honor was the *don of dons,* Roberto D'Aubuisson. The actual and literal father of El Salvador's death squads—the country's worst butcher since the *generalissimo.*

Ajax beelined toward Gladys, thinking they should be presented together. Thinking the sphinx had given him the first clue, the first thread to pull on. *Everybody knew him.* He scanned the room for Gladys, excited to tell her the game was on, when his roving eyes fixed upon a face that stopped him dead in his tracks. Literally, dead.

Between him and Gladys his eyes met the eyes of the boy with the long eyelashes. Ajax stopped so quickly he stumbled a step. He checked left and right to see if anyone else could see the blood-spattered specter in their midst. But all attention was on the front door, awaiting the great entrance. The boy looked right at him, but otherwise made no move.

The guests erupted into cheers as El Mayor and his entourage made their entrance. Ajax moved away from the crowd, hoping he might draw the ghost away, but the boy stood his ground, yet his eyes tracked Ajax. Gladys was on the far side of the room and he went to her. When he got close, he halted again. The crowd had surged around her to get close to their champion, but she was rooted to her spot, petrified, like Lot's wife. Her face blanched white as salt. White, like she was about to pass out. White like *she* had seen a ghost. *His ghost?* Was that possible? But she was looking in the wrong direction to see the boy.

He stalked closer to her, on full alert, for the first time feeling the Needle strapped to his calf. He was feet away when he finally saw what had so transfixed her—the gorgon she'd looked upon. And when Ajax saw, the sound went out of the world, replaced by the rushing of blood from his head to the bottomless chasm that had opened in his stomach.

It was another ghost.

Her ghost.

And her ghost was as transfixed as she was—mouth open in shock and astonishment.

Ajax dropped to one knee, slid the Needle out of the sheath on his calf, and stood up with it cupped in his hand. As he did, Gladys's ghost blinked its eyes and shook its head. Then the eyes met Ajax's. The bewildered disbelief of before became hatred, as quickly as the dark of night is illuminated by a lightning bolt.

Gladys's ghost pointed a finger as accusing as that other ghost had at Macbeth.

"*Piricuaco!*"

Krill.

18

"Piricuaco!"

Krill's voice rang out like the bell of doom: *Peer-e-cwa-cooooooo!*

It's an old saw that time slows down in combat, and combat had commenced. Ajax grabbed Gladys's arm and rather than run, plunged them into the crowd of people so that Krill's finger would not aim at them. He had a few seconds to save their lives, and they were owed to jargon. *Piricuaco,* the Nicaraguan slang for rabid dog, was the Contras' name for Sandinistas back home. But it was not familiar to Salvadorans, and while the crowd heard the alarm, they did not yet know what, or who, it meant.

So Ajax gave them one they all knew. *"Asesino!* Assassin!"

Bedlam.

The few civilians there bolted at the word, the wives and girl-friends panicked and fled in all directions, their screams drowning out Krill's voice. The hired guns and bodyguards drew pistols and Uzis. Ajax bent low to get lost in the crowd, but Gladys was still so stunned by the sight of her tormentor that Ajax had to grab the back of her neck and force her down and drag her along with him.

Screaming *Asesino!* in the ear-splitting pitch howler monkeys use to warn of jaguars, he made his way through the stampede to the stairs at the far side of the big *sala,* near the *generalissimo*'s portrait. He'd noticed before a hallway he was certain led to the kitchen, and beyond, to the servants' quarters. No matter how high the security in a house like Max's, Ajax knew there had to be a separate entrance for the servants.

He peeked back over the stairs. Order was descending on the chaos. Colonel Benivides and the officers were retreating in order out the door. A dense scrum of bodyguards surrounded El Mayor and was doing the same.

But Krill, fucking Krill, dressed in civvies, holding two .45s, was screaming into the ear of one gunman. He'd lost Ajax and Gladys in the rush, but as soon as he made them understand what was going on . . .

Ajax wouldn't finish the thought, so he turned to Gladys and backhanded her, snapped her head halfway around. Then he held her face.

"Gladys! Live or die, now!"

She blinked her eyelids a million times at near the speed of light as a nasty welt rose on her cheek.

"I'm okay. I'm okay. Whatta we do?!"

She didn't ask how Krill had materialized as surely as Ajax's ghost had, which was a good sign. Then a pistol barrel appeared in his peripheral vision. Monkey Man, the batterer. Ajax was about to open his throat with the Needle when Gladys threw her arms around him.

"Thank God! Please help us, we're the *Americans*! Please save us!"

She kneed him in the nut bag. Ajax caught his pistol as he accordioned to the floor. He had one second to spare, and used it to kiss Gladys on her bruised cheek.

"You're a good man, sister."

Then he fired three shots into the *generalissimo*.

They fled down the corridor to the kitchen. Terrified servants cowered in their rooms. They were moving so fast Ajax almost missed the doorway to a small courtyard and the iron door leading out.

"Stop!"

Ajax whirled, twisting down as he brought the pistol up to bear. For a split second he thought it was *another* ghost chasing them.

Jasmine, in a floor-length white dressing gown, ran down the corridor to them. When she was a few steps away she ripped her gown open, showing her breasts, and stopped before them.

"Hostage."

The sphinx!

"Okay."

He pushed her first into the courtyard to the door, and escape. The door was a solid three inches of iron with a crossbar to secure it. Ajax opened it and reconnoitered the outside. There was a ten-yard wide strip the length of the wall that had been cleared as a free-fire zone, on the far side of which began the dense growth of the tropics. Ajax saw no one in either direction and drew his head back inside.

Jasmine gestured to go up the hill, away from the road, its cars, and armed men. Ajax nodded agreement. Gladys turned her palms up.

"Jasmine, this is Gladys. Gladys, this is Mata Sofá."

"No fucking way."

"Way," Jasmine said. "I'll go first."

The three of them hugged the wall and dashed up the hill toward the edge of the wall, and, hopefully, out of sight of the squat guard tower. But a spotlight hit them, and bullets ripped the ground just ahead of them.

Hope is a fickle cow.

"*Alto! Quien son?*"

Who indeed?

"Don't shoot! It's me. Doña Jasmine!"

Ajax put Jasmine in a choke hold, careful not to hurt her, stepped away from the wall so the guard could see her, and aimed his pistol at the center of the light, knowing that at any second he'd see the small muzzle flash that would be the last thing he ever saw.

And he did. Although the flash was somewhat larger than he'd expected. So large in fact it engulfed the entire guard post which exploded into fire and flying concrete. Then it seemed the small muzzle flash he *had* expected did appear, except all around them and by the dozen. Ajax was certain Krill had rallied the godfather's minions and was lighting them up. He pushed Jasmine to the ground.

"What the fuck!" Gladys joined them eating dirt.

"It's the Farabundos," Jasmine shouted over the gunfire. "They're attacking the house!"

"What?" Things were moving too fast for Ajax.

"They're after El Mayor. Benivides, this is your chance! Up the hill!"

Ajax had questions, but none more pressing than living.

They rose to a squat and ran for their lives.

The fugitives kept slogging up the hillside. After half an hour they'd left the house and the firefight far behind, and their breath too. They panted and sweated, at times having to crawl on their knees reaching out for one handhold after another to ascend the steep hill through the dense undergrowth. But death is a great motivator, life even more so, and they kept on, in silence, to the top.

But Ajax was not silent in his mind. *WHAT THE FUCKING SWEET JESUS MOTHERFUCK JUST HAPPENED!?!?*

Krill? In El Salvador? Turning up at the very same soiree as he and Gladys? And Gladys seeing him? He recalled the look on Krill's face: it wasn't anger, or hatred. The only word that came to mind was— *relieved.*

Krill had actually looked relieved, like seeing someone you thought lost in a fire walk out of the inferno.

And Jasmine. The sphinx. He followed close behind her, her white dressing gown a ghostly apparition in the dark.

Too many goddamned ghosts.

And what she'd said: *the Farabundos are attacking the house.* A strange phrasing. If she was with the FMLN rebels she'd've called them compañeros or *muchachos.* Against them, she'd've said *terroristas.* But Farabundos? It seemed an almost neutral term. Too neutral for a country where social conditions, ideology, or a gun in your face made everyone take a side.

As suddenly as his world had turned upside down, the hill flattened out as they reached the summit. He dropped to his knees, panting hard, the stitch in his side feeling like an appendectomy on the fly. All those months playing catatonic opossum he'd kept his muscles iron hard deadlifting his weight off the plastic chairs or balanced on his toes for hours. But he had the wind of an emphysemic.

He could hear Gladys panting too.

"Gladys?"

"I'm okay, okay. You?"

"If I don't die of a heart attack."

She reached for his hand. "Ajax. You *saw*?"

"I did. I can't explain it."

"God help us, look!" Jasmine called out from the dark and Ajax leaped up, pistol at the ready.

She stood at the rim of the canyon they'd climbed, her ghostly outline in the dark, finger pointing like a phantom. Below them the teeming city of San Salvador, home to a million souls, was in blackout. Firefights could be seen all over the city, dozens of them. Explosions flashed like strobe lights, followed by *Booms!* muffled by the distance. On the ground red tracer bullets split the black, ricocheting high into the air. While from the sky denser streams of red fell as helicopter gunships answered with their own tracers, looking like angry angels peeing death on the city.

"Jesus save us," Gladys murmured.

"The Farabundos," Jasmine said. "It's the offensive. They've begun. The final offensive."

And somewhere down in that cataclysm was young Peck. Dead or alive.

As Ajax watched the combat roil over the city his blood chemistry changed as his lungs finally delivered enough oxygen to his corpuscles.

His heart steadied and slowed as his muscles ceased screaming for sustenance. And a great, deep, malevolent calm settled over him, as dawn settles all the fears of the night. For the first time in three years, Ajax Montoya felt truly at peace. At home.

19

Gladys Darío/Batista fell to her knees and puked. And puked again. For a minute she retched in rhythm to some internal beat: spew, pant, pant, pant, spew, pant, pant, pant. After that minute she stopped and Ajax listened to her catch her breath, a panting steadiness under the staccato sounds of the distant gunfire, and the bass grinding of the helicopters' mini-guns.

"What is *he* doing here?"

He didn't need to ask who.

Ajax squatted next to her. "I do not know. But are you gonna be alright?"

"No! I'm not alright! Jesus Christ, Ajax, it was fucking Kri." She stammered the name, retched one last time. "Fucking Krill! How did he know?"

"About us?"

"Of course!"

"He didn't. I saw his face, he was as amazed to see you as you were him."

She shot him a look as violent as the combat below, but much closer.

"Not like that, but as surprised as you were. The question is, what *is* he doing here at all?" Jasmine stared over her city; Ajax could not read her face in the dark. "Jasmine, when D'Aubuisson came in he had a Nicaraguan with him, a Contra named Krill."

But the sphinx was mesmerized by the faraway chaos.

"Jasmine!" Gladys was up on her feet, angry—at the wrong person, Ajax knew, or hoped—but right now he'd take Gladys angry over any other variety.

"What? I'm sorry, a Nicaraguan? I don't know. Why does it matter now?"

"Because we're . . ."

Ajax slapped her arm to shut her up. "Because we know him and he knows us," he said.

"I'm not following."

"You know we're here undercover."

"To find Jimmy, yes. But, you mean you aren't private investigators from Miami?"

"We are but we have history with that guy, bad history, and if we hadn't gotten away . . ."

"If I hadn't helped you get away."

"If you hadn't helped us get away, we'd be dead right now."

"Or worse." Gladys spat it out.

Ajax knew she was right. "Our cover's blown, and this . . ." He gestured to the city below. "We might not survive the night."

Jasmine turned back to the city where the steady flicker of fires illuminated the night. "None of us might. See down there," she pointed off to the west where they could see a cluster of white explosions and red tracers, "that's the Quartel, army headquarters. And there," another cluster of red and white, "that's the presidential palace, poor Freddy, not even a year in office."

Ajax knew *Freddy* was Alfredo Cristiani, a gray-suited, American-educated banker D'Aubuisson's ARENA party had chosen as a front for last year's presidential elections. He'd won too—not hard when most of the opposition were rotting corpses with their thumbs tied behind their backs.

Freddy. Ajax shook his head. How much damage has been done to a nation's soul when all the devil has to do to win the popular vote is don a smiley-face mask.

"And there," Jasmine pointed to large area in the blackout, "down there is the American embassy. Just go there, or any hotel. The Farabundos won't attack the hotels. You'll find a lot of Americans at the Camino. You'll be safe there."

Ajax and Gladys moved away from Jasmine, still transfixed by the deadly pyrotechnics engulfing her city. Ajax tried to count the days since he'd left Kilometro Cinco, but it was lost in the gap between experienced time and the calendar. "Well, this is another fine mess we've gotten ourselves into."

"I wish I believed in God."

"Why?"

"Then I'd have someone to blame. How do you explain this *inexplicable* coincidence?"

"Karma?"

"Is ours that bad?"

"Mine is, wouldn't think yours was. But Reynaldo did say that back in Miami."

"What?"

"The cease-fire in Nicaragua . . . he said rumor was some of the Contras were out freelancing."

"But why Krill and why here?"

"Krill, 'cause he's Krill. Here? It's where he started."

"What?"

"Back in seventy-nine Krill and his unit were the last of the Guardia to keep fighting. When they were finally cut off they commandeered a fishing boat out of Chinandega, made it across the Gulf of Fonseca. As I heard it, the officer wanted to put into Honduras, Krill didn't trust the Hondos, so he put the officer over the side. The last five days they were without food or water, floating on currents. They washed up here, boatload of corpses. Krill made it. Supposedly he got his start with El Mayor and ORDEN, until the CIA picked him up. He must've told you this?"

"You think I was *listening* to him?"

"No, sorry. But that might be why he's back *here*. Maybe he's undercover too."

Gladys's hand moved through her purse like a snake in a sack of cornmeal. She fished out a towelette, fingered it in such a way that he knew it was her last.

"Ajax, when I saw him . . ."

He could sense more than see the tremblers zigzag through her body.

". . . I froze. He could've shot me and I wouldn't have moved. He could have shot you and I wouldn't have lifted a finger."

"So? You were in shock."

"You weren't."

"I had an early warning."

"How?"

Who?

Boo!

The ghost.

It was not the first time the boy with the long eyelashes had appeared just before trouble. The last time, on a coffee *finca* in northern Nicaragua, he'd woken Ajax the moment Malhora's henchmen had arrived to assassinate him and Gladys. Ajax still didn't know what the ghost wanted, or even if it was a real phantasm or the hallucinations of a failed mind. But he hadn't told Gladys then, and he sure wouldn't confess it now. She was on the verge, on a precipice over a void—she would step back or over. He couldn't bring her back. But neither would he nudge her forward with ghost stories.

Then it hit him: it was *all* just one big ghost story. The boy, Krill, the Pecks. There was no mission, it was still 1986, and he had only opened and closed a single door to be here.

"Ajax? What early warning?"

"Jasmine's right. The embassy and back to Miami."

"Abort the mission? You think I can't handle it? You think I'm afraid?"

"I don't care." He shook his head. "It doesn't matter." His head shaking sped up slightly as all the pieces came together in a centrifugal motion. "You need to go, Gladys. This is all on me."

"What?"

"You asked what Krill's doing here. He's here 'cause I'm here. It's all because of that, because of . . ." He shook his head. "It's still 1986, Gladys. I've been stuck in this eddy of time, pushed up against the bank while the rest of you went on. Think about it: all that time as a somnambulist and it's the Pecks reading Amelia's letter who wake me? Horacio who gets me released? Even El Gordo back at Kilometro Cinco? And this . . ." He plucked the Needle from its sheath on his calf. Its long, elegant, devilish blade as familiar and as repulsive as a goiter on his soul. He flipped the blade and as it spun he knew the steel and rawhide handle would slap flawlessly into his palm as it had ten thousand times before. "I come here, with this, and find Krill?" He slipped it into its sheath without looking at either. "No time has passed. I just closed a door in Managua and opened one here. Young Peck's not the mission. There is no mission. Or unfinished business is the mission. I am the mission. You need to go."

Gladys looked at him a few moments without judgment, like someone waiting for the simultaneous translation to catch up. Then she stuck the still unopened towelette in his face. "Here."

"What?"

"Take it."

"Why?"

"You need it more than I do, you're a fucking hysteric."

The statement was so unexpected it pulled Ajax out of the trance he'd slipped into. "Don't be ridiculous."

"Ridiculous?" She put the towelette back in her purse. "Listen to yourself! 'I'm trapped in an eddy of time.'" For some reason while mocking him, she put her hands by her face and waved her fingers like whiskers, or like Kafka's cockroach would its antennae. "You list all the actors in your little sci-fi story, but what about me? Horacio called *me*. The Pecks came to *me*. *I* took you out of Managua. And *I* am here now. *Listo. En pie.*"

Upright and ready. It made him smile. It was an old saying from the old rebel days. No matter how dog tired, sick, or even wounded, when asked by a commander how you were, it was the only answer. It had become the slogan of an increasingly exhausted revolution.

"But you've had a life, Gladys. You've got a life. Miami, your mother, the missing persons. You need to let the Revo go, let Nicaragua go. Go home. Do what you have to do to get a green card, then your private dick license . . ."

She shoved him so hard he was on his ass before he knew it. Gladys looming over him, her bony fist in his face. "You are such an asshole. Ajax fucking asshole Montoya!"

"Umm. Guys?" Even Jasmine was pulled from her trance watching the ruin of her city.

"I have a life?" Gladys hadn't even heard her. "I do? I go to bed with Krill every night and wake up to him every day. For three years. And you know what? I *am* afraid. Right here and now I am afraid. But I've been afraid for three years and for the first time I'm okay with that. Right here! Right now!"

Her face was only inches from his now. And he saw all the truth of her life there. He reached out and rubbed a smear of dirt off her cheek, but really, he just wanted to touch her.

"You're a good man, sister."

He held out his hand and she pulled him to his feet.

"And you're a good sister, brother."

He brushed of his pants. "You caught me off balance, it's why . . ."

"Yeah I had to push you outta that time vortex."

They looked at each other for far longer than most friendships between a man and woman would allow. Ajax nodded his head. Gladys nodded hers. He held out his hand. She took it.

"So we have a mission, Lieutenant."

"Yes we do, Captain." She counted on her fingers. "Stay alive. Kill Krill. Find young Peck."

"And Liam Donaldson."

"Him too?"

"Somebody dropped him into our laps."

"Okay. But what do we *do*?"

"What do we got? You?"

"My purse," she opened it, "passport, some money, my mother's credit cards."

"Mami gives you her credit cards?"

"Fuck you. Whatta *you* got?"

He searched his pockets.

"Passport, pistol, some cash, maybe fifty U.S." He didn't list the Needle, the same as he wouldn't list two arms and two legs. "And this." He held up the ORDEN ID Little Max had given them. "It's our get out of deep-shit free card. Got yours?"

"Yeah. Wait." She moved closer to see him in the dark. "Get out of deep shit? We're not already in it?"

Ajax took her arm and moved her to the rim of the canyon they'd climbed. "That shit storm down there is the best cover we could have. Without it, granted, Krill would have them all looking for us. But now? Gladys, they don't know which way the tide of battle will go . . ."

"*The tide of battle?*"

"Yes, the tide of battle. It'll be three or four days before it shakes out, maybe a week. In the meantime, chaos. We've got American passports for one side, ORDEN IDs for the other."

Gladys turned her back on him. Surveyed the combat below them. There was no letup in the explosions, the red tracers slicing the black. After a few seconds she held out her hand.

"I get the gun."

He slapped it into her hand like a nurse passing a scalpel to the surgeon. It was a Browning 9mm. She slid out the magazine, checked the load, checked the chamber, put the safety on, and jammed it into her purse.

"I won't be taken alive by him."

"No, you won't."

Gladys seemed to flinch. "I don't mean I want to . . . to . . . you know . . ."

"Yeah, I get it."

"You're sure?"

"Yes, Jesus," he said. "Now, where to begin?"

"Claribel."

"Who?"

"The *puta* at the party. You sent me to the bathroom to talk to her."

"Right."

"She knows Peck, called him *Himmy*. The asshole that hit her?"

"Monkey Man?"

"Yeah, she and Monkey Man partied with Jimmy."

"With that flat-footed gofer? He's a hit man at best. We know Young Peck knows Jasmine, Little Max. They're upper class—parties, soirees—it makes sense. Monkey Man's street-level assassin." Ajax could feel the weirdness of the time vortex slipping away as he stirred his cop's brain. "Good intel. She just volunteered all this?"

"You know, bathroom talk. We exchanged lipstick. I think she's got the hots for me."

"Ooookay."

"You got a problem with that?"

"No! It's just, you know, she's a . . . *puta*?"

"And?"

"Nothing." He looked down the hill to the besieged city. "How do we find her in all that?"

Gladys pulled a slip of paper from her purse. "We could call her."

"You got her number."

"Yeah, I used . . ."

"To be a cop, I remember."

He walked over to Jasmine, rooted to the lip of the ravine they'd scaled, still transfixed by the sounds and sights of destruction. He took her by the shoulders and gently turned her away from the edge.

"Jasmine. We need shelter, a phone, a car, a driver, or a damn good map."

She nodded and waved vaguely over her shoulder. "Doña Estela."

20

Krill explored the ruins of Max's villa looking for a glass of water. The smell of cordite—of combat—was still strong over the place as the first bloodred rays of dawn smeared over the embattled city. Krill was both exhilarated and desolate. The firefight with the Farabundos had been fairly brief, but warm work. The most violence he'd experienced since those treacherous *hijos de putas* in Miami had agreed to the cease-fire with the *piricuacos*. *La cupola,* the leadership. Leaders? Rich, soft pussies with no stake in Krill's war had sat down with the *piris* and decided Krill's war was over.

He stopped under the portrait of the *generalissimo*. Now there was a man, he thought. *Un varón*. A man's man. But those shit-eating sons-of-bitches in Miami? Calero? Chamorro? Robles? Their names were like a stroll through Nicaragua's society pages! Only one of them ever wore a uniform under General Somoza, and he, "Colonel" Bermúdez, had spent the fight against the Sandinistas in Washington, D.C. Civilians. Chicken-shits. And they had all given in to the gringos and signed the peace accords that castrated Krill's army.

"*Mi general.*" He saluted the portrait, saddened to see the old man had taken three bullets to the chest. "Over? They tell Krill his war is over! *A la mierda hijos de puta!* is what I told them. Krill will go back to *his* men and we will go back to *our* war."

He could not tell the *generalissimo* the next part. Could not say it out loud. *They arrested me. Arrested! Put chains on my hands.* And told me I could agree with the cease-fire or stay in Miami in *protective custody*. But it was they who needed protection, he knew it and so did those soft-handed, white-skinned *vendepartrias*. They had sold out Krill, sold out their country. Sold out their souls for green cards.

He knew he'd had to restrain his impulses, so rather than slaughter them all, he'd acquiesced. For the moment. Then taken a bus to New Orleans and a plane to San Salvador, the last refuge of the *varón*.

Krill walked on, turned down a corridor that led to the kitchen; he'd forgotten momentarily about the water. The house was quiet, the servants had fled. The sporadic sounds of combat came from far away. Maybe the Farabundos hadn't known how many armed men would be at Max's party. Their initial attack had been well-executed, he could admire good tactics even from communist shit-eaters. But they had either been undermanned for the attack, or only meant it as a hit-and-run. Less than half an hour after the assault began, they'd fled. There was a handful of dead on his side, mostly the poor bastards outside with the cars or the guys in the guard towers. They'd found no Farabundo dead. Mostly, Krill reckoned, because El Mayor's men were just civilians, coked-up assassins who were good against some campesino or intellectual with their thumbs tied behind their backs, but they clearly knew nothing about fields of fire or how to maneuver against an ambush.

He stopped.

On his way to the kitchen he spotted the small courtyard and washbasins in the servants' quarters. And the steel door leading out. He found the door ajar and pulled it open, not yet ready to stick his head out in case they'd left a sniper behind. He would have.

This is how she got out.

He stepped back in and secured the door. As he did he caught his reflection in a mirror over the washbasin. *Look at yourself.* Jeans, a Tex-Mex cowboy shirt, shoes, not even boots!

"Fucking faggot!"

The sight of her, his *angelita*. No less miraculous than had it been

Gabriel himself. His reflexes, his infamous reflexes froze. Infamous? *Impotente!* She had unmanned him. It was only when that motherfucking Montoya had shown himself that Krill had recovered. But he'd lost the two seconds he'd needed and they had slipped away.

"*Maricón.*"

He pointed his .45 at himself and pulled the trigger. Click! Empty.

"*Hijo de puta!*"

He needed ammunition. No, he needed weapons, ammunition, and transport. El Mayor's assassins and the army had their war. Krill had his own fight to finish. But first he had to finish with Max.

He filled a bucket with water and went back upstairs. He'd found that ridiculous piece of shit coming out of his safe room—a closet-sized mini-bunker hidden at the back of his actual closet in the bedroom. Krill had tied him to a chair for interrogation and found him there when he returned with the water. He tossed the bucket into Max's bruised face and revived him.

"Please." Max's speech was a little slurred. "Please, my friend, we are on the same side."

Krill leaned over, almost nose to nose. "You brought those *piricuacos* here."

"I didn't know, no one did! They have American passports. No one knew. Please."

"You didn't know they were Sandinistas! Who does your intelligence?"

"They had contacts in Miami, Cubans, friends who vouched for them in Miami!"

Fucking Miami, Krill thought. Not for the first time he pledged to burn fucking Miami to the ground.

"Again: Where were they staying?"

"Here, I told you."

"Who were their contacts?"

"Only me. And my cousin Jasmine."

"Jasmine. And their mission?"

"Relief supplies, medicines, toys. But listen, listen." Max wet his lips and tried to catch his breath and calm his voice. "We were using them, we didn't take them seriously, we were using them for propaganda! Please. I have money, more than you could imagine . . ."

"Shh. Shh." Krill patted Max's cheek. It was time.

"It's okay. Don't worry. *No se preocupa*, Don Maximiliano."

Max stopped blubbering. As Krill knew he would. Change from the informal "*tu*" to the formal "*usted*," put a "don" in front of their name, and these rich *pendejos* would feel safe every time. He could sense Max relaxing. As he did, Krill took stock: the house was full of weapons, money, cars in the garage. Krill had two passports, a Salvadoran identity card, and one lead: this Jasmine, if Montoya or the Farabundos hadn't already killed her.

Krill looked around, he needed a place. "That safe room, it's very good, yes?"

"Yes."

"The Farabundos didn't know about it, eh?"

"No. No one knows."

Krill saw the dawning realization on Max's face as clearly as dawn crept in the windows. But for Maximiliano Hernández Martínez III it was the last dawning. Krill tipped him back in his chair and dragged him into the closet. Any port in a storm, he thought, any room for a tomb.

Krill finished searching Gladys's suitcase. There was nothing that hinted at where she might be, or go. He'd found nothing in Montoya's room either. He had found the little hidey hole in the suitcase and wondered what he'd needed to smuggle in. Could it be that blade that had carved so much carnage in Krill's camp? He picked through Gladys's things and watched a brief war between his hand and head—he picked the blue blouse up, put it down, picked it up, and put it down. Then he let the hand win and pressed the cloth to his face. He inhaled deeply. The smell was unknown to him, new. But it stirred an old longing.

Weakling! Weakling! Weakling! He'd been searching the house for an hour or so, and in that time he had murdered Montoya many times. Butchered him. Hung him upside down so he couldn't pass out and inflicted every pain in his well-stocked repertoire, and some even Krill had only ever heard of. But he had not so imagined his *angelita.*

Cobarde!

He hurled the suitcase into the mirror and shattered himself into a hundred pieces. He hurried out, down the hall to Jasmine's room. It was even more than he'd expected.

Ricas! Rich girls. Max had said she'd only stayed here occasionally but her closet held enough clothes to outfit a brigade, enough shoes to shod a battalion. Enough purses . . . Purses. Lined up by the dozen like sentries. But one set apart, already on duty. He scrounged through it and came up with what he'd hoped for: a beautiful red leather notebook attached to what Krill knew was a real gold-plated pen. He flipped through it, her address book, page after page of names, numbers, and addresses.

It was the only lead he needed.

21

The news was good, Gladys thought. Good. Well, maybe not if you were Salvadoran, or if you were a noncombatant. Or if you were with the government, given the pictures they were watching on the TV news. Of course, if you were with the FMLN the news was not so good either, given the images of helicopter gunships laying waste to entire city blocks. But at least for her and Ajax the news was good, as no mention had yet been made of them and their faces had not appeared on the news. But they might, at any moment.

So maybe the news was not so good.

Doña Estela was a glorious grand dame, who, much like her house and household servants, was aging divinely so long as you looked in the right light. Too close an inspection revealed the decades of built-up dust, water stains, and cracks in the foundation.

She clucked her tongue at the images flashing across her TV like a stern librarian shushing noisy teenagers. She was a graying matron, widowed, and lived in a large house just half a mile from Max's villa. They—Gladys, Ajax, and Jasmine—had made their way down the ravine to doña Estela's back door just as dawn stole their cover. She'd welcomed them like they'd been survivors from the *Titanic* washing up on her porch. *They're Americans,* Jasmine had said, and the old lady had clucked her tongue, *Pobrecitos, que desgraciada.* What a disgrace, as if she were embarrassed that strangers had gotten caught in a family feud.

She'd ordered her clearly terrified servants to feed them and within an hour they'd been fed, coffeed, and washed.

"Jasmine!" Estela leaned forward into the television as the news cut to a press conference. "Jasmine, come here! It's Freddy."

Jasmine hurried in, looking, Gladys thought, stunning even in an old lady's housecoat that she'd cinched tight around her waist with a slit of cleavage showing, like a cleft in a very soft rock. Ajax came in, too, down from the roof where he'd been following the combat with a practiced eye. Not for the first time Gladys was relieved to be with him. There was just something about him, a confidence, and a cool that wafted off him like body odor. Only instead of pinching your nose at the smell, you wanted, like a dog, to roll around it, get that scent on your own body, to be able to at least smell like you have that much composure.

She'd been horrified by his penchant for violence, since the first time she watched him beat up two State Security agents in Managua because he objected to their presence at a crime scene. True, much of the worst of it had been done out of her sight. The massacre at Krill's camp, even El Gordo at the hospital. Once, they'd been chasing leads at a coffee farm way up in the mountains when Vladimir Malhora had sent assassins to finish them off. Ajax had woken from a dead sleep and worked out a counterassault that had gone exactly as he had said it would. At least until Gladys got shot and Krill had arrived with his men.

And then his rescue of her from the Contras. He'd explained it as simply as a housewife would a favorite recipe: Ajax had staked out Krill's camp for two weeks. He'd noticed the big Jeep Wagoneer coming and going, had deduced who might be in it, and one day Ajax had put on a sentry's uniform, taken his post, stopped the Wagoneer like he was in need of a light, and seized two high-value hostages.

Pop it in the oven and wait half an hour!

Cool. Cool was the only way to describe him. Cool under fire, cool under pressure. Cool.

And yet. And yet.

When Ajax told her he'd taken over the sentry post, she'd known he meant he slipped the point of the Needle into the man's throat and sliced it out through arteries, veins, and voice box. She wondered if all that cool did not disguise a coldness, a glacier inside of him that entombed a very vulnerable part that, while it might weaken you, also made you human. Even at Max' s party—and all she'd wanted was to flee Krill—she'd grabbed Monkey Man around the neck, knowing that if she hadn't Ajax would've killed him on the spot. But so what? They were alive, again, thanks to him.

She watched him come into the room, lean, alert, hair unkempt, and for some reason she recalled a line someone had said back in Managua: diplomacy is the art of learning to say "nice doggy" while bending down to pick up a rock.

Ajax could be that rock. He could also be the dog.

On the TV, Alfredo Cristiani, president of the republic, took the podium at the presidential palace press room. He had the haggard look of someone who's been startled awake by such bad news, the shock of it was imprinted under the bags in his eyes. Freddy was dressed in a white, long-sleeved guayabera and flanked by military men—generals, colonels, and Benivides, whom Gladys remembered from Max's party.

"He's wearing body armor," Ajax said. "The president, under his shirt."

Gladys looked, and he was right.

"The officers are, too, look at their epaulets, you can see the indentions on their shoulders before they took them off."

She leaned in to see, and sure enough. Ajax the rock.

". . . thousands of our citizens are in danger from this illegal attack. The FMLN bears sole responsibility for the violence, the deaths . . ."

Ajax grunted.

"What?"

"How long has he been at it?" Ajax tilted his chin at the TV.

"A few minutes." Gladys checked her watch.

"Hmph. So the press got there before him."

"So?" Gladys could not see where this was going.

"So the Farabundos are watching television too."

"I think you might be right, young man." Doña Estela watched the screen but nodded her head vigorously.

Gladys turned her palms up. *What?*

"If I was the Farabundos I'd lob some mortar shells right about now."

As if saying made it so, the TV image went wobbly, like a small earthquake shaking the ground. But it was the TV cameras rocking from the explosion. The president—it would be said later—stumbled from the impact and was steadied back on his feet by the generals, but Gladys could see he'd really been headed face-first for the floor and his wiser officers had held him back by his elbows.

"Chicken-shit," doña Estela spat, much to Gladys's surprise.

Estela slowly rose and headed for her bedroom where she would, eventually, put together enough of a persona to present to the world. "The Cristianis have all always been chicken-shits. The whole family. Shopkeepers."

When the old lady had tottered off, Jasmine laughed into her hand. "Isn't she something? She was the first female doctor in El Salvador and her husband was a colonel. Killed in the Soccer War."

Gladys observed Jasmine as she watched the hurried conclusion to Freddy's press conference. Ajax looked at Gladys and drew a question mark in the air—begin the interrogation.

"Jasmine," she said, "we can't stay here much longer. We've got to find Peck. What can you tell us?"

"Jimmy?" Jasmine seemed lost in the TV, which had gone back to live images of street battles. She shrugged, as if to say, *What does it matter now?* "Everybody knew Jimmy, he was kind of popular. I saw him at parties, he and Max did the nightclub scene, which, I am not completely naïve, meant cocaine and whores."

"But how could he hang out with . . ." Gladys politely did not finish.

"With the *escuadrones*?" Death squads.

"From what we know it doesn't fit. Friends with these death squad Charlie types, no."

"I don't know, Gladys, maybe men make truces when it comes to carousing. But he had a lot of friends, Max and his type. But the Fathers too, I met him there."

"Fathers?"

"The Jesuits at the UCA," the University of Central America. "Six of them. They're about the only professors we have left, teaching the few students who still attend at the only university that's still open. It's a highbrow group, Spaniards mostly."

An explosion muffled the air and the concussion a second later rattled the windows. They all went out to the veranda where a mile or so away they saw a massive, fiery cloud ascend to the sky. Jasmine pointed.

"That's Escalon, near the Salvador del Mundo statue." She grunted. "I think they just took out the McDonald's there." She clucked her tongue. "Estela will be upset, she loves their apple pies." Jasmine wandered off, seemingly in midsentence. Off, Gladys assumed, to tell Estela she'd need a new dessert place.

Ajax and Gladys were alone on the veranda.

"This make any sense to you? This sound like the young Peck his parents described?"

Gladys shook her head. "No. They said he was a firebrand, hated the government and the death squads. How was he partying with Max?"

"Can't see him whoring with those berserker boys. Maybe he was a switch hitter? Playing both sides?"

Whoring. That reminded Gladys. She dug in her purse, took the pistol out, and found the crumpled-up paper on the bottom. "Claribel."

"See if the phone's working."

22

Moving through a city at war is a counterintuitive experience—at least when you're a noncombatant. Every fiber of your body, as the hack would say, is screaming to stay low, creep along, peek around, duck, and dart.

But those are precisely the moves the *combatants* are trained to watch for and kill. So there was nothing for it but to brass it out right down the middle of the street, nice and slow, a white flag flying.

Ajax had seen it over and over again in Nicaragua in the late seventies when he and his compañeros of the Northern Front had been closing in on the capital. Red Cross jeeps did it all the time, rolling through barrios, speakers blaring: "Bring out your wounded. Bury your dead where they are." Civilians, desperate for help, for food, would walk right down the middle of the streets, white flags flapping, hoping to get to the bodega before a bored sniper took up his scope.

He and Gladys drove along a street slowly snaking downhill, right down the middle, doña Estela's white pillowcases hanging as limp as they were probably useless.

The phone had been working, and strangely, so was Claribel. She'd agreed to meet them for what she claimed was her regularly hourly rate, but which Ajax was sure was the "gringo rate." He was a gringo, again. "El Gringo" had been his first nom de guerre in Nicaragua when he'd first gotten to the mountains, to the storied Sandinistas, who, when Ajax arrived, looked more like half-starved refugees than revolution-

aries overturning the world. But what else would they call the kid from
Los Angeles? Didn't matter that Ajax's father had made sure he was
better read and more versed in Nicaraguan history, poetry, and politics. He'd grown up in los Estados Unidos and so he was *el gringo*. The
memory disturbed him and he brushed it away, hurriedly, like a
cobweb you walk into in the dark.

They'd driven out of the tony section of town, where Max and
doña Estela had houses, and down into Escalon, still an upscale barrio,
but in the heart of the city. The streets were not as deserted as he'd've
thought. Some solid citizens were already cleaning up the rubble, or
at least sweeping it out of their doorways. Small groups stood around
corpses frozen in their last moment on earth. A few groups had already taken up the public health business of burning the rebel dead in
small pits they'd dug along the roadways—burning the bodies no one
would come for.

But one thing was very different. There were no soldiers anywhere.
On the ride in from the airport there had been police, National Guard,
and army everywhere—on street corners, foot patrols, or manning
roadblocks. They were conspicuously absent now—except in the air
where helicopter gunships zoomed low overhead. But Ajax knew this
did not mean they were safe, it just meant even more was hidden from
them.

But they weren't bad off either. They had a car, money, and guns—
good ol' Estela had thrust the keys and a bag into Ajax's hands as
they were leaving. The keys started her BMW from the early seventies, the bag was filled with banknotes from the sixties and a pistol
from the 1948 Pan-American Games. It was a mere .22, but a target
pistol and so was both well-balanced and not a sidearm you'd expect
a guerrilla to carry in case they got stopped.

They climbed down from Escalon into the main traffic circle—
dominated by the statue of Salvador del Mundo, Jesus with His arms
outstretched like a traffic cop. There were no buses, no civilian traffic
at all. A Red Cross ambulance with red light flashing but no siren

wailing passed them by. The driver gave them the once-over and shook his head, as if to say, *I'll be back for your bodies later.* As they entered the traffic circle Ajax had a small laugh.

"What?" Gladys perked up.

"The McDonald's."

Jasmine had been right. The golden arches lay in a ruin like the Philistine's pillars toppled by Samson, if Samson had used an RPG.

Ajax steered them slowly through the big traffic circle, no sign from Officer Jesus that he should not, and pointed Estela's Beemer down the hill. (Ajax had taken to calling the car Chicken-shit, as that's what Estela dubbed her driver when she found she could not raise him on the phone and have him come chauffeur Ajax and Gladys through a war zone. *He's just not picking up. Chicken-shit!*) He and Gladys rode with their doors unlatched but held closed with their arms so that if they took fire they could eat dirt without having to remember the door handle.

"You sure you can find it?"

"Jasmine said just roll downhill from the statue to the Metropolitan Cathedral." It was where Claribel had insisted they meet.

"Interesting choice," Gladys said.

"'Cause she's a whore?"

Gladys cut him a look. "No, not because she's a *whore.* The cathedral. You don't know whose church that is?"

"Enlighten me."

"Romero's."

"Ah!" That caught his attention. Archbishop Oscar Romero had been a living saint, one of those Latin American prelates whose humility, whose genuine concern for the poor bordered on devotion. It had put him in direct conflict with the powers-that-be and was one reason why, in El Salvador, after *communist,* being a priest was grounds enough for execution.

"I still remember that last homily he gave in 1980. You know?"

"Gladys, in 1980 I was still hunting the Guardia in the mountains."

"I mean I heard some of Fidel's speeches at the Academy, it was required listening, but he was always preaching to the choir, you know. But man, listening to Romero talk to the military . . ." Gladys leaned forward, looked through the windshield at the empty streets and lifted her hand like a stage actor. "'In the name of humanity I beg you, in the name of God I order you! STOP THE REPRESSION!!'"

She sat back.

"Man, I still get goose bumps remembering it."

"And they shot him a week later."

"Killed him while he was saying mass."

"On the orders of Roberto D'Aubuisson, whose hand we almost shook. It was a good shot too. I remember that."

"A good shot? Jesus fuck, Ajax!" She looked away, truly disappointed it seemed. "He was a great man! You talk like a fucking assassin."

He tapped the brakes just hard enough to whiplash her, but he kept his eyes on the road.

"Or a cop. It's called forensics, Lieutenant. From fifty feet one shot to the head with a small-caliber gun, something like the twenty-two Estela gave us. On my best day I couldn't've made that shot, could you?"

Ajax knew Gladys was a dead-eye shot, it was what he'd admired most when they were first partnered.

"No."

"So it wasn't some death squad Charlie type like Monkey Man, but a real pro, probably not even Salvadoran. That eliminates a lot of suspects."

He let her stew for a moment. "Yeah, I used . . ."

"To be a cop, I remember."

He hit the brakes for real now. He'd come around a corner and they'd run into the war: a heavily defended intersection, two small tanks, a .50 cal, and what seemed a battalion of troops.

"Hands out the window."

They stuck their arms out as far as they would go. After a moment a soldier stepped forward and motioned them back. Ajax put the car in reverse until they came to a line of cars, parked before the fighting began and now bullet-riddled.

"They gonna let us through?"

"I think so, they're worried about a car bomb, is my bet. Hide your passport, show them the ORDEN card."

"The guns?"

"Gonna have to leave them."

"No."

Her face showed she meant, *I will not be taken alive by him.* And maybe the soldiers would accept the greater need for a woman to be armed, what with marauding *terroristas* on the offensive. Ajax had learned long ago that little helped the clandestine agent so much as the opposition believing their own propaganda.

"Okay, keep it, but try not to look so . . . you know."

"What?"

He freed the white flag he'd tied to the door.

"Fierce."

"You were gonna say butch, weren't you?"

"Right down the middle of the street, hands up."

He hoisted their white flag in one hand, his identity card in the other. Gladys joined him, walking slow and steady toward the roadblock and its many guns and jumpy soldiers.

"I wasn't gonna say butch. I was gonna say look vulnerable, in need of a gun."

"You like them vulnerable, soft and sultry. Jasmine's your type, with her cleavage like a cleft in the rock."

"Did you just say that?"

"Cleavage? You want me to say *tetas*?"

"No, 'cleft in a rock.'"

"*Alto!*"

They were ten feet from the blockade and a sergeant stepped forward, his pistol pointed at Ajax.

"We're trying to get away from the terrorists," he said, hopefully.

"*Papeles.*" The sergeant had a steady eye and a steady hand when he took their identification cards. He seemed to recognize the significance of the ORDEN stamp of approval, but he searched their faces again, matching them to their photos. Ajax knew it was best in such situations to just put his passport face on and let the man look.

The sergeant looked back, found an officer, and said, "Orden." The officer nodded in return.

"*Pasan.*"

As they passed through Ajax looked the soldiers in the face. The men did not seem frightened. Many of them looked angry, which meant they'd already been in the shit. And they didn't look beaten.

Ajax nodded at the few who would make eye contact, thinking, *Just nod back you sons-of-bitches.*

"Wait."

Ajax could hear Gladys's breath catch, he hoped no one else did. A major stepped forward, wearing a different insignia than the others. Ajax guessed military intelligence.

"Identification."

They handed them over.

"You two are not Salvadoran."

Ajax could see Gladys's hand slowly go to her purse and he reached for it, like a protective lover, but squeezed her fingers in a soft vise.

"No, *mi major.* We are not."

The major looked their cards over, front and back.

"You're the Americans. The *cubanos-gringos.*"

Gladys didn't flinch, bless her. Ajax kept his passport face on.

"Passports."

They handed them over, the major inspected them, compared them to the ORDEN photos.

"I saw you at the party. At don Maximiliano's. Last night."

"Was it *only* last night?" Gladys freed her hand and ran it through her hair like *I must look a sight!*

"It seems a long time ago." The major smiled at her. "The airport might be open tomorrow, you should leave the country."

"We'd like to," Gladys jumped in, "but it is important we bear witness to this communist aggression, so the people back home can know what it is you fight for."

Damn, she is good! Ajax almost heaved a sigh of relief.

"You better hurry then." The major smiled. "There won't be any communists left soon, this"—he waved at the bullet-scarred walls— "has given us permission to take care of them all!"

"Good luck, Major." Ajax took Gladys's hand. "Good luck to all of you!"

Hearts pounding and breath ragged, they walked on to the next block in silence.

"You can let go my hand now. What the fuck was that?"

Ajax released her.

"We just walked over our own graves," he said.

"No shit. He didn't know?"

"Which means either they're all too busy or communications are fried, or . . ." Ajax turned back and waved at the soldiers, but also, strangely, to make sure he and Gladys were actually where they were and not being stood against a wall. Some of the soldiers waved back, but the major was not watching them.

"Or?"

"Or Krill didn't tell them."

"You think?"

"Not if he wanted us to himself."

She blanched. Krill's feet walking over her grave.

23

The Metropolitan Cathedral of San Salvador was packed to the rafters with the homeless, the hopeless, and the terrified.

Ajax and Gladys had made their way through increasing numbers of soldiers until they reached Plaza Morazan—a square with a government ministry on one side, which explained the soldiers, the cathedral on another, and a small park anchored by a bronze statue of a man astride a horse, which, like all such landmarks, had become a target for pigeons and a rendezvous for lovers.

The vaulted-roofed church was alive—hundreds of people full to overflowing. Families, refugees, the scared, the devout, and no few rebel sympathizers and army informers, Ajax was sure. Some families had staked out small areas with mats and bundles of their possessions, here for the duration. Others sat in the pews looking stunned, some knelt in prayer, some made the Stations of the Cross, or prostrated themselves before a painting of their patron saint—the martyred Romero. Ajax crinkled his nose—the tang of unwashed bodies, a whiff of fear, and the comforting aroma of rice and beans simmering and tortillas warming.

The wretched of, if not the Earth, then at least of San Salvador, the savior. Redeemer. One mortar round would kill them all.

"Any antidote to the inferno."

"What?" Gladys was scanning the crowds.

"You see Claribel?"

"Yep. Tenth pew back, far side."

"Walk by her, lead her over there." Ajax nodded to a side chapel off the nave. "Meet you."

He wandered the long way around to the chapel, inspecting the crowds. There were some children with schoolbooks, the older siblings helping the younger as it was clear their parents could not. He found the source of the rice and beans, a few long tables with young men, maybe altar boys, ladling out victuals with tortillas. On the other side of the chapel some nuns tended wounded civilians, although none seemed badly hurt. But through a side door he caught sight of at least one body under a white shroud. He made his way around to the front of the church, before the main altar, a huge bronze cross bearing the body of Christ—El Salvador. Ajax turned his back on the Risen Carpenter to face the congregation packed cheek by jowl, waiting. Waiting for peace, or just a cease-fire. Waiting for a handout or a boost up. Waiting for the Messiah to return, or just for Romero to be canonized so they would have their saint to appeal to and be cared for.

La gente humilde. He'd been reminded in Miami how such a phrase would not work in English, or at least not in America. *The humble folk* would seem condescending, an insult. Maybe *salt of the earth* was the correct translation. But what did that mean anymore? The discovery of salt, he'd read somewhere, its effect on stamina, the ability to preserve meats, had revolutionized human culture. Almost as much as those first ancient farmers who'd figured out how to cultivate maize in the Americas, or rice in Asia, wheat in Europe. Humble farmers.

But somewhere along the way someone had harvested more than someone else and he'd become the headman, then chief, king, emperor, *presidente.* And salt had become some base, common commodity you wouldn't stoop to pick up off the ground. Salt of the earth. Wretched of the earth. Wretched salt of the earth.

He spotted Gladys and Claribel entering the side chapel and joined them. They flanked her on each side like the good and bad thieves had Christ on Calvary. They knelt as if in prayer.

Ajax slipped a fifty out and passed it to Claribel. She sniffed at it like it was thirty pieces of silver and she was no Judas.

"No money, I do this for Gladys." She took Gladys's hand. Ajax shot Gladys a look, she shrugged like, *What? I inspire loyalty.* "She was so nice to me in the bathroom. And she said she kicked Kiki in the balls."

"Monkey Man," Gladys explained.

"I like that name better. She said you wanted to cut his throat?"

"Well . . ."

"Well if you ever do I'll give *you* fifty dollars, that fucking *pendejo*." Claribel made a quick sign of the cross and muttered an apology.

"You want to know about Jimmy?"

"Yes," Ajax said. "You knew him?"

"Professionally? No. But he was with Kiki sometimes. He and Jimmy came to the club I work at, he would party with us."

"Claribel, what were Jimmy's politics?"

She stiffened and flicked a Judas look over her shoulder.

Ajax pressed: "Was he with the Farabundos? *Escuadrones? Gringos?*"

"Shh. I understand. Jimmy had no politics, he liked partying and powder." She sniffed, rather dramatically, Ajax thought.

"Did he go with girls?"

"Never. Kiki used to make fun of him: '*Ni varón, ni maricón.*'"

Neither macho nor fag.

"But he liked girls?"

"What does that matter? Lots of us like girls."

Gladys sniggered, and Claribel gave her a look. *A look.*

"But Jimmy came out with one girl sometimes."

"Did you know her?"

"Sure. So do you. Doña Jasmine."

"Jasmine?"

"What, you think she's such a lady?"

Ajax, in fact, did. "She partied with you?"

"Drank beer. She was slumming, checking out La Sucia."

"The what?"

"The Unwashed," Gladys explained.

"Claribel, do you know where Jimmy is? What happened?"

"The Farabundos, they killed him. He partied with the wrong people. They probably thought he was military, *la cia*. He's dead. I saw his body. Kiki had me go take pictures. *Pobrecito*. It was terrible what they did to him."

So that was where the morgue photos had come from.

"Claribel, do you think he could have been *with* the Farabundos?"

"Jimmy? *Imposible, hombre*. He was stupid." She pointed at her head. "*Ignorante*, you understand? Like only gringos can be." She turned quickly to Gladys. "Not *all* Americans, *amorcita*."

Another *look*.

Suddenly something changed. The air, the vibe of the church altered. Ajax looked around and saw a squad of soldiers stroll in. They were heavily armed—automatic weapons, bulging ammo pouches, grenades dangling off their combat web. And to each man's back was strapped a machete.

Weapons for the rebels, Ajax thought, machetes for the people.

But the arms they bore were nothing compared to the faces they wore. They'd painted themselves with camouflage sticks, like snipers used. But these soldiers had painted masks, and not Halloween masks but demons from Indian lore. One had a frog painted on his chin so it seemed to emerge from his mouth, another a dozen eyes all over his face, a third a vampire monkey with fangs. They reminded Ajax of the visages he'd seen in books about the Aztecs. Their executioners—those who'd cut out the hearts of uncounted thousands—would paint their faces to resemble demons so the souls of the dead would be too terrified to pursue them in the afterlife.

These soldiers were not hiding, they were not afraid of the afterlife either, yet the masks were disguises that would prevent anyone from identifying these soldiers once the paint was off.

They strode through this holy place, this refuge, to remind this huddled mass in the cathedral of their martyred archbishop that while their priests told them they *might* make a Heaven on earth, these soldiers were from Hell.

Claribel whimpered. *"Atlactl."* She knelt down so low her forehead touched the floor. Ajax looked around, all of the hundreds there suddenly got to praying real hard, kneeling, dozens of hands flying, making signs of the cross, and all eyes were not on the cross which bore Christ, the son of God, but on the floor.

The Atlactl (*At-la-cat-l*) Battalion was notorious, meaning they scared the shit out of everyone. Ajax felt a little twinge in his own balls. In a country long synonymous with slaughter, the Atlactl had carried out the worst massacre of the war. He'd read about it in the Nicaraguan press, hell, even the *New York Times* had covered it. The Atlactl was raised as a special counterinsurgency unit, only the best of the best had been selected and sent to the School of the Americas at Fort Benning, Georgia, for the kind of first-class training third-world soldiers only dreamed of. Drilled in the most state-of-the-art weapons and tactics, the Atlactl had also been schooled in human rights, and the need to win the hearts and minds of the people to defeat the insurgents. A thoroughly modern military unit recruited and trained by America as a sign of its commitment to defeating communism in Central America.

And on pretty much their first mission they'd committed the single worst atrocity since the *generalissimo*'s genocide. El Mozote.

Atrocities are a funny thing, Ajax knew, for those not directly touched by them. In Nicaragua, for all the war and the tens of thousands of dead overthrowing first the Ogre, and then battling the Contras, there had been few actual atrocities other than war itself. When people read about children's heads dashed against rocks, and pregnant women's wombs ripped open, their brains go into a kind of protective shutdown—the information is processed like the images of a movie, instead of in that part of the brain that copes with actual sensory stimulus.

Ajax recalled that once, in high school back in North Hollywood, his English teacher had had the class read a memoir by a Hungarian teenager who'd survived Auschwitz. Upon arrival at the camp, the author recorded, he had been marched by a massive flaming pit, as big as a football field, filled with burning bodies. The author reported how he, as a teenager himself, watched camp inmates pour barrels of diesel into the pit to feed the fire, while other inmates hurled the bodies of recently gassed children into the flames. All this in his first hour in the camp.

For two days Ajax's teacher had read this section out loud to the class and had the students read it aloud to each other. Eventually his classmates, mostly working-class Mexican kids, but a few Anglos, had protested, complained the author was rubbing their noses in it, and the teacher too. But Ajax had understood: the reality of the evil was so unfathomable most of the students had flipped a switch in their brains and talked about the hellish images as a literary choice by an author, a metaphor for hell on earth, rather than the plain and simple recitation of literal facts their imaginations could not assimilate.

The teacher had also assigned an essay, the students had to write a letter to their "family" back in Hungary explaining how to pass the selection process at the camp, and thus "survive." Ajax had written his "family" persuading them that as none would survive, they should all kill themselves and die with dignity in the arms of loved ones. He earned his only ever A+.

It had taken the Atlactl an entire day, twenty-four infinite hours, to slaughter the people of El Mozote. Massacres like that are the opposite of a sinking ship, he thought. On the ship it's always women and children first, the "most vulnerable" to the boats, and the men must face the worst alone. In a massacre it is the men who are killed first, and the women and children face the worst, because the very act of murdering all the men unleashes a bloodlust in the killers so profane it is a seamless segue to the smashed skulls and butchered bellies of the most vulnerable.

The entire town had been wiped out as thoroughly as that boy's Jewish ghetto had.

Ajax watched the soldiers make their rounds through the cathedral—the Stations of Humiliation—not strutting like peacocks, but striding like panthers. They went by the food tables, where the altar boys folded their hands and dropped their heads like the Eucharist was passing. One of soldiers looked into a pot of simmering beans and gobbed his spittle into it.

"I need a cigarette," Ajax decided, and got off his knees.

"No, Ajax . . . Martin!" Gladys reached for him, but Claribel seized her hand.

"Please, Gladys. If they find out I'm a *puta* they'll take me to the barracks."

Ajax marched over to the soldiers. His one unrestrained pleasure in life had once been the Marlboro Reds he'd extorted from a cigarette smuggler in Managua. He'd kept himself in plenty of them in the Honduran jail, but smoking didn't go with the catatonic opossum so he'd given them up. He was jonesing for one now.

"*Oye! Soldados!* Anybody got a cigarette? One of you guys must have a Marlboro Red!"

As one, the soldiers turned on him, shocked, it seemed, that anyone would address them at all, let alone bum a smoke.

"Hey man, I know you guys!" He scanned the soldiers and found the one with a lieutenant's bar. He reached out to the officer and pinched the patch on his shoulder. "Atlactl, right? You guys are bad-asses!"

The lieutenant pulled his shoulder away as his men encircled this fool.

"Who are you?"

Ajax stuck his ORDEN card in the officer's face and kept prattling to the soldiers.

"Man, if we had you in Miami we could've gotten rid of Castro and all them communist *hijos de putas* long ago. And their whore wives and retard children too, right? Now who's got a Marlboro and I don't mean them Mexican knockoffs, they're shit. You, *teniente?*"

The lieutenant was none too pleased, Ajax was pleased to see. But in the hierarchy of El Salvador one crazy-ass death squad civilian out-ranked one bloodied uniformed officer. Reluctantly, like dipping his hand into a pile of shit, the lieutenant reached into his pocket, drew out a pack of Winstons, and shook one loose.

"Not my brand." Ajax took the butt, set it loosely in slightly pouted lips.

And just stood there.

The four-hundred-plus refugees packed into the church, Gladys on her knees, Christ on his cross, and Romero in his painting all seemed to hold their collective breath for possibly the longest five seconds ever recorded.

Then the lieutenant relented, yielded, surrendered—he took out his Zippo and flipped it into fire. Ajax still waited, the cathedral still held its breath, until the officer held the flame under the cigarette. Ajax inhaled, held the smoke in his lungs—the nicotine and cornucopia of chemicals rushing through his blood until he felt that glorious buzz of the first butt of the day. The people themselves seemed to exhale as one and slip Medusa's gaze. Ajax even clocked some actual movement: Gladys leading Claribel to an exit.

And then Ajax languorously exhaled straight up so that the smoke hung in the ripe, humid air like a cloud, and then descended around the lieutenant's head like fog settling around a pumpkin. The cathedral and its congregation held its collective breath, again. Even Claribel stopped her hasty retreat.

Ajax looked at the burning ember, flicked his head. "Not bad. Hey!" He turned on the rest of the squad like he'd had a brainstorm. "You soldiers must be hungry! YOU!" he screamed at the altar boys behind the food table. "Serve these heroes some victuals, you fucking morons!"

The altar boys stayed immobilized in seeming prayer, terrified,

Ajax knew, that he was the only one who had not seen the communal pot fouled.

"Fucking retards!" Ajax looked to the lieutenant for comfort, stuck the butt in his mouth, and dished up a heaping plate of beans and tortillas. He held it out to the officer.

"You hungry, Lieutenant?"

Ajax swished the tortilla in the beans and wolfed it down.

"Fucking shit. But what do you expect from peasants? Better than nothing." He offered the plate to the soldier who'd gobbled the beans. "You?"

The lieutenant turned his gaze away from this crazy-ass fucker as if he'd never even seen him. He passed his eyes over the congregation one more time, to make sure *everyone* still looked away, and then slowly strolled out with his patrol.

Ajax kept the butt in one hand, and fed beans into his mouth with the other as he followed the soldiers a few paces.

"Hey, Lieutenant!"

He stopped, but would not turn around, just rotated his contemptuous face over a resentful shoulder.

"Leave me a butt, for later. Fucking terrorists got all the stores closed, communist sons-of-bitches."

The lieutenant made an invisible signal, and the last man in line fished a beat-up pack of Camels from a pocket. He shook one loose, but Ajax slipped the whole pack out of his fingers.

"Thanks, bro."

And strolled back to the tables. He felt the congregation's eyes on him. Some watched, befuddled by the miracle of a man who'd not been executed for the worst crime of all: insolence. Others looked on with smiles in their eyes, they knew when bullies had been bested. Yet more would not look at all, afraid of the man more powerful than the murderers of Mozote. Ajax stopped at the food tables where the frozen altar boys showed signs of thaw. He held out the plate. "Please, señores, I'd like some more."

．　　．　　．

Claribel slipped her tongue into Ajax's mouth and lightly ran it under his upper lip.

"You, *loco,* get freebies for life!" She playfully pinched his nipple.

"*Gracias, amorcita.*"

She turned to Gladys, touched her face. "You'll call me, *won't you?*"

"Of course."

They pecked each other on the cheek, but Ajax saw Gladys give Claribel's left nipple a pinch. The *puta* moaned and dashed down the steps and out of sight. Gladys had a strange half-smile on her face.

"What was that?" he said.

"What?"

"That!" He made a crab pincer.

Gladys just shrugged.

"Wait a minute. *Es lesbiana?*"

"Something wrong with that?"

"No, Gladys, but, you know, she just offered *me* freebies for life."

Gladys shook her head. "Jesus, after what you just pulled in there I have to explain to you that prostitutes are always faking *it?*"

"No! But . . . she goes with men."

"*Faking* it!"

"Okay, *claro.*"

"Now, you want to tell me why the fuck you just almost got yourself and maybe all of us killed?"

Ajax shrugged. But some of the refugees leaving the church passed close by to them, whispering "*Dios te bendiga.*" God bless you.

Gladys pulled a face. "Fucking Saint Ajax. Do you want to get martyred?"

Ajax pointed at his left leg where the Needle was strapped to his calf. "I would've got the spitter first."

"Lot of good that would've done."

"Shine, señor, shine?" A scrawny gawky boy with quick eyes, faster hands, and a shoe-shine box was bent down in front of them with

Ajax's boot up and a brush going over the leather before he or Gladys had realized it.

"*Oye, muchacho.*" Ajax lightly flicked the kid's ear. "*Ve te.*" Get outta here.

"No, señor, please. 'If a man cannot see his face reflected in his shoes, then he has no soul.' Saint Thomas Aquinas said that."

Ajax smiled. "Really?"

"He is the patron saint of shoe-shine boys." The kid held up a cheap, paper scapular hung around his neck, but it depicted Christ's resurrection.

"That's not Thomas Aquinas."

"Who can afford medallions in an economy like this?" The kid flung his hands into the air. Then touched a finger to his nose. "But when I hold the scapular, I pray to my patron saint."

Ajax was disarmed—the little shit was good. "Alright."

The kid went to shining and Ajax switched back to English.

"What do you make of Claribel's story? Young Peck the party animal?"

"She was telling the truth." Gladys seemed defensive.

"I know, but it doesn't jibe with his letters home to his folks. 'Kind of a lefty firebrand,' his father said, but he's a great pal of these death squad Charlies?"

Gladys grunted.

"What?"

"Maybe it runs in the family." She blanched as soon as she said it, and held up her hands. "Sorry, Ajax. But those Republican *pendejos* in Washington, would they have believed Amelia was, you know . . ."

"Fucking a Sandinista?"

"I was gonna say having an affair with a minion of the Evil Empire."

Ajax looked down at the shoe-shine boy, his hands flying like a magician's over Ajax's once scuffed, dirty boot. He *could* almost see his reflection.

A stolen season. Star-crossed lovers. The obvious clichés had occurred to him even in the moment of greatest passion, while he'd moved his brown, calloused hands over Amelia's pale, flawless thighs. Of course Romeo and Juliet were just a couple of bratty rich kids. Still, like them it had ended pretty much in death all around. Except for Ajax.

"Or maybe Claribel got it wrong." Gladys seemed to sense where his mind had gone, and wanted to draw him back. "She said young Peck brought Jasmine to the club. Maybe Jasmine brought him—you know, bored rich girl likes a bit of rough trade, but needs a proper escort."

The boy lifted Ajax's other boot onto the stand, hands flying again.

"Could be. Plausible. It's just . . ."

"Someone's lying?"

"No, not that. Jasmine and Claribel told the truth." He watched the boy's hands at work. "It feels like . . . misdirection. You've been to a magic show. Magicians don't lie, they misdirect: 'Look over here' while they make the switch over there. Misdirection."

"So who's the magician?"

"All done, *jefe*!"

The kid patted Ajax's leg, touched the Needle strapped to his calf. Ajax snatched his foot away, shot the kid an evil look.

"Hey, it's okay, boss." The kid held up his hands. "In these times we all need protection." He lifted his shirt to reveal an old paring knife with a taped handle. "I even sell it." He lifted the top off his shoeshine box. Inside were a couple dozen condoms, all of which looked older than the kid himself.

Ajax smiled and winked. "Me and my girl brought our own."

The kid eyeballed Gladys and sniffed. "Yeah, right."

"What's that mean, you little shit?" Gladys gave his box a kick.

"Watch it! You need to go to the confessional."

"I might confess to kicking your barrio-rat ass."

The kid gathered up his box and leaned in close to Gladys, all this hustler bonhomie replaced by a quiet menace beyond his years. "I didn't' say 'confession' you dyke bitch." He looked right at Ajax. "I said confessional."

And he was gone. Ajax and Gladys looked at each other. *What the hell?*

Ajax looked over this shoulder, through the tall doors of the cathedral to the far side of the church. The confessional was there. Two draped entries for the penitents, between them a solid wood door for the priest. Above the door a small amber light was on.

The padre was in.

24

Ajax drew the heavy curtain in the confessional and knelt at the wooden lattice screen that separated the sinners from the ordained. He could hear a faint murmuring. The confessional smelled of old wood, the wool drapes in the too-humid air, and the sins of the thousands who had knelt here before him.

The divider behind the lattice screen slid back. Ajax peered into the darkness. Only a few inches separated them. There was a shape on the other side, the vaguest of outlines, a chin, a nose. There was a long pause.

"Have you forgotten how to begin, my son?"

The Spanish was not local, but then many priests were foreigners. Still, Ajax was confused, had the shoe-shine boy been messing with him? Sins? Where to begin? Why bother? What was the ruse here?

"My son?"

"Ahh. Bless me, Father, for I have sinned?"

"Yes, go on."

"It has been, ahh . . ." He could not actually make out an image of him on his knees confessing. That boy was as lost in the darkened past as Ajax was in this hot confessional. ". . . maybe thirty years since my last confession and these are my sins."

Ajax waited.

"What are your sins, my son?"

"I think there's been a mistake, Father."

"But you have sinned, haven't you? You have walked in the sun and so cast a shadow, haven't you? Have you lied, for example? Deceived?"

"Not so that you'd notice."

"Pride is a deadly sin. You were showing off to the people, provoking those soldiers. You have magical papers that protect you, but you endangered these people with your spectacle."

At first Ajax had thought the padre was helping, offering items off a sin menu, the day's specials to get him started. But he was sounding more like a prosecutor.

"Hubris is excessive pride. It is an affront to God. Do you know why?"

"Tell me, Father."

"Because pride is a function of human ego; it inverts God's natural order and places the individual over Creation. That is what the Serpent gave to Eve in the apple, not knowledge, but self-awareness, which led to ego, vanity, hubris."

"I've not eaten an apple, though I've seen a serpent or two."

"Listen, Martin Garcia . . ."

"How do you know . . ."

"Silence! You have come to a forsaken land. Evil stands on two legs here, has hands and a mouth. Your mission was one of kindness, but do not let pride overcome you. Do not further endanger those who already walk in the shadow of the Valley of Death. Do not place your mission, yourself, over them."

"I haven't . . ."

"You have come searching for a corpse. In disguise, deceiving people. Some of those people know who you are. How many of the living must die for a corpse?"

"Wait, Father, do you mean Jimmy Peck? Do you know where he is?"

"Get out. I have sinners to confess."

"What about my sins?"

"Bear them yourself."

The divider slid shut and Ajax knelt alone, in the dark. He contemplated his sins for a moment. He laid a hand on the lattice divider, it gave a little. Knowing it was a sin he nevertheless gave in to anger and shoved his hand through the divider. It came off its wooden rail and tumbled into the priest's lap. Ajax reached for him, thought to pull his head right through the hole he'd made. But the darkened confessional flooded with light as the padre fled.

Ajax dashed through the drapes and straight into the arms of a tiny woman who hugged him around the waist in a vise of gratitude.

"Thank you, señor. God bless you. God bless you."

"Yes, yes." He dragged her along with him, wanting to catch that smarmy priest but not wanting to shove the little woman to the ground. He broke her grip and ran after Father Smartass. He turned a corner in the nave to a side chapel and caught a glimpse of a tall man and flash of a cassock legging it around the corner. And for one millisecond, he was almost certain, a lock of red hair, almost orange. *Son-of-a-bitch!*

Then two arms encircled, the grateful *mamacita* was back.

"Oh, señor!"

"Okay, okay!"

Ajax broke her grip and pursued. But at that moment, like in a zombie movie, every *mamacita* and her kids in the chapel turned to him, their arms out as if to embrace him—but Ajax knew it was to entrap him, delay him. The whole goddamn thing was a setup. He ran to the side exit, dodging the zombie grateful. He ran up the alley over uneven cobblestones and caught the toe of his newly shined boot on a drainage grate and took a tumble, skinning his knees as he went down, but thinking, *That fucking shoe-shine boy.* He rolled haphazardly and got back to his feet.

He spilled out of the alley doing a running limp into the street along the plaza across from the cathedral. It was full of soldiers and civilians, but no priests he could see. He slowed to a walk and scanned the crowd as he made his way back to Gladys. She spotted him the same time he spotted the boy. Ajax gave her the high sign—*get a grip on that kid*. Gladys walked over and set her shoe on the boy's little stand. Ajax could see the surprise on his face, and when the boy scanned the crowd he looked right into Ajax's eyes, grabbed his box, and took off. Gladys and Ajax were right behind him.

But all three of them were aware of the soldiers and none would break into a run that would draw their attention. It became a kind of slow-motion pursuit, the boy walking as fast as his legs would go. Gladys doing the same, a few steps behind him, doing a kind of walk-skip to catch up as Ajax did the same to gain on the two of them.

The shoe-shine boy turned a corner just a few steps ahead of Gladys, but once out of sight he'd break into a run and Gladys might not catch him. He saw her go around the same corner and it was excruciating to walk the final half-block until he, too, made the corner.

And the street was empty.

A city under siege could be like that. A plaza crowded with people could be surrounded by empty blocks. A city's streets were its veins, its boulevards arteries, and people moved through them like corpuscles. Combat cut off the blood vessels and pooled people into precincts or neighborhoods. Ajax jogged down the empty street as fast as his bruised knee would carry him. As he passed one long alley he saw Gladys at the other end, peering around the corner. He legged it up to her, but tripped over another drain and another searing pain went through his knee.

Gladys turned when he cursed.

"Lost him." She indicated the empty street. "He came up here, thought I had him for sure." She looked at Ajax. "What's up with the barrio rat?"

"The priest, in the confessional. It was Peck."

"No."

"Yes. Smarmy son-of-a-bitch lectured me."

They turned and walked back down the alley.

"Watch that drain . . ." Then it hit him. Two drains, two alleys. There are no coincidences. He grabbed Gladys's arm and pointed down.

"No."

"Got to be, how else did he give you the slip?"

"No, I mean, no, I'm not going down there."

But Ajax had the heavy grate off. It occurred to him that had he been in Nicaragua the job would've been much easier or more difficult. In Managua, things were so tight that the heavy metal drains or manhole covers had to be removed or welded down so people wouldn't steal them for the iron. He would just about fit.

"Come on, it's the dry season."

He dropped down into the darkness. It was the dry season so the sewers were not flooded, but the stench was correspondingly overwhelming. Ajax felt distinctly like someone had shit in his mouth. He gagged several times and heard Gladys scrape the drain back into place. She gagged and pulled a hanky of some kind from her pocket and doused it in perfume. *Perfume?*

"Claribel," she muttered. Ajax held out his hand and she sprinkled some on his palm which he clapped over his face.

It was a coin toss, so Ajax decided to head in what seemed downhill. The sewer had a small ledge on either side, about six inches off the ground, by putting a foot on each ledge they were able to waddle without actually walking in the bilge of the city's effluvium. After what Ajax reckoned was about six blocks, they came to a tunnel, at the end of which was a light. But a light shining down from above. This was the worst part—they had to crawl so Ajax could not cover his nose. Gladys, he noticed, tied the hanky around her nose, and not for the first time Ajax realized that, in general, a woman was always better prepared for such happenstances than a man.

He crawled along the tunnel, got right under the grate, and could hear soft voices, the sound of many people it seemed. He lifted the grate as quietly as possible, when it was yanked out of his hands and replaced by a flashlight in his eyes.

"You fucked up my shine, didn't you?"

25

The sewer had led them into a warehouse that was a staging ground for over a hundred Farabundos, by Ajax's count. And they were not militia: AKs, M16s, Belgian FALs, RPGs, and hand grenades both manufactured and homemade. These were the core of the FMLN, brought in from all over the country, and he and Gladys had walked right into them. They'd passed a few tough minutes bound and gagged while a vigorous, if near silent, argument had broken out, not so much what to do with them but how to kill them. Ajax had quickly told them their true identities and purpose. The shoe-shine boy had pointedly not vouched for them, and their American passports, ORDEN ID cards, and the Needle strapped to his calf had landed them in a world of shit much deeper than the sewers.

After a while they were taken to a room sealed with plastic where a young woman sat with a field radio that looked fifty years old. She was introduced as the commander, but Ajax noticed she had an M40 grenade launcher strapped to her back—more something a soldier would use.

"Kneel," she said.

They did. She drew a pistol and put it to Gladys's head.

"You have American passports and ORDEN identity cards but say you are Nicaraguans."

"We do, and we are. I was a *comandante guerrillero* for the FSLN.

I led the Northern Front." Ajax did his best to sound calm and hoped the young woman knew a little about her brother revolutionaries in Nicaragua.

She pushed the gun into Gladys's temple. "You?"

"I was a lieutenant in the Policia Sandinista. Graduated the Academia Policia de Havana. Class of 1985."

The woman looked at a crib card in her hand, then at Ajax. "Where and when was Sandino born?" Augusto César Sandino, the George Washington of Nicaragua who'd given his name to the Sandinista Front. The FSLN.

Ajax wasn't sure he'd heard it right. "What?"

She cocked the pistol at Gladys's head.

"Okay. Okay. May eighteenth, 1895. In Niquinohomo, Nicaragua."

She checked his answer. "When did he die?"

"He was assassinated. February twenty-first, 1934, in Managua."

She went back to her crib. "What was your nom de guerre?"

"Spooky."

There were two sharp knocks on the adjoining wall. The young *guerrillera* holstered her pistol and went back to monitoring the radio. An older woman slid through the plastic wall and Ajax thought he could've immediately fallen in love. She was as tall as he, far from beautiful but handsome in the way careworn women were. She had two .45s in shoulder holsters over her fatigue jumper. God, but he still loved a woman in a uniform.

"Nora." She held out a hand as muscular as her pistols.

"Ajax Montoya."

"Gladys Darío."

"You can imagine the inconvenience you have caused coming here at this time."

"We can, compañera," Ajax said. "And we are sorry for it. We're looking for an American, James Peck. He's here with you. I'd like to talk to him."

The commander seemed to do a mental roll call. "No. Not here. I've got two Swedes and a Frenchman. No gringos. Except maybe you two."

"The shoe-shine boy. He sent me to him."

"Who?"

"Ernesto," the radio operator said.

"Get him." She turned to Ajax. "Ernesto told us what you did, in the cathedral. Why did you interfere with the soldiers?"

He shrugged. "They spit in the beans. I was hungry."

Nora nodded. "That hunger saved your life."

"Fuck! You two, again!" Ernesto was none too pleased.

"Report" was all Nora said.

"I was at the cathedral. Some guy gave me ten dollars, *American*, to send him," he shot a thumb at Ajax, "to the confessional."

"You were on *duty*, Ernesto."

"Yes, *compa*. *Undercover*. What kind of shoe-shine boy passes up ten bucks?!"

Nora shook her head. But a snort escaped the radio operator. Nora held out her hand, and the shoe-shine boy, after appealing to heaven, handed over the ten-dollar bill.

"He have red hair?" Ajax asked.

"Didn't see him, he was already in the confessional. I thought he was a priest."

"A gringo?"

"Don't know. He sounded foreign, lots of priests are."

"Ever seen him before?"

"Didn't see him at all, genius, I told you."

The radio operator silenced them with a hiss and held her hand to the earpiece. "They're moving."

Nora gave a low whistle and a *Mount up!* hand signal. In a disciplined silence Ajax watched the hundred or so Gs line up at three drains and drop rapidly into the sewers. A smaller column headed out a side door. In less than a minute the crowded warehouse was empty.

Nora and the radio operator packed up her gear. Nora handed one of her .45s to the boy. "They try to leave before it begins, kill them."

"And if I don't have to?"

"Let them go when it's over." She pointed her finger at Gladys. "Don't underestimate short pants, he'll do it."

She was about to duck out when she turned back to Ajax. "Aren't you married to Gioconda Targa?"

The mention of his ex-wife's name was so unexpected Ajax almost choked, and stammered. "I . . . I was."

"I met her once. In Managua. She's good people."

"I'll give her your regards."

Nora snorted. "You got about as much chance of seeing her as I do."

Five minutes later all hell broke loose about three blocks away. Ajax could make out small arms, RPGs, and the M40 he'd seen. At the moment of contact he'd thought he'd heard the squeal of brakes and assumed Nora and her men had hit a convoy. Maybe the one he'd seen back at the cathedral.

Ernesto seemed anxious, but maybe not so disappointed to have been left behind.

"They hit a convoy?"

He pointed the pistol at Ajax. "Shut up."

"They don't tell you much."

"Shut up!"

"It's alright, kid." Gladys smiled. "I know the feeling."

Ernesto was going to turn the gun on her when the first helicopter gunship arrived.

The deep bass grind of a gunship was not a noise forgotten once heard—in peace or war. It was like the engine of an enormous truck trying to turn over. GRNNNNNNNNNNNNNN! GRNNNNN-NNNNNNNNN! Ajax counted each time. About a three-second burst.

"He's good." Ajax pointed to the sky.

"How would you know?" Ernesto's teeth were clenched tight.

"Listen."

GRNNNNNNNNNNNNNNNNNNNNN!

"About three seconds each. Controlled bursts." Ajax pointed a finger gun at the kid. "Means he's aiming at what he's shooting at. Three seconds is about six hundred rounds each burst."

GRNNNNNNNNNNNNNNNNNNNNNNNN!

Ernesto blessed himself and kissed his scapular.

"Don't worry, *mijito*. If you can hear it they've already gone by you."

They didn't hear the rocket. Just felt the explosion when it took half the roof down. The second one went straight into the floor. The concussion sent them flying. It's thought by those who've never been in one that an explosion makes you feel like you're coming apart. But Ajax knew it was the opposite. The first thing an explosion does is suck the air out of a room and out of your lungs for a fraction of a second. So the first sensation of detonation is suffocation. That's what Ajax felt as he went flying across the room—that he would suffocate.

But he was on his feet in the next second.

"In the sewer!"

The three of them dashed for the grate. Gladys got there first, yanked it off, and was down it before the grate hit the floor. Ajax stuffed Ernesto down it like a rabbit into a hat and dropped straight in.

"Go! Go! Go!"

"*La* pistola!"

"Forget it, we gotta move!"

"It's Nora's. She'll kill me!"

Ernesto was back up the ladder before Ajax could even move. He started up when that deep bass grind let rip. The 20mm cannon shells peppered the floor above, shaking concrete loose in the sewer. Four long bursts and it stopped, flew off, and left them mostly in silence.

"Ernesto!"

Ajax climbed back up into the ruined warehouse. It seemed there was not a two-foot square without at least one cannon hole in it. Ernesto stood in one of them, shaking like he would break into pieces. A deep gouge was between his feet, his legs were powdered in concrete dust up to his crotch. But he had Nora's pistol. Ajax went to him, and lifted the cheap scapular around his neck.

"Boy, you have a powerful patron."

The kid tried to speak, but the only sound he made was his teeth chattering like a bag of bones.

Ajax scooped him up in his arms and carried him away.

He and Gladys made their way back to where they'd come into the sewer. The shoe-shine boy'd gone off to find his unit. When they got to the grate, Ajax saw a gunship directly above them. With each burst hundreds of black aluminum casings fell. They were the links that held the bullets in their long belts. The shells struck home far away, but these links fell straight down out of the gunship's belly, like black rain from a cloud. They even bounced off the ground and danced like raindrops, cascading down into the sewer and onto his head.

When the gunship moved on he and Gladys climbed out of the sewer. But not out of the shit. The air was heavy with the reek of cordite. Nora's battle was blocks away but the smell of it followed them as they made their way back toward the cathedral. They stopped at a broken water main to clean the sewer off their shoes if not their skins. The plaza around the church was now almost empty of soldiers. They melted into the crowd as quickly as they could and copped a squat on the stairs. Gladys let out a sigh so long she sounded like a balloon.

"You alright?"

"Yes, fucking yes. Stop asking all the time."

He smiled. She was alright.

"Gladys, I think that was young Peck, in the confessional."

"You *saw* him?"

"No. I thought. But . . . Shit!" He remembered. "He knew my name, called me Martin Garcia."

"Who knows us as that?"

"Jasmine, Max, Michaelson at the embassy . . ."

"Teal."

Ajax snorted. "But Reynaldo? And whoever Reynaldo works for."

"I thought he worked for Teal."

"Teal's an idiot. He might be president someday, but he doesn't run someone like Reynaldo." Ajax stood, in sudden need of straightening out the kinks. He stretched out as high as his hands could reach, and then bent at the waist to touch his toes. He felt three pops in his spine as the vertebrae realigned. He patted his calf where the Needle was still strapped, and stood upright.

"Something's not right, Gladys. But I don't know what. Like an unseen hand hiding something." He shook his head, there was a disconnect between his mind and instinct.

Gladys stood up. "So what's next?"

"We go see the padres at the university."

"Now?"

"What time is it?"

She checked her watch. "Jesus, it's only ten thirty."

"Yeah, and of the same day no less."

"Why there? It's on the other side of town."

"How many times we hear the word 'priest' today? If that was young Peck he pretended to be a priest. Ernesto said a priest paid him. Jasmine knows the priests. Peck knows them. Priest. Priest. Priest. Let's go see the priests."

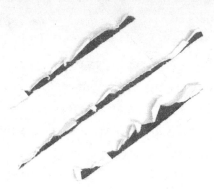

26

Their trek to the University of Central America, Gladys felt, was long, dangerous, and strangely monotonous, like riding a tortoise through a minefield—each step might be your last, but after a while it was just *Get the fuck on with it!*

She and Ajax had made their way from the cathedral back to Estela's car, walking each block right down the middle of the street, their white table napkins waving, and offering about as much protection, Gladys felt, as a prayer in a plague ward.

She'd begun to wonder if Ajax was *her* white flag, her table napkin—offering more of a psychological shield than a refuge from actual arrows. His stunt at the cathedral had been reckless. That he'd pulled it off did not reassure her as much as his impulse to do it worried her. It was the Miami coyote all over again, but one branch higher on the crazy tree.

When they'd reached the car she'd insisted on driving, a need to be a little bit more in control. Ajax had surrendered the keys, but would not be drawn on his motives for confronting the Atlactl soldiers.

Now they were two hours into what was a fifteen-minute drive during peacetime. It was an odd experience, to say the least. They moved slowly, the cautious tortoise, windows down, listening for the sound of gunfire, flinching when they heard it. On some blocks people were out—sitting amidst rubble or tamping down fires in one spot that had been hit. On other blocks people just stood in the street, talking, waiting. Occasionally a squad of soldiers, government or rebel, would scurry like iguanas on a hot zinc roof across the street and disappear down an alley or over a wall. Gunfire would erupt, or not. It was, Gladys thought, like being a minor character lost in a performance—the major players would dash on and off the stage, but the main action was always elsewhere. They could locate the battle only by sound—the rapid popping of small arms and machine guns overlaid at times with the deeper bass grinding of the helicopter gunships.

They passed through three army checkpoints—each time Max's calling cards got them through with no more than a caution about the "*terroristas*" up ahead. But so far the Farabundos had not shown themselves, except off stage.

They journeyed like this—stop, start, halt, wait, bail out, get back in, and all over again—always rolling southwest until they got to Colonia Sultana. But the closer they got to the UCA, the more sporadic the sounds of war got, until they petered out except as far echoes. The university was bordered by several broad avenues in a leafy lower-middle-class section of town.

They circled around the neighborhood once, looking for an approach, but most of the main streets leading to the campus were blocked by the army—the UCA, merely as a university, was considered a natural ally of the FMLN. In truth it was, which was why, Gladys reckoned, the rebels let it be and the government locked it down.

They rolled by the main entrance, crowded with soldiers and armored vehicles with .50 caliber machine guns. Gladys tapped the brakes.

"Want to try the front door?"

"No! Go, go, go."

She drove on. "What?"

"Look in the mirror, clock the civilians."

She did. Four, maybe five men. Sunglasses, leather jackets with big bulges. Paramilitaries.

"Got 'em. Where do they learn to dress like that?"

"*Miami Vice?*"

"Death squad Charlies?"

"Gotta be. Turn right here."

She swung around the corner.

"Pull over here."

Gladys parked at the base of a hill on Albert Einstein Avenue. She watched Ajax stare out the windshield while slowly rubbing his thumb and forefinger.

"What?" she asked, to break the silence.

Ajax turned his palms up. "Creepy feeling. The army's up to its throat in Farabundos. But if Krill has told anyone about us, it'd be them, the *escuadrones*. All the checkpoints we've been through today, we never saw one paramilitary. This place is crawling with them."

"The one place all day there's not much combat."

"Yeah, but they're not cowards; well, they are. They're the tail that wags the dog. That's why our ORDEN cards got us through the army checkpoints. Anyone questions us here, show the passports. We're frightened, hopelessly lost Americans trying to get to the embassy."

They got out and walked a few blocks. Ajax checked the streets for an approach. They stopped at what was more a long alley than a street. The sidewalks were lined with a couple dozen *comedores*—a small charcoal barbecue under a bit of plastic roofing. Pork and chicken grilling, tamales. The kind of joint that made Gladys want a Handi Wipe. She was surprised so many people were out, so many cooking. But as the micro-restaurants were all attached to the cooks' homes, it was just a matter of opening your back door and blowing on the coals. The alley was full of soldiers and even civilians.

"This'll do," Ajax said, lingering at the mouth of the alley. He took out a cigarette from the pack he'd clipped from the soldier. "Got a light?"

"You smoking again? Things'll kill you."

He held out the cigarette, a little too dramatically, she thought.

"Got a light?"

"No."

"Pretend you're looking in your purse, we'll peruse the alley."

"Oh." It was a prop. Gladys made a little show of searching for a lighter. "Crowded up there, we can find an emptier street."

"No, this is better. The *comedores* push all the pedestrians onto the street, easier to keep an eye out."

She held up her hands, *No lighter*. "What're we looking for?"

Ajax patted his pockets, saw the food vendors and their customers eyeballing the strangers.

"Anyone dressed in civvies, not obviously cooking, eating, or keeping someone company, and is male from sixteen to twenty-eight is suspect. It's the undercover guys we've got to watch out for."

Ajax drew a book of matches out of a pocket. *There they are!* And he sparked up the Camel, took a long pull, exhaled, then held the cigarette between thumb and forefinger, and held it in front of him like a Prussian fop would a monocle. "It's a college, try to blend in."

Gladys's eyes rolled so hard it made her head spin. "You think that is a disguise?"

"I'm the old-world professor, try to look like an adoring student, mesmerized by my erudition."

"I'd rather be your cleaning lady."

They strolled up the alley, carefully parsing the faces for hostility. The Salvadorans are a handsome people, Ajax thought. More Ladino than Nicaragua, generally lighter skinned. *Aquiline* was a word you'd use to describe the *salvadoreño típico*. They were a lean people, shorter than Nicaraguans, who tended toward pudginess in middle age, the women as well as the men.

The vendors and customers eyed them back. No matter who they might be, this strolling couple was an unknown entity, and therefore dangerous.

Ajax stopped at a couple of places, got some mystery meat on a stick and a little bag of *pupusas,* the rough corn tortillas stuffed with cheese and meat that was the national dish. Each stop made Ajax and Gladys a little more familiar—pleasantries exchanged, money counted out and change counted back. The small interactions of giving and taking back that closed the distance between them. It was silence that fed fear.

"*Gracias, profesor,*" one of the vendors said with the coins he dropped into Ajax's hand.

Gladys grunted her disapproval that he'd actually carried the ruse off. They carried on up the alley. Ajax still scanning the faces, searching for the serpent in this greasy garden. They reached the apex of the hill. It curved steeply to the right and back down toward Einstein Avenue. The sloping driveway up to the left was the entrance to the UCA. As they crested the hill Ajax spotted the viper. But not the one he expected.

Fifty yards ahead, and slightly down the hill, the boy with the long eyelashes stood in the middle of the street. Ajax stopped and turned his back to the ghost.

"What?" Gladys was on full alert.

"Not sure." He held out his cigarette. "Take the butt, throw it on the ground, and stamp it out, like you're mad."

Gladys did just that. Ajax flapped his hands in protest, gestured to the ground. "Now we're gonna have a little argument over my smoking." He pointed at the mangled butt. "You look over my shoulder, slightly downhill."

Gladys took a peek. And blanched.

"Shit."

"You see it?"

"Monkey Man."

"What?"

"Isn't that who you saw?"

"Right. Right." Ajax took his cigarettes out, pointed once at the ground, and waved a rebuking finger at Gladys. He looked around and caught someone's eye, shrugged, *Women!*

"What's he doing?"

Gladys peeped. "There's a jeep, a uniform in it. Monkey Man's folding up a map. Shit, he's coming this way."

"Your gun?"

"The car. The Needle?"

"My calf. If he makes us, he's dead, we bolt to the car, try to make the embassy."

"Shh." She put her finger to his lips. Slipped a cigarette out of his pack and lit it for him.

"What are you doing?"

"Playing the infatuated student." She pecked him on the cheek. "He's gone. Got into the jeep."

"Who with?"

She shook her head. "Officer. He got some salutes on the way out."

Ajax had a look back. The coast was clear, except for one more army checkpoint just inside the entrance to the university. That's where he saw the ghost. Slowly treading up the hill toward the padres.

Ajax hooked his arm through Gladys's and they strolled by the soldiers, one of whom nodded, muttered "*Profesor.*" And they were in.

27

The priests, the Seis Padres, Ajax had come to call them, lived at the top of the hill, in a house behind the campus chapel. The campus was mostly deserted—all the students and most of the faculty had fled. Which made sense, given that the university had in the past been the scene of unspeakable violence and repression. There were a few workers about—gardeners, cleaners, clerks—who had either been trapped there last night, it seemed to Ajax, or stayed for the protection the university might offer.

One such laborer had escorted them to the padres' house. After his *confession*, Ajax was not hopeful these priests would be of any more help, and the last thing he wanted was another lecture on the seven deadly sins.

What he found inside was a den of iniquity. Or at least the din of a raucous poker party.

The door was opened by a smiling, middle-aged man who was the living definition of the frumpy professor—only this one was in a bathrobe and the kind of leather slippers that should only be sold with a pipe.

"Who is it?" someone else called from inside.

The frumpy priest looked Ajax and Gladys over, frowned. "Well, it's not the army, but it's not dinner either. *Pasen*." He stood aside and let them pass.

He led them into what seemed a fraternity get-together on a lazy

Saturday afternoon. The rectory was an old elegant building, and the walls of the smoky room were heavy with framed photographs, stuffed bookshelves, and primitive art and pottery, Ajax saw, from each of the five Central American countries. The six Jesuits sat around their dining room table, which was strewn with cards and poker chips, glasses of beer, and ashtrays overflowing with cigar stubs.

They were dressed like frat boys too—from the 1950s. One was in a wife-beater and his boxers, two wore bathrobes that dated from the seventies, one was in black slacks and a white shirt, the other two, with unkempt beards, were in equal states of half-undress.

It was a desultory game too. Two of the Jesuits seemed intent on playing, one strummed a guitar, the fourth had let them in, and the other two—looking like bearded teddy bears—argued with an unseen someone in the kitchen.

"You're all going to hell!" the someone in the kitchen shouted like a street preacher. Ajax guessed it was their cook.

"Yes, doña Elba," said one of the beards, "but we can absolve ourselves of our sins." He turned to the room, made the sign of the cross, "*Les absolvo . . .* "

"That's sacrilege!" Elba pronounced it like an inquisitor.

The priests finally took note of their visitors. They did not, Ajax thought, seem embarrassed at their informal state, nor make any move to become more presentable. Instead they reconnoitered their guests with practiced eyes.

"I am Ignacio Ellacuría," said the Jesuit who'd let them in. He went around the room. "This is Segundo Montes, Juan Ramon, the other Ignacio, Joaquín López, and Amando." Each nodded as they were pronounced. Ellacuría turned toward the kitchen, "And that cruel hellion blockaded in the kitchen is doña Elba."

"This is a den of iniquity," she shouted. "Get out while you can!"

Father Ellacuría tightened the belt on his bathrobe and motioned for Ajax and Gladys to sit. The priests might have been divided in their loyalty to the game, but they all took their places at the table and studied the strangers. A silence fell over the tableau, but a surprisingly comfortable one.

"I am . . ."

"Martin Garcia," said one. "That is Gladys Batista."

"You're the *cubanos-gringos*," said one of the beards.

"Jasmine told us to expect you," said the other beard.

"Doña Elba," said the guitar priest, "we have guests, can you not relent and bring our weary travelers some refreshment? Some Christian charity?"

"No! You are gambling in the House of God!"

"We are gambling in *our* house, God's House is next door in the chapel."

Silence.

"Celina!" The guitarist mouthed *Elba's daughter.* "Would you please bring some refreshments?"

There was no reply, but Ajax heard the sound of glasses and cups being laid on a counter. The six all sighed with relief.

Ajax and Gladys made a circle around the long dining room table—which would have held half a dozen more guests—shaking hands. By the time they were done a very plain girl, about sixteen, brought a tray of coffee and *pupusas.* Celina looked happy to do so, wearing none of her mother's opprobrium. She paused to serve Gladys first, seemingly delighted at another woman's presence. Then she served Ajax.

"What do you think, Celina? Are the fathers wicked?"

She smiled, Ajax thought, with a forbearance beyond her years. "It's a poor enough sin, they play for pennies."

"Ten *centavos* ante," Ellacuría objected. "There's almost five *colones* in that pot." About two dollars. Ellacuría took a sip of coffee, looked at his cards, tossed them onto the table—a busted flush.

"Do you play poker, Martin?" He'd switched to English.

"God understands English!" Elba eavesdropped.

"Yes, my darling, but you do not!"

Smiles darted around the room, linking the faces in the same con-spiracy.

"Poker, Martin?"

"Yes."

"You're a gambler?"

"No. But I like cards."

The guitarist leaned forward. "And what is the first rule of poker?"

Ajax paused. "Never open on your own, never lead, always raise someone else's bet."

The guitarist threw his palms up at the two beards, as if to say, *See?*

"And why is that, Martin?"

"Because poker is a game of misinformation. The winning hand should always appear to be following someone else, the leader, until the final raise when the leader realizes he's not been leading, but being led."

"And then it is too late."

"Too late."

A silence fell over the Seis Padres, they all seemed to quietly con-firm something.

"You've been on the streets?" This from the padre in his boxers and wife-beater.

"Yes." Ajax nodded, as if reviewing all that he had seen.

"What's it like?"

"Deadly." Gladys jumped in. "Lots of combat, though we didn't run into any, or not head-on. Firefights, explosions, those gunships flying low over everywhere. The whole city seems locked down."

"What's that tell you?" boxer shorts asked.

"The battle's not lost nor won yet."

"And who does that benefit?"

Gladys paused, and Ajax was sure she didn't know she was being raised by the winning hand.

"The rebels. They don't have to win, not yet, just not lose."

Another round of glances wended its way through the padres' eyes.

"Any army around us, the university?"

"You're pretty much locked down too."

"See any civilians?"

"Civilians? On the street . . ."

"He means paramilitaries," the guitarist added.

"Oh, well, ah . . ." Gladys cut her eyes at Ajax. *Do I tell them?*

"Call or fold, Gladys" was all Ajax had to offer.

"We did spot one guy, we saw him at Jasmine's, Max's house. He's with D'Aubuisson."

"Well, El Mayor needs his own intelligence." Ellacuría seemed almost sympathetic. "Jasmine speaks highly of you." He addressed Ajax.

"And of you, all of you."

"So, you want to know about Jimmy Peck?"

"We do," Ajax said.

"But you come here in disguise?"

"Not really." Gladys just couldn't be left out of the conversation, the poker game, Ajax thought. He studied the walls, the books, art, mementos of their lives and time in each Central American country.

"We know Peck's parents." Gladys unfolded their cover story. "They asked us to ask around while we were here. As guests of the government they thought we might find some answers . . ." She trailed off, her story stopped by the impish expression of the priests.

A not unfriendly silence followed, until the priests' eyes were on Ajax.

"We fold, Fathers." He smiled at Gladys. "They know who we are."

"We know who *you* are," boxer shorts said.

"Jasmine," Gladys hissed.

"No." Ajax pointed at the walls, naming the Nicaraguan artifacts arrayed there. "That painting is from Solentiname. Three volumes of poetry by Cuadra, Belli, and Cardenal. And those heads"—he pointed to three very antique but crude clay heads—"I'd bet are from Isla Muerta in the big lake." He surveyed the priests. "Who's lived in Nicaragua?"

The guitarist and both beards raised their hands.

"Before or after the Triumph?"

"After."

"Before."

"Both."

"Oh," Gladys said.

"Poker," Ajax replied.

"I was actually in Managua when you captured that serial killer," said the guitarist. "I remember he escaped. Didn't he? Did you ever recapture him?"

Ajax cut a quick glance at Gladys. " I got him eventually."

Ellacuría poured his guests more coffee. "We will not speak your names," he nodded dramatically to the kitchen, "but of course we know them. So, you want to know about Jimmy?"

"Yes!" Gladys set her cup down with more force than dexterity. She seemed nervous to Ajax—maybe the priests as college professors reminded her of her own school days.

"Why?" boxer shorts asked.

"I knew Jimmy's sister in Nicaragua a few years ago," Ajax said. "She was murdered, it was my fault. Jimmy's parents came to me. To us. They want us to find him or at least bring his body back, something to bury."

"Do you think he's dead?" the guitarist asked.

"Do you think he's alive?"

Another glance went round the table, like some Jesuitical telepathy, and agreement was had.

"Jimmy was . . ." Ellacuría paused, inviting adjectives.

"Innocent."

"Naïve."

"Reckless."

"All of the above."

"You know he worked for the Democratic Party back in Washington, gathering information for the certification," Ellacuría said.

"Counterfactual information," Ajax said.

"Yes. But he was playing a dangerous game. There are many people here, groups of people who risk their lives chronicling the depravations of the army and death squads." Ellacuría lifted his hands to take in the whole country. "There is no secret to what happens here! Disappearances, the murders. That the Americans continue to 'certify' this monster's progress on improving human rights is not a lack of information . . ."

"It's an abomination."

"Yes, it is, my friend. Jimmy was naïve, innocent, and reckless, because he thought he could uncover other information, that he could *infiltrate* the death squads and provide some *truth* that would sway the American Congress to cut off aid."

"The Lone Ranger," the guitarist said.

"Batman," suggested boxer shorts.

"Tubbs and Crockett," said the padre in black slacks and white shirt, the first time he'd spoken.

"Who?" Gladys jumped in.

"*Miami Vice*," Ajax explained.

"You know it!" Black and white seemed delighted.

"Caught a few episodes."

"Except those are all television shows," Ellacuría reminded them. "Some good, mind you, I wanted to *be* Batman until I went to the seminary. But . . ."

"But playacting can get you killed," Gladys concluded.

"In El Salvador many things can get you killed; being too loud . . ." Ellacuría seemed to pass a ball around the table:

". . . being too quiet . . ."

". . . demanding too much . . ."

". . . wanting too little . . ."

". . . knowing the wrong people . . ."

". . . knowing the right people."

There was a long silence around the table.

"What about Jasmine?" Ajax said. "She work with Jimmy?"

"Work?" Ellacuría was baffled. "Jasmine has no side in this war, she is one of the few. Why would you ask that?"

"She and Jimmy partied with some death squad Charlie types, Max too—discos, drink, coke. Could she have been helping him? Robin to his Batman?"

A round of head shaking passed through the padres.

Ajax looked each man in the eye—they were the honest, decent, bighearted types that often were found in some of the world's worst places. The exalted of the earth.

And they were lying.

"Who killed Peck?" he asked, feeling more cop now than shy guest.

"The *escuadrones,* there are no other suspects."

"There are always other suspects," he corrected. "But how is it possible there is no body? We know there were morgue pictures. Where's his body?"

"There is no lack of bodies here." The guitarist sat forward, showing some anger. "There is not even a lack of disappeared Americans. You're the second ones to come looking for a gringo who fell off the edge of the earth."

"Another?"

"A college student from Notre Dame, it's a Jesuit school, we're Jesuits. His family contacted us, asked our help."

"That's in Indiana," Gladys jumped in.

"Why, yes," Ellacuría said. "You know it?"

"Missing person poster at the embassy, had an Indiana phone number. Liam Donaldson."

"That's him. His father called. He was backpacking through

Central America. Can you *imagine*? Does no one in America read a newspaper?"

"You have any luck?" Ajax asked.

"No. We are not actually equipped for that sort of thing."

Ajax and Gladys shared a look. She flicked her eyes to the far side of the room, to the phone and the big beige fax machine sitting next to it.

"You're saying you don't know Liam Donaldson is the spitting image of Jimmy Peck? Tall, pasty white skin, red-orange hair? His family contacted you but didn't send any photos over that fax machine?"

"They did," Ellacuría admitted. "We put some pictures up around campus, but they're in black-and-white. What are you suggesting?"

"Liam Donaldson is dead. Jimmy Peck is alive. I saw him today, in the confessional of the Metropolitan Cathedral."

Ellacuría seemed genuinely surprised. He turned his palms up and again went around the table. All the padres signaled they were equally clueless. That, at least, Ajax thought, was the truth.

"I will not look upon your sins!" Doña Elba interrupted and entered with a big tray of victuals and her eyes closed. "But if you need food to sustain you in your *prayers*, I will not be the one who denied you it!"

There was a round of *Gracias a Dios!* as the Seis Padres switched back to Spanish and ladled out the *carnitas, pupusas,* and beans in cream. For a half hour or so the eight of them feasted on Elba's cuisine, teasing her lovingly as she condemned them for their sins like the house mother she had become to these garrulous bachelors.

Food was followed by beers, snuck in from the guitarist's room. The table talk shifted from Peck, death, and disappearances to poetry, anthropology, and the pros and cons of Jheri Curl like Detective Tubbs used. They were all Spaniards, the priests, but had been so long in Central America, their Spanish was utterly colloquial. Ajax felt at home for the first time in years, and he was pleased to see Gladys relax into the conversation too.

The sun had begun to tilt dangerously low by the time he and Gladys gave their thanks and made their good-byes; the dusk-to-dawn curfew in the city was enforced to deadly effect by both sides. They found the padres' phone was working and called doña Estela. She relayed a message from Jasmine to meet them at Max's. She assured them Jasmine had said it was safe.

The padres escorted them to the door. Ajax found the ghost standing there, like a bottle of wine he'd forgotten to bring in. Or a mangy junkyard dog who'd followed him and stayed. Ajax scanned the eyes of the others to see if they too saw, but none did, only wondered at his wavering.

"You've got to go back to Jasmine's before curfew."

Ajax hesitated again. "Fathers, what do you do for your security?"

"You mean are we pistol-packing padres?" Black and white made finger pistols.

"I mean, do you have any security? Just a lookout?"

Ellacuría took his arm and led Ajax to the lawn surrounding their rectory, lavish as it was in bougainvillea and honeysuckle. He pointed up. Ajax followed his gaze to the bronze cross atop the chapel.

"Best lookout in the universe."

Ajax had a quick look at the ghost; the boy rarely had proven wrong as a herald of trouble. "You'd do better with a pair of eyes up there."

"The army has us locked down and locked up. This, too, will pass. Go with God, my son."

Blessings and handshakes were passed from one to another and they left.

"What do you think?" Gladys spoke once they were back on the street.

"They're lying about something."

"Yeah, but what?"

"Not Donaldson."

"No. They seemed straight about Peck too. So who?"

"Jasmine."

"She's the only one left."

They made their way more quickly down the hill than they had coming up. Night was coming and they needed to get off the streets. Ajax kept looking back. They soon outpaced the boy with the long eyelashes.

28

"Why is there evil in the world? I don't know. If God created evil, then is evil good or bad? Why would He create it? Maybe He made evil as a measure, to measure how much good we can create? So it's a test, right?"

Krill turned from the portrait of the *generalissimo* to see why Jasmine was not answering him. Did she think he was asking the general? He meant these questions, damn it! They vexed him. He was sincere. Fucking *ricos*! So much fancy schooling, so much time to ponder these uncertainties and what did it get them? Did they know more than Krill? Did they *care* more? No one had ever taken his search for answers seriously. Not his father, that broken-down donkey working the harvests of other men for *centavos*. *The land is our life* was all the answer he'd ever had while running his machete over a stone to cut cane or maize on someone else's land. And the day he'd brought a machete home for Krill? For his only *son*. Not even a new one, but one his father had found in a field. Krill'd known that day that his family, his life would not be in service to the *ricos*. He'd taken that machete and walked fifteen miles to the nearest army post, sat outside until the sentry finally took him to see the commanding officer. Krill had buried the machete into the captain's desk and demanded a gun to fight the Sandinistas. After the captain had almost shot him, but hadn't, they shaved Krill's head and gave him a uniform. He had become his own man then. But even his comrades found Krill's questions laughable.

Or had until they learned the price for laughing at him. All those peasants had wanted were three meals, a bed, and a little pay at the end of the month.

Krill wanted answers. What was evil and how did one serve God doing good? Communism, capitalism, nationalism, faggotism. What were these things? Who made them? His questioning had made for a lonely youth—his barrack-mates had scorned him as social climber; his officers had condescended to the uneducated peasant. But once he had become Krill, *Comandante Krill,* his search only intensified, even if command had made him lonelier still.

There was no answer from Jasmine. It should make him angry, her silence. But maybe being rich gave you nothing but things, no knowledge.

Krill gazed at the *generalissimo* and ran the machete over the whetstone. The blade passed lightly, smoothly, and fast over it. The timbre of the sound told all. A dull blade made a scratchy sound. The more honed the blade the smoother the sound. This machete made barely a whisper. When the feel of the steel on stone was right, when the sound of the blade told him there was no more edge to be gotten, he turned to Jasmine to make her answer.

"I'm so sorry, señorita." He'd left the gag in her mouth. *Idiota!* "Apologies."

29

Ajax told Gladys to turn the engine and headlights off, and roll Estela's car downhill until a few houses from Max's. Night had come on fast and they'd just made it back as the last of the light died. They got out without making a sound, quietly clicked the doors shut, and made their way to the iron gate, pocked with bullet holes like zits on a dead teenager's face.

They peered through a couple of zits to case the house. No lights in front, maybe one in the back. He signaled Gladys to chamber a round in her pistol and go around the side and check the servants' entrance.

He put an eye to a zit. If there'd been danger, if Max or Monkey Man were waiting for them, he'd felt sure Jasmine would've let them know. And the padres had given him no reason to think their secret was not safe.

Ajax had found the priests charming, had felt at home in their company far quicker than most—not that his choice of company over the past three years had been much to brag on. But young Peck was an enigma whose mystery only deepened every time they spoke to someone. His sister, Amelia, had been an open book—direct, honest, and naïve like most gringos. He knew now he'd expected her brother to be the same. But young Peck was fooling someone—either the priests had him all wrong, or Max and Monkey Man did.

He had a feeling it was the latter. Young Peck as a cowboy, trying to play at spy, working Max and the *escuadrones* for information he thought might tip the balance in the war between good and evil.

"What is it with Americans?" He looked around, startled, until he realized he'd spoken out loud. Then Gladys reappeared, shook her head.

"Locked. What do we do?"

"Ring the bell."

So he did. A buzzer sounded far away and after a few moments the iron gate slid back to let them in. They approached the house warily. Sticking to the shadows. The front door was unlocked. So they walked in.

The foyer was dark. Down the hall a light was on in the dining room, illuminating little.

"Jasmine?"

There was a pause, which suddenly put Ajax on alert. Jasmine stepped into the hallway, but did not approach. Did not move from the door between dining room and hall.

"Come on in, Max will be right down!"

Ajax put an arm on Gladys, mouthed *Max*? He held up a hand and waved Jasmine to them. She shifted her hips ever so slightly to the left—someone was in the dining room with her.

"Max is changing," she called out. "We've got *nacatamales*! Made them myself!"

Nacatamales was a Nicaraguan dish. That was all Ajax needed to know.

He put a hand on Gladys's shoulder, mouthed *Krill*. She tensed and Ajax feared she might charge. He pointed to the wall separating them from the dining room. He pointed to a likely position, put his mouth to her ear. "When she moves shoot through the wall, between here." He held a hand at shoulder height. Gladys nodded her assent. Her gaze was steady.

Ajax held up his hand to Jasmine, signaled her first to bend low, then run. He gave her the thumbs-up. She made no move at all. Silence equals consent. He flipped his hand at her.

"Now!"

Gladys started blasting, making a tight pattern as Jasmine folded over and sprinted to them. It was only a moment later when a hand appeared around the corner and fired back, blind. Jasmine sprawled to the floor, bullets smashed plaster loose. One shot was dangerously close to Gladys's head. Ajax drew the .22 as Gladys reloaded her only other clip. He put a couple shots about where he hoped Krill might be, but the *Pop Pop* of the dinky gun would do little to deter Krill.

"I've got men outside," Krill yelled.

"You're alone and we're coming for you!"

Ajax signaled Gladys to go left, covering the hallway. Ajax would go right and come up behind the fucker—the .22 wasn't much use, but he didn't want Krill dead right away. As he and Gladys made their move, a hand appeared, or rather, a hand grenade. The sphere, black in the gloomy light, made an arc. Ajax saw the spoon flip off as it went live, hit the floor, and bounded toward him. He and Gladys both hit the deck, Ajax pushing himself against the wall. But the grenade bounced toward him like it had his name on it, and came to a stop inches from his face. He froze, only for an instant, expecting oblivion when, like a viper, Gladys's hand lashed out and swiped it away. The little orb of death flew back down the hallway, only to slam into Jasmine's head and come to a stop, almost in her ear.

Then Krill flew out of the dining room and down the hallway toward the kitchen and the servants' quarters, Gladys chasing him with her last three shots. Ajax closed his eyes, tried to shield his face from the blast, from death. That fucking Krill, they were all dead.

Or not.

"Why didn't it go off?"

The three of them had lain there for a full minute before they realized they weren't going to die. Ajax had checked the servants' quarters, found the door unlocked as Krill had left it, secured it, and rejoined the others around the dud grenade.

"Why didn't it go off?" Jasmine repeated.

Ajax picked it up, weighed it in his hand. "Clever bastard." He quickly loosened the top of the grenade and unscrewed the head. Turned it upside down and shook it. "He took the explosive out. I've seen it before. When your back is against the wall, you make it look like you're going to blow yourself up, toss the grenade, everyone ducks, and you slip away."

"Why would Krill want to do that?" Jasmine took the grenade and had a look in its empty belly.

"He wants us alive." Gladys said it to no one, or to all of them. Ajax thought she might be saying it to Krill.

"Are you alright?" she asked Jasmine.

"I'm okay, he didn't . . . I mean, all he did was talk, for hours. Sometimes to me, sometimes to the general." She nodded to the portrait. "Does he always call himself 'Krill'?"

"He does. Tiresome, isn't it? Why'd you come back here, Jasmine?"

"I couldn't wear Estela's bathrobe forever. The phones were working for a while, I called, got no answer, assumed Max had fled to safer ground. I came up the same way we went down."

Gladys checked the load in her pistol. "I'm spent."

Ajax searched her face, he saw no outward sign of panic, but Gladys had an edgy, restless feel to her. She was jonesing for a wash, he could tell.

"We can't stay here" was all she said.

"We can't be out after curfew either." Ajax was willing to risk a lot, but not a night on the street. "Can we make it to doña Estela's?"

"We don't have to." Jasmine tossed the empty grenade to Ajax. "Max has a safe room upstairs. Bolts from the inside. No one knows about it but him and me."

"It'll withstand bullets?"

"Anything Krill's got short of an RPG."

The three of them went upstairs. Ajax kept watch until he heard Jasmine's cry when she found Max's garroted corpse in the safe room, still tied to his chair. Ajax went over the body, signs of some torture, a cloth belt, maybe from his bathrobe, still looped around his neck. It made Ajax think briefly of El Gordo Sangroso's strangled body. Ajax and Gladys dragged Max out, laid him on his bed, and covered him in his own bedding.

They packed pillows and bedding from Jasmine's room, some water from the sink, and entombed themselves in the safe room. The last thing Ajax saw as he pulled the heavy door closed was Little Max's outline under the blankets.

All over the city people were trying to do the same—hunkering down. Claribel in whatever hovel she lived in was settling under the mattress she'd propped onto two chairs. The fast-talking shoe-shine boy made a pallet of old newspapers under the one table in his room. Nora and her troops stretched out on whatever ground was under their feet. The padres and their housekeepers were safe in their beds. Krill did the same at Estela's house, to where he'd tracked Gladys and Ajax. There was plenty of room for him now.

San Salvador—the Holy Savior—was sheltering from Death, a figure so familiar to its people they called him uncle. Tio Death walked the city's streets that night, not alone, not in El Salvador where there were so many helpers already fanning out through the dark lanes of the Savior's neighborhoods.

30

They killed the housekeepers first. I don't know why they killed us first. I was in my bed when I heard the trucks stop, the squeal of the brakes like my own scream. I climbed into bed with Mami, holding my St. Agnes medal so tight it broke off the chain. Praying, praying, praying, *Please God, don't let them come in.* But that light in our faces, poor Mami was crying, she held out her rosary like it was a safe-conduct pass. But the soldiers only yelled at us, dragged us into the garden with the fathers.

Pobre padres. Some of them were in their underwear or bathrobes. Barefoot or in slippers. Two of them held Bibles. All of them held hands. Father Ellacuría tried hard to make it all normal. Telling the soldiers not to worry, they were always ready to cooperate with the army. He'd even tried to send me and Mami inside to make refreshments. "Don't fear, doña Elba," he'd said, patting my mother's cheek. "Soldiers are always hungry."

But they had shouted at him to be silent, and pushed him to his knees. All of us to our knees. We held hands and prayed, Father Ellacuría led us in the Lord's Prayer, but I whispered Hail Marys. The Blessed Mother has always been my favorite in times of trouble.

Some of the soldiers had painted faces, faces like demons. Others wore bandannas, like God would not recognize them in the afterlife. They were civilians. *Escuadrones.* They were rude to us, especially one.

He called me and Mami whores and the priests subversives. I'd rather have been a subversive.

Matan los, he said. I closed my eyes then, when he said to kill us. They shot me first, I don't know why. Poor Mami. She'd had her eyes closed too. But the gunshot scared her and she opened them in time to see me die. And then to see her own death coming. Just like that they shot us, one by one. First the housekeepers and then the priests. Father Ellacuría last. He held his Bible out and a bullet ripped right through it. The rude civilian stepped forward and shot the father in the face. It was the only time he fired.

They left us where we fell, then ransacked the house. Father Ellacuría was right, soldiers were always hungry and I watched three of them carry off all the *pupusas* I'd made for the *cubanos-gringos* who'd played cards with the padres. They grabbed a lot of papers and things they carried off. Then they took some money from the big box the fathers kept. Most of the soldiers had left by then. The last few went through the priests' clothes, looking for money. But the padres didn't carry their money in their bathrobes and underwear, not even in their slippers or Bibles. That's when one of them saw the gold chain clasped in my hand. He pried my fingers open. I tried so hard to keep my fist closed, but the body down there was not mine anymore.

After that they were gone. I stayed a little while watching Mami, the padres. Even myself. Then a boy came. He was terrible to look at. The soldiers must have caught him somewhere and killed him to be silent. His clothes were all bloody. But he was a beautiful boy. He took my hand and led me away. I don't know where, yet.

31

The next morning broke clean and clear. Gladys had a few nerve-racking moments while she and Ajax cleared the house. No sign of Krill or anyone overnight. Max still lay in his bed-coffin and the *generalis-simo* had stood guard overnight, notwithstanding his own wounds. When they'd assured themselves there was no immediate danger, they'd brought Jasmine out. She paused over her cousin's body but seemed to have no need to mourn or weep and wail. Gladys thought her a tough bird, unless there was something hidden in her family history with Max.

Gladys checked the lights and water as she made her rounds. Neither was working. She lingered by the dining room wall where she'd tried to kill Krill last night. It was a tight shot group—six shots at about shoulder height. But the wall was concrete and none had passed through. Still, the dining room floor was littered with pieces that had exploded off. Maybe that's why Krill had fled. But why he had come at all was a mystery she did not want to solve. Even more so his reasons for tossing a dud grenade at them.

Or, his reason.

What did he want if not to kill her? Them? She shook her head and kicked some of the debris on the floor. But she wasn't saying no so much as refusing to consider the evidence: what Krill wanted was *her*. The thought of it made her heart pound in her temples. A tremor from her stomach ran through her. She held out her gun hand and watched the fingers twitch like a palsied old drunk. They had twitched like that three years ago, every time she'd felt his tread through the floors of her cell. She would not . . .

"Gladys."

She had her pistol in Ajax's face before the least little thought had told her to. "Jesusfuckingchrist, what are you doing!"

"Easy, Gladys."

He reached out and pushed the gun down. He gave her the once-over, and she didn't like it.

"Maybe you should go home."

"What?"

"Home. Miami. We might get you to the airport. You can wait there for the flights to resume."

"What the fuck are you talking about?"

"Look at you, Gladys. Krill's freaked you out."

"Fuck you Ajaxfuckingfuckyoumontoya." She gave him a little push into the hallway and pointed at the holes in the wall. "Look at that shot group, that look like I'm freaked out?"

"He's hunting you."

"I know what he's doing and what he wants. And if he wasn't hunting me that grenade he tossed would've been live and you'd be splattered all over the fucking wall! Yes?"

"NOOOOOOOOOOOOOOOO! NOOOOOOOOOOOOO!"

Jasmine was screaming upstairs.

They bolted passed the *generalissimo* and up to her bedroom where they found her on her knees banging her head on the floor.

"NOOOOOOOO! NOOO! NO!"

"Jasmine, Jasmine." Ajax bent over her and lifted her to her feet. "What is it? What's happened?"

"They've killed them. They killed them all!"

She lifted up a transistor radio that was broadcasting the news. They stood in a small circle listening as the names of the Seis Padres were called. The housekeeper and her daughter last.

"Not Elba and Celina too!" Jasmine dropped her head in her hands, as if the weight of just thinking about it was too much.

Gladys conjured the faces of the two women—the women who had nothing to do with these men, neither priests nor assassins. "God-damn, Ajax, where are we?"

"Satan's waiting room," Jasmine said, wiping tears and snot from her face. "They will kill us all."

Ajax said nothing, just walked to the window overlooking the street. Gladys watched him for his reaction, she could tell how much he'd liked the padres. He stared into the street, then his head popped up, like he'd seen something, or someone. He nodded his head as if answering a call.

"What is it?"

He whipped his head around, cut his eyes back to the street as if checking on something.

"What do you see?"

"What do *you* see?"

Gladys scanned the empty street. "Empty street."

"Good."

He looked into the street again. Gladys followed his line of sight, he was staring at the middle of the street, but there was nothing there. Still, he nodded his head as if acknowledging a signal.

"What're you thinking, Ajax?"

"Monkey Man."

"What?"

"We saw him at the UCA. He did it, or was with those that did."

Gladys scanned the street again, as if looking for the script he seemed to be reading.

"So?"

"You still got Claribel's number?"

"Why?"

"She'll know where Monkey Man is."

She pushed past him to stand between him and the street. "Hey, *loco*. Look at me. It was crazy enough coming here to look for Peck."

"Young Peck."

"*Young* Peck. But now all hell has broken loose, our cover's blown, and Krill is out there hunting us. *Us*, Ajax. And I am . . ." She checked over his shoulder that Jasmine would not hear. "I am sorry about those two women and the priests, but you are going off mission here."

"No, we have to question Monkey Man about Peck."

"*Young* Peck."

He smiled and she saw him there, saw Ajax in that smile.

"Even in Satan's waiting room, a hit like that, they'll be lying low. Claribel will know where he is."

Gladys studied his face, like cutting for sign. She shook her head, but all she could think to say was, "I need bullets."

"I need a real gun."

"Max has both." Jasmine was on her feet now. "In the safe room."

And he did too, bless the dead bastard.

Ajax sorted them in Jasmine's room while Gladys made the call. There were three M16s and four different types of pistol, including, to Ajax's delight, a .357. Not a chrome-plated Python like the one he'd carried in Nicaragua all those years, ever since he'd killed the boy with the long eyelashes to get it, but the grip and the heft were old friends in his hands. He flipped the pistol's cylinder open, all the chambers were empty. He closed it, spun the cylinder, pointed the pistol in the air, and pulled the trigger.

Click!

"That's one."

Then he loaded it, two .45s, and an M16. He set Krill's dud grenade out too. He checked over his shoulder occasionally, back into the street to make sure the ghost was still there.

He was.

Gladys came in, surveyed the arsenal, picked up a .45, weighed it. Holstered it down her back.

"Okay, I'm feeling better."

"Claribel know where Monkey Man's holed up?"

"She's going to him, same place she says after every hit. They lie low, party, she brings the girls and coke."

Ajax smiled. "She say where?"

"Yeah, Jasmine showed me on a map."

"Jasmine." Ajax said the name like he'd forgotten about her. "She can't stay here. We gotta bury Max, but she can't stay here. This is a night op, Gladys. We'll get into place early enough to beat the curfew, then wait for dark. But we'll have to stick out there until daylight tomorrow. She can't stay here overnight."

"She won't. She's going to doña Estela's."

Gladys stood on the balcony overlooking the street. She'd counted six army patrols racing past in the last half hour. Once they were gone there was only silence on the street, but the sounds of combat rose up from the city below them like a smell wafting uphill. In between she could hear Ajax digging Max's grave out back. Her eyes kept going back to the street, the spot he'd been looking at. What was it?

"Gladys."

"Jesus Christ!" She leaped out of her skin. Jasmine stood just behind her. "Why is everyone sneaking around!"

"Sorry. I . . ."

"It's okay, just, you know."

"Jumpy."

"The whole country must be. How is it you're not all on anxiety meds?"

"I suppose that those that can afford it are, the rest . . . well . . . what are you doing here?"

"Keeping an eye on the street."

"No, Gladys. *Here*. El Salvador."

"Looking for Jimmy Peck."

"Like hell you are. When was the last time you spoke of him or even thought of him?"

Gladys swept her arm over the city. "Things got a little, you know, complicated."

"And you're going to go with him?"

"Who?"

"Ajax! After this Monkey Man you're talking about. You're going with him?"

"Go? He probably couldn't find the place without me. Man's got no sense of direction."

"You think it's funny? These men are all professional killers, the most professional in all the goddamn continent. Father Ella . . ." Jasmine stopped, swallowed hard. "I can hardly say their names. Father Ellacuría lived in Nicaragua during your insurrection. He was there a few years ago when that whole thing went down with you two. He knows all about Ajax. Do you know how many men he killed in Krill's camp?"

"Yes, I do."

"Eleven! Eleven men with a knife. Do you know how many died during that 'case' you worked with him? Including the firefight where you were kidnapped?"

"I was in that firefight!"

"Yes, you were. And how many men did *you* kill? How many people have you *ever* killed?"

Gladys knew the answer, and knew Jasmine did too.

"He was a *guerrillero,* you know that."

"That war has been over for ten years. Death follows where he goes, it covers the ground like guano."

"What's your point?"

"Do you feel safe around him? Really?"

Gladys swept her arm over the city. "As opposed to?"

"Not here, not in a war. When the two of you are alone, do you feel safe?"

Gladys had had enough. She pushed in on Jasmine until their pelvises almost touched. Jasmine made a quick two-step back—straight girls were like that, all female solidarity until you got a little too close. Gladys took another step until Jasmine found herself against a wall. She was sure she knew so much about Ajax, Gladys was going to fill her in.

"You ever been taken by a man, Jasmine?" Gladys leaned in until their lips almost touched. "Taken against your will?"

"No."

"I was in hell. Listening every day for Krill's footstep to my cell. It was only three weeks but it lived like three eternities. He would talk to me, quietly, softly." She reached out and stroked Jasmine's hair. "He'd touch my hair, tell me about our lives together. What we would do, the little *finca* we could have, our *children*. But I never answered, I couldn't. Do you understand?"

"Yes."

"So I decided when the day came that I'd bite his fucking manhood off and swallow it before he buried a knife in my brain. And the day came, but instead of death, there was Saint Ajax, holding a hand grenade. A division of our best troops could not have dislodged me from that camp. But he did. And for that he spent three years in hell."

"Yes, he did. The prison and the insane asylum, Gladys. Who has he killed since he got out?"

Gladys didn't want to answer but her eyes flicked away from Jasmine's as she thought of El Gordo, and she knew she'd given herself away.

"He's not going to interrogate this Monkey Man. He's going to kill him."

Gladys took a step back. "But not Claribel. He won't hurt her or the other women."

"And what does that mean? Isn't that what I am talking about? Look around you!" She pushed Gladys back onto the balcony. "I am not some bourgeois girl. This is a country of killers. I know them, I live with them, they are my family. And Ajax is a killer. I'm not saying he is a bad man but you don't seem to know who this man is. He is *broken*."

"Ladies."

Gladys flinched, again, but was finished showing it to others. Jasmine, apparently, wasn't. Ajax stood in the doorway, caked in sweat and dirt from the grave digging. For a moment all three just stared at each other.

Ajax broke the silence. "You want to say some words over Max?"

Jasmine looked from one to the other, and swallowed hard. "Yes. Thank you."

She slipped past Ajax, taking care not to touch him. He and Gladys stood in silence. She knew he could feel what they'd been talking about. He made his way to the balcony, resumed the same post she'd found him at before. His eyes going to the same spot as if some invisible sentry stood vigil there.

"So," he said. "What's going on?"

"Thanks for digging the hole."

"I like it. Digging. You got ground, earth, one shovelful, two, keep at it slow and steady, you get a hole."

"That's weirding me out."

"Holes are useful. You can put a body in it, treasure, guns, shit."

"Can't argue with that. Let's go say good-bye to Little Max."

She began to brush by him when he put his arm out. "Claribel?"

"She'll be there with her girls. There's a green light by the pool, when it's on, the men'll be out."

"How does she know?"

"She says they always get all fucked up after a kill. When the girls get tired of them they slip some kind of barbiturate into their drinks. Out cold, but it seems like sleep."

"Tell her to double the dose."

"We can't interrogate Monkey Man if he's out."

"Then everyone but him."

"And we can't interrogate him if he's dead."

"What do you want to know?"

"You're going to kill them?"

She squinted imperceptibly to take in every facet of his face. He did not blink. Not a muscle twitched. Not a hint revealed. Immobile and impassive. But in his eyes, somewhere deep inside, she sensed the shift to that part of him that always had been hidden, alien.

"Every goddamn one of them."

"Why . . ."

"Did you sit at their table last night? Did the girl serve you? Did her mother cook for you?"

"No, why *you*?"

"Me?"

He looked into the street again, always to the same spot like his lines were written there.

"Because I can. Because Claribel will lead me to them, right now, tonight! You want to leave it to the Salvadorans? The gringos? The U.N.? Or wait forty years until they're shriveled old men like them fucking Nazi camp guards that keep turning up?"

"What's that got to do with Peck?"

He leaned in close to her, until her back was against the wall. "Nothing. Not one fucking thing." He leaned back. "But we'll interrogate Monkey Man first. Or I will."

Now she stepped forward, made him take one backward. "Stop doing that! Assuming I won't go, or I'm not in or I should fucking go home. I'm in. Besides, I got to make sure Claribel and the girls get out safe."

Ajax put his hand over his heart, the move so quick she flinched. "What's that mean? You think I'd hurt her?"

"No! Of course not. Look, you want Claribel's help, I have to be there to reassure her. Okay? Now, let's go. Put Max in the ground and go get cleaned up, you look like a fucking yucca farmer."

He brushed some dirt off. "Yeah, death's a dirty business."

32

The jaguar looked into Ajax's eyes. And he looked back. The animal crouched, perfectly still. It might have been made of clay, or salt. Ajax slid the Needle from its sheath on his calf, fingered the point, and slid a finger along the honed edge until he felt it slip beneath a single layer of skin. The Needle was his claw, his fang. There was something inevitable about it now. This creature, this place, this night. Only a few feet separated them.

He wasn't sure if he should kill it or worship it.

The screech of a quetzal split the night. Still the big cat did not blink, nor did Ajax. He could hear all the animals of the night, smell the dung, feel ponderous feet pacing back and forth. Even Gladys coming up behind him. But he wasn't ready for the monkey head that sailed over him. The jaguar was, and leaped like a ballerina assassin into the air and came down with it in its mouth. The cat cracked the skull open in one bite.

"The fuck did you find that?"

Gladys shrugged. "Most of the monkeys are dead, someone's been butchering them, heads and hands and feet scattered all over."

The Parque Nacional Zoologico was closed, to say the least. There might be some zoos somewhere, he'd thought, say in Belgium, that tried to look like natural settings for the animals they caged. But like a lot of third-world zoos, this one was more gulag than park. Ajax reckoned the cage was just big enough for the cat to take four strides before having to turn about. Just big enough to pace yourself into a psychosis.

The zoo was their staging ground for what was to come. He and Gladys had left the car as close as they could, then scaled a fence at dusk and hunkered down waiting for night. It seemed fitting that Monkey Man's post-massacre safe house was only two blocks from the zoo. But if Gladys was right then someone had been coming during the day to butcher the monkeys for meat. That is a city under siege.

Ajax sheathed the Needle, checked the load in his .357, and then rechecked the magazine in the M16.

"You're not going to kill it."

"Thought never occurred to me." He looked up to find Gladys holding an armful of monkey limbs. "What are you doing?"

She waved a paw in his face. "Hi, Ajax."

He slapped it away. "Get that shit away from me."

She held up another one. "Give me five, bro."

"Stop it. And be quiet."

Gladys threw a paw to the cat, which set about cracking it and licking the marrow from the bones.

Ajax shook his head. "You want to be charitable? Here."

He handed her an M16. Gladys slung it over her shoulder. "No way." She tossed another monkey paw in. "We could open the cage."

Ajax chuckled. "You know how the road to hell is supposed to be paved with good intentions?"

Gladys flicked a paw over the fence. "I sense a rhetorical ambush, but I'll say yes anyways."

"Well, I always thought the road to hell should be paved with the skulls of do-gooders."

Ajax took a monkey skull from her and shot-putted it to the big cat who leaped and caught it and cracked it in one movement.

Now it was Gladys who shook her head. "You won't let it go, but you're going to kill five men."

"You let it go and it's just another killer on the loose. You think once free it'll just hang around here? Someone's kid will be dinner and then what?"

Ajax stood, he was restless like the jaguar and tired of the small talk. "If you're not going to kill it, leave it be. You think he's better off in a cage?"

"Better off than dead? Sure. Weren't you?"

Ajax considered it. "My cage was for a different purpose."

"Was it?" She tossed another paw over the bars.

"The jaguar wasn't brought here to be punished, but put on display. The cage restrains its natural desire to run back to the jungle and kill whatever gets in its way."

Gladys tossed the last of the slaughtered remains to the big cat. But she made no reply. Neither did Ajax.

"Let's go" was all he could think to say.

33

"I'm not prejudiced, you understand?" Krill cut another length of rope. "*Mi general*, General Somoza, he gave me *everything*. Everything I have become came from him. And he was rich, rich as a king! So I am not prejudiced against *ricos*. But in '79 when the *piris* came, the rich ran, all of them. Miami, San Jose, Mexico City." He measured the length of rope—he wanted them all to be exactly the same. Precision was important to him. It's why he wanted these two to understand him precisely. "When they ran, I stayed. Krill stayed."

He studied his captives. It hadn't taken much time to find the old lady's house. It had been his refuge since he'd fled Jasmine's. That decision still troubled him. He could've killed them all with that grenade—but he had to speak to *angelita* first. Just talk! He tied Estela's feet. She tried to kick him! What a character! He'd hated hurting her, he really had. But there was no other way to get Jasmine to talk, to tell him where to find his *angelita*.

"No, *abuela*. No kicking Krill. I'm not prejudiced. But you *ricos*, you're just not strong enough, you need people like me. Not as a servant, but a protector!" He tied Jasmine's feet. "But your cousin, doña Jasmine. He was just too weak. Too weak to live. I am sorry."

Jasmine said nothing, well, she was gagged. But she communicated nothing. Still, Krill could tell by the look in her eyes that she was not such a weakling. Krill fetched the car keys from the pocket of Estela's dead driver. Then he hoisted the old lady over his shoulder. She was so light! Like a bird.

34

When night was well settled over the city Ajax and Gladys scaled a wall at the far end of the zoo and made their way up an alley that connected to a street only five blocks over from Monkey Man's safe house. The sounds of gunfire were far off, but close enough to remind them the city was still under siege. Gladys knew this was the dangerous part: no matter the ID cards or passports they carried, nothing would save them if they were caught by either side armed and creeping around at night.

She and Ajax scoped the street and dashed across it. They crept down other alleys and dashed across streets until they found the green light Claribel had said marked the house. The rear entrance was a heavy steel door set in high walls topped with concertina wire. Ajax nodded for her to try the bolt and at the first touch it gave a little screech. She grimaced at the sound, took out a small bottle of olive oil she'd brought from Max's, and poured it over the bar. She gave it a second and tried again. It slid almost soundlessly out of the catch. Gladys took a breath and pushed. The door popped open.

The both slid the safety off their M16s and stepped in.

The door led to a yard big enough for a small swimming pool surrounded by deck chairs and a cabana for changing. The yard was dark, but the house—a two-story bungalow with lots of windows—was lit up. The brusque hum of a generator came from somewhere. Good, she thought, a generator meant gasoline.

They crept behind the cabana and watched the house.

"Time," Ajax whispered.

"Nine thirty."

"They should be out by now."

But shadows moved inside the house. Gladys couldn't tell whose. Ajax signaled for her to go right, he'd go left. "Get the girls out, bring them to the cabana."

She turned to go when he grabbed her arm. "Don't come inside until I signal."

She crouched and made her way along the wall, circling toward an entrance that should lead to the kitchen. She got to a wooden door with a small window, turned the handle, and it opened silently. She stepped inside to find a pistol in her face. But then Claribel kissed her.

Gladys gave her enough tongue to reassure her, took the pistol, and put her lips to Claribel's ear. "Where are the others?"

Claribel gave a tiny whistle and four young women appeared.

"The men?" Gladys asked.

Claribel dropped her head to the side and stuck her tongue out—they were passed out. But then she pointed one finger up. "Monkey Man's upstairs, he was on the phone."

"He out?"

"Should be."

"Where's the generator?"

Claribel pointed to a door at the far end of the kitchen.

"Okay, get the others."

Claribel disappeared back into the house. Gladys had a quick peek in the garage and found, as they'd hoped, fifty-five-gallon gasoline drums for the generator. Claribel returned with four others. They did not look as scared as Gladys thought they'd be. She indicated the back door and led the *putas* out and through the yard to the cabana.

Ajax crouched behind a rolling bar near the house. He crouched so still he might've been made of clay, or salt. But he could see movement in the house where none should be if the girls had spiked the killers' drinks. He'd counted four men splayed out on couches and chairs. Someone was moving amongst them, more shadow than man. He hoped it was the boy with the long eyelashes and not one of the killers. He slipped the .357 down his back and drew the Needle out. He ran the blade over his palm, then put it lightly to his nose and breathed in the smell—the light coat of oil clinging to the steel, the rawhide strips covering the handle. They say olfactory memory is often the strongest, but the scent of the Needle did not bring up things past. Ajax had read somewhere that maps are not a record of where you've been, but where you mean to go. The Needle was like that—the smell did not remind him of what he had done, but what he meant to do. And if he was right, if the shadow moving inside was not a man but the boy with the long eyelashes, then it was time to cleanse them all.

That's when someone touched his shoulder. He spun and had ahold of Gladys and the Needle under her chin without, it seemed, moving at all. She blanched, her mouth open and eyes like two moons.

"You're supposed to stay with Claribel," he whispered.

Her mouthed quivered, but no sound came out. He gave her a light slap on the cheek. "*Comprendes?*"

Gladys swallowed. "She says Monkey Man is upstairs."

He nodded. "You see anyone moving around inside?"

Gladys seemed unable at first to take her eyes off of him, but then she scanned inside the house.

She swallowed again. "No."

"Good. Now go."

But Gladys was wrong. There was a shadow. Not inside, but creeping around outside on the street. Testing doors and concertina wire for a way in.

Gladys made her way back to the cabana. Her heart pounding in her ears, breath coming short, her hand would quiver if she held it out to see, but she wouldn't, she didn't want to see and didn't want anyone else to either. It was not so much the Needle poised to prick her skin, a millimeter or millisecond from drawing blood, as the look in Ajax's eye. It wasn't him. It wasn't Saint Ajax holding a hand grenade, it was . . . she couldn't keep El Gordo Sangroso's name out of her head.

Then the lights went out. And in the darkness the silence of the generator escaped her. Claribel gasped. "He knows!"

Gladys put her finger to Claribel's lips. "Stay here."

There was enough moonlight for Gladys to make out shadows as she moved quickly back to the house. Ajax was gone, he must've moved inside. But why had he cut off the generator? She crouched outside the window looking in on the main *sala*. The shapes of the four men on the couches and chairs were still there. But their postures had relaxed somehow. Through the windows she could see a shadow moving. She let herself inside, pistol at the ready. She'd not taken three steps when her foot slid. That certain tang on the back of her teeth. It was blood. What she'd thought were shadows on the floor were pools of blood. He'd already killed them all. Across the room there was a shadow moving up the staircase. Through a sliver of moonlight she caught Ajax's profile on the stairs.

"What the fuck!" Monkey Man shouted from above. "Put the generator back on, you stupid fucks!"

She saw Ajax stop. Gladys knelt to take aim and felt her knee slide in the gore pooling on the floor. She pushed her disgust away and took aim. If Monkey Man came to the top of the stairs he'd catch Ajax, but she'd nail him. She tried to signal Ajax but . . . but what? Later she wouldn't be sure what happened, but as she heard Monkey Man's steps coming to the top of the stairs she saw . . . she saw . . .

Ajax disappeared.

He just disappeared. One moment he was right there, or a sliver of his face was and the next he was just . . . gone. Disappeared into the darkness.

Then Monkey Man appeared at the top of the stairs.

"*Oyen! Idiotas!*"

She took aim. It seemed impossible he hadn't seen her. He came down the stairs, disappeared for a moment, then stepped into the pool of moonlight where Ajax had been. But he was alone. He grabbed the banister and seemed about to shout again. Monkey Man opened his mouth, but no sound came out. Instead a black stream poured out and ran down his chin like all his sins streaming out of his black soul.

It was blood.

Monkey Man hung there a moment, blood running out. Then his head gave an odd jerk backward and he fell over the banister with a wet thud.

Ajax stood on the stairs, rematerialized like some ghost. A shape shifter resuming human form. Gladys gasped in fear and tried to stand, but she slipped in the blood under her feet and half fell. Her hand went down to steady herself and came back covered in black gore in the darkness.

Ajax looked right at her. Or behind her. But he was seeing something else.

"Get away from her," he shouted. "Get away!"

He rushed down the stairs at her. "Get away from her!"

Gladys spun about, expecting an assassin, but there was no one, nothing but dead bodies and moonlight.

"Get away from her!"

She turned about, slipped again in the blood pool, went down on one knee. Ajax, the Needle in hand, charged her.

"Stop! Ajax, stop!"

He disappeared into a pool of dark.

Gladys stood, wiped her bloody hand across her shirt, moved back toward the door, and raised her pistol. She suddenly had to get Claribel and the others out of the house, away from . . . away from . . .

Ajax emerged into another pool of light.

She pointed her pistol at him. "Stop."

"Gladys?"

"Stop." She cocked the pistol. "Stop!"

"I told you to wait outside. This had to be done. You know that."

"Who're you talking to?"

"Put the gun down, Gladys."

He kept coming at her, slower, but he wouldn't just stop.

"You said 'get away from her.' Who're you talking to?"

"Gladys." He put his hands up. To her horror they were clean. Clean! He'd slaughtered five men and his hands were as clean as if he was sitting down to table. He was no longer a man, no longer her friend, but a butcher in an abattoir and he was coming for her.

"Stop!" She took a step back.

As if in an ambush every light in the house snapped back on with the small grumble of the generator. The suddenness of it was like a slap, she slipped on the blood and in reaction she pulled the trigger.

Bang!

The report struck her like a sonic boom. The muzzle flash merged with the lights coming on and she was blinded for a moment. When her vision cleared Ajax was gone, again. Gone to the floor on his back.

"NOOOOO!"

She dropped the pistol and ran to him, knowing what she would see. In her panic, in her new horror she missed the silhouette sliding down the hallway from the garage and the generator that had so fatefully come back on.

"No. No. No. No. No."

She'd hit him a few inches below the nipple on his right side. The stain! THE STAIN! Oh God how it spread across his chest. She reached for him but the sight of her already blood-covered hands froze her a moment. In that second Ajax opened his eyes, but he seemed not to see Gladys.

"Get away from her."

She ripped his shirt open. Had only enough time to see the blood pooling on the floor from an exit wound when a pistol barrel nuzzled her ear, then the click of the hammer.

"You've killed him, *angelita*."

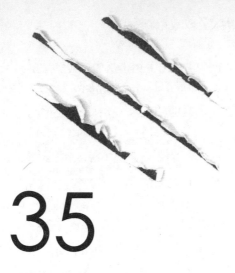

35

It is time to die.

Gladys had no time to think, or at least no time to reckon. *I am caught between the Devil and the deep blue sea. The Devil and a bloodred sea. A rock and a hard place. A cock and a hard-on. Goddamn all men!* None of this did she have time to actually think. Ajax was bleeding to death and Krill had a metal phallus stuck in her ear.

"You two are like a *telenovela*, I swear, *angelita*!" Krill looked around the room at the slaughtered men. "And they say I am a butcher."

Gladys had her hand pressed over the hole she'd shot into Ajax. Her fear of Krill was nothing compared to her dread that Ajax would die, right here and now. His eyes fluttered open. He looked at her, looked up at Krill.

"You."

Krill smiled. "Me. I told you I would see you again. And here we are. You should have left her with me."

Gladys leaned over him. "Ajax, I'm sorry, I'm sorry, I'm sorry. Forgive me. I . . ."

Ajax lifted his hand, Gladys was afraid he would strike her. But he took her chin more gently than she believed he could, and he gave her a little tug. It was so gentle, so weak, that tears sprang to her eyes.

"It's alright, don't worry. You can fix it. Stitch me up, like knitting a sock. All you need is thread and a needle."

And then she got it, he was not reassuring her, he was pointing her face at the Needle, still in his hand, half hidden under his thigh. Could she? Her eyes went to his. "Wash your hands."

That did it. Gladys snatched up the blade and whirled like an angry dervish, burying it into Krill's thigh.

"AHHHHHHHHHHH!" Krill recoiled but still managed to knock her on the head with the pistol grip before stumbling backward.

But through the pain, through the tears, through the blurred vision from the blow Gladys was on him, like a python on a staked pig. All her fear was now anger, all her shame was a burning rage. Her hand clamped on the Needle like coils on a delicate neck. She rolled into him, twisting and turning both her body and the Needle. She got her other arm around his legs and took him down. Krill hit hard, his head bouncing off the tiled floor. She ripped the Needle out, feeling it slice muscle and blood vessel before tearing through his skin. But Krill was from generations of campesino stock breaking their backs on the land and his head was as tough as a dirt clod. He got one hand on the wrist wielding the Needle, the other on her throat.

"No, *angelita*, not like this, not like this."

Krill's face seemed a mask of confusion. She could see the killer in him, the set of his mouth, the teeth grinding each other, governing the vise he'd clamped on her throat. But the eyes, the eyes implored something else.

"Not like this."

No, not like this.

She gave in. Gave in to those eyes. And it wasn't, she knew, the blood and air he was cutting off to her brain. She wanted it, this, to give in to him as she had never done in the dark dungeon in which he'd kept her. No. This was the surrender she needed, and he wanted.

She opened her mouth, not to speak, but to offer it to him. He had taken it before, her mouth, but there would be no end if she did not, this time, offer it to him. Her head shook with the violence of his grip, but she parted her lips and forced herself down on him, even though it meant colluding in her own strangulation.

Look at me. See me!

She could not speak but she could tell him nonetheless. *Like this. Yes, like this.*

And he saw, God bless him. He knew. His heart willed his killer's mind to let her come, come closer as he had wanted her always to come. His hand was still on her throat but he let her come. And she longed for that too. *Let me do it, please!*

Her lips reached for him. He reached back. His grip still locked on her throat but he let her come down, come down to him until their mouths were inches apart. And then, and then, at long, long last they touched. The kiss. That longed-for kiss.

Then Gladys locked her teeth on Krill's lower lip and ripped, tore, rent that quivering piece of flesh from his face.

"AHHHHHHHHHHHHHHHHH!!!"

It seemed shock as much as pain as Krill instinctively let go of her throat as Gladys rose up from his chest, a piece of him in her mouth, finally the piece of him she wanted in her mouth and she spat back into the motherfucker's face.

In the same gesture she stabbed the Needle into his neck to the hilt and held it there, like a thermometer up his ass.

Krill's face was now all about the dying. All about the knowing that every moment of their joint existence had led to *this* moment. All he'd ever had or could have expected was this moment. But he could not speak, the blade had gone through his jugular right through his larynx. All he could do was gasp like a fish and cough blood.

Gladys leaned in close until their noses almost touched. "Like this, *angelito*. Always like this."

And then she sawed the Needle up and out of him, his blood spraying her and the world like the first rain of a long-delayed deluge.

36

It is like a call, like Gabriel's trumpet. I don't know why, but I can't resist it. It beckons and I answer. But this time it is not Señor Ajax who summons me, but the woman Gladys. She holds the trumpet, she has been anointed and I see her now. I can see them all, the flesh ones, but as if through a veil. But Gladys is now as clear as Señor Ajax used to be. Now he is veiled, too, not like the others, but I cannot see him as he once was. He is more like me, like Celina and doña Elba. The padres.

They're all gone now. Most of us just go like that. Like cows following each other to the barn, most of us just go, not knowing where, we just follow. Some know where they're going. The padres did. Celina stayed awhile. She wasn't lost, just reluctant. The men Señor Ajax sent, they are gone now too. Soon he will follow. I think he knew that, when he saw me standing behind Gladys. It's why he told me to get away.

Gladys now calls me so I come. There are others, the girls like the ones from my town who used to tease me. They are all saying many words, the words I used to know. There is fear, I can hear that. The other girls are afraid of Gladys, as she was once afraid of Señor Ajax. The lamentations I can also feel. Señor Ajax will come with me now. We will go with Señora Gladys.

37

"Get me some plastic! Get me some fucking plastic!"

Claribel and the girls looked at her in horror. She thought they were horrified by Ajax lying near dead. She slapped Claribel. "Get me some fucking plastic, anything, a shower curtain!"

Claribel recoiled at the slap but she went into action. Gladys kneeled over Ajax. She pressed her hand over the wound on his chest, slid her hand under him to seal off the exit wound. She knew from the pink foam blowing on his chest the bullet had pierced his lung—a sucking chest wound. If she couldn't seal the hole he'd be dead in minutes, and she would not let that happen.

"Ajax! Ajax look at me! Open your eyes and look!"

But nothing. Claribel was back in a moment and Gladys used the Needle to slice two patches off the shower curtain and pressed them over the wounds.

"Come on, come on, come on. COME ON!"

It was the longest half minute of her life, but the plastic re-created the vacuum in his lungs and his chest rose ever so slightly and fell. After an agonizing moment it rose and fell again. He coughed up a mouthful of blood and she turned his head away to let it seep out.

"Claribel! Check Krill's pocket for car keys. You!" she shouted at one of the girls. "Get me some pillows, raise his feet up. And you, bring sheets from the bed!" Gladys saw that Ajax had not lost a lot of blood—

if her calculation of where Krill's blood stopped and Ajax's began was correct. Shock was her main enemy now.

Claribel held up some keys.

"Go outside, find the car they belong to, Krill must've parked nearby. Pull the car inside the gate, we're going to a hospital."

"We can't, Gladys. The curfew, the army, they'll shoot us."

"Do what I say!"

But Claribel's sense of self-preservation was stronger than her loyalty to these two *cubano-gringos*—stangers passing through the hellhole of her country. The other girl was back with the sheets. Gladys got another of the girls to keep pressure on the wounds while she slit the sheets to make bandages. If she could tie down the plastic she could rig it to hold long enough to get him to a hospital, but all the while she wrapped and tied she knew Claribel was right—driving to a hospital would likely get them killed, staying would likely see him dead. She wouldn't allow that.

She took the keys from Claribel and made her way to the street to find Krill's car. She'd made her choice: better to die with him than let him die alone.

The street was empty and dark. About half a block away was a Ford LTD, about ten years old and as big as a boat. She'd seen it somewhere before. That had to be it. She rolled the iron gate back and dashed to the car. Red tracers suddenly arced into the sky, but they were a long way off, ricochets from a firefight she'd not heard. She crouched and made the final dash to the car. She was about to open the door when muffled voices made her freeze. *Damn it!* She'd not brought her gun, had only the Needle. The voices must be near but in the blackout streets she could see nothing. She heard them again, muffled but very near. *The trunk?* She crouched next to it. She heard them clearly. She tapped twice on the trunk. The voices stopped. She tapped twice again and someone tapped back. Gladys fumbled for the key and unlocked the trunk, knife at the ready, little good that it would do her.

What she found was as surprising as it was miraculous: Jasmine and doña Estela were trussed up like chickens. She slit their bonds and yanked off their gags.

"Gladys!" Jasmine reached for her.

"Shut up! Estela, thank God. You've got to help me. Ajax. He's dying!"

"Then get me out of this trunk!"

"Stay there." Gladys shut the trunk, gunned the old boat to life, and plowed into the driveway, where Claribel shut the iron gate. Gladys helped Estela out of the trunk, and then sprinted back into the house, her mind clocking the next steps: a stretcher, the car, a hospital. She ripped curtains off the windows—a stretcher. She knelt by Ajax, put a hand on his chest, and waited the longest moment of her life until his chest rose ever so slightly and fell again.

"Jasmine! Help me roll him onto this, we've got to get him in the car. Where's the nearest hospital?"

She slid some of the curtain under him, the roll onto it would be a delicate thing but . . . but . . . She realized no one had spoken nor moved.

"Jasmine, help me!"

"Gladys, we're not going out there now. No one can move on the streets, you'll hit someone's lines and they'll kill you all."

Gladys leaped at her, all the anger, the guilt, the shame at what she had done surged like amphetamines through her blood. She had the Needle against Jasmine's throat, her hand, her entire body shaking in rage, in helplessness.

"He needs a doctor. I'll take him. I'm taking him!"

To Gladys's surprise doña Estela's hand came into view, set itself on her own hand. The old woman's skin was cool, soft, papery-thin. With the slightest, lightest of touches Estela pushed Gladys's hand down, and slipped the Needle from her desperate grasp.

"We are not going anywhere, young lady. Neither are you, neither is he."

"He needs a doctor," Gladys begged.

"I am a doctor."

"What?"

"She was a doctor, Gladys." Jasmine touched her shoulder. "I told you about it."

"*Am* a doctor," Estela said. "You think because I haven't practiced in twenty years I've forgotten? My husband was a soldier. I served in the Soccer War."

"Gladys? Gladys?" Claribel's hand trembled as she clasped Gladys's arm.

"What!"

"Upstairs."

"What about it?"

"They," she gestured to the slaughtered men, "they keep kits upstairs, in case they are wounded. Trauma kits. I've seen them. They snorted the pain pills in them."

"Do they?" Estela seemed delighted. She took Claribel's arm. "Now, honey, you and the others go upstairs and find all that you can, bring it down here. Okay?"

"*Sí, señora.*"

"*Doctora.*"

Estela looked around the *sala*. "We can't keep him in this butcher's palace. My God, what happened?" She saw Krill's body. "And this one!" She spit on his corpse. "Talk, talk, talk! *Hijo de puta!* Got yours, didn't you?" She turned to Gladys. "Is there a table? Tables are better than beds for the wounded."

Gladys wasn't sure what was happening. She wanted action, she wanted to race through the streets, she wanted to be as dead as she was certain Ajax was. She hadn't really expected him to live.

She and Jasmine rolled Ajax onto the curtain and gently dragged him into the next room where a dining table sat, covered with the detritus from Monkey Man's last supper. They swept it clean and levered Ajax onto it. Estela set about checking Ajax's vitals. Claribel came in toting a box with a red cross. The other girls brought in two more.

"Wonderful!" Estela seemed delighted. "What's your name, *amorcita*?"

"Claribel."

"Claribel, you and the others will be my nurses, okay?"

Claribel seemed dubious at best. The clock was ticking and this safe house was no longer safe.

"Do you know this man, Claribel?"

"Yes, *doctora*."

"He a good man?"

Claribel looked around the room, around the house, around her life. "Yes."

"Then help me save his life. God knows there's few enough good men in this shit world, *verdad*?"

"Yes."

"Good. Now go through the aid kits, look for saline, plasma, and trauma bandages."

"What should I do?" Gladys felt her control of the situation slip away, and with no death race to make to the hospital she felt lost.

"You!" Estela clucked. "Go clean yourself up, you look a disgrace."

She let Jasmine lead her up the stairs to the master bedroom.

Gladys Darío did look a disgrace. She studied herself in the mirror. No, she thought, not "a disgrace," but *disgraced*. She had the blood of one man splattered all over her face and clothes, and the blood of another man on her hands. She held those hands up. Coward. Stupid little girl. *Cobarde!*

She hadn't meant to shoot, had she? The way he came at her. The blood, the slip, the lights coming on. That'd been Krill, firing up the generator. And she had just fired.

And now she'd killed him.

"Take your shirt off."

Jasmine helped her peel off the bloody top.

"We still have to get him to a hospital."

"And that still won't work, Gladys. Think! Any man of fighting age showing up with a bullet in them is a *guerrillero*. At best he'd wind up in an army hospital and only then until he was well enough to be interrogated and killed."

"They wouldn't dare . . ."

"Dare what? Kill an American? You're not Americans, not even Cubans. And I'm pretty sure Krill has alerted the *escuadrones* to your ruse."

"We could get him to the embassy."

"How? There's a dozen checkpoints between here and there."

"I can't let him die!" She furiously scrubbed her bloodied hands.

"Oh my God, *you* shot him?"

Gladys looked into the mirror. She couldn't look into Jasmine's eyes. She scrubbed the blood off her face. "I've got to try."

"There is an aid station not far away. We can get him there. It's one of ours."

Now Gladys looked into her eyes. "Ours? You're . . ."

"A Farabundo? Of course. What did you think? I was a silly little rich girl?"

"You don't look the *guerrillera* type."

"I'm not. The technical term would be 'spy.' I've got impeccable right-wing credentials, and I travel a lot. A lot."

Gladys looked at herself in the mirror. She was clean. *Clean*. And for the first time since she'd pulled the trigger she saw a sliver of hope. Of a future.

"How?"

"I'll make a call, someone will come. We've got to go at first light, this house isn't safe. The murder of the priests is rebounding badly on them. They'll want Monkey Man and the others out of the country. We'll take you and Ajax to the aid station, and you'll be evacuated out of the city when our troops go."

"When?"

"Well, I'm not a *guerrillera*," she smiled a teasing smile, "but I think soon. The battle's not lost, but it's not going our way. We've taken parts of the city, but that's all. We're holding our own. But that's all."

"You're losing?"

"No. We've made our point. To the government, and the gringos. Ten years of counterinsurgency and billions in *yanqui* dollars and they get this: total war. The cowboy Reagan is gone, your President Bush . . ."

"He's not my president."

"Then the American president Bush doesn't have the *ganas* for endless war here. The Soviet empire is going, it's a brave new world for the gringos, they can't enjoy their victory over communism with a dirty war here. In a few months there'll be peace talks. All this was to strengthen our hands before that happens."

All this, Gladys thinks. *All this?*

"Okay. We do it your way."

Back in the dining room Gladys found Doctor Estela had her own MASH unit going. She had two of Claribel's girls holding bags with tubes sluicing into Ajax's arms. A fresh bandage leaking a less than alarming amount of blood secured the wounds.

"Estela."

"Well, now, Gladys, you look less like a side of beef."

"How is he?"

"One ornery son-of-a-bitch. My husband the colonel would've liked him. I've saline going into one arm and plasma into the other. But he needs blood. Do you know his type?"

"No."

"Well, we'll go with O positive, the universal donor. As long as he doesn't have some freakish type he should be alright. I assume you've got a plan to get him out of here?"

"Yes," Jasmine said.

"Call some of your Farabundo friends?"

"How did you . . ."

Estela cackled like the wise crone she appeared to be. "You young-sters. You think you invented everything!"

"Gladys."

It was the smallest of croaks, but froze them all. Ajax's eyes were open.

"Ajax! Ajax! Yes! It's me. I'm here!"

"Gladys. Water."

Estela shook her head. "Water's no good for you. I need your stomach empty. Suck it up, young man."

"Gladys."

"Yes. I'm here."

"Krill . . ."

"He's dead. Dead."

Ajax smiled, tried to raise his hand to her face. "You're a good man, sister."

Tears sprang to her eyes.

"The Needle . . ."

Gladys pulled it out of her belt. "Right here, Ajax, right here."

"Did . . . you . . . use it . . . ?"

"I did. I got him."

Ajax seemed to try to shake his head, but it just lolled around on his neck. "Too bad. Didn't want . . ."

"It's okay, I got Krill."

"No . . ." He pointed his finger over her shoulder. "The boy . . . the boy . . . the boy . . ."

38

Ajax died sometime that night. But he didn't mind, he didn't mind at all. Death was a rewrite of bad chapters.

He and Amelia Peck had a farm in Miami. Great tentacles sluiced down from the clouds and filled their cistern with the purest of water. They grew pages of poetry on trees like giant knitting needles and every day he would harvest some verse to bring home. Amelia would meet him at the door of their house and their pet jaguar would rub up against his legs and nuzzle its head in his lap while Amelia brewed a few stanzas. He would set the rest out to dry on long racks made of bone, and they'd bring them to market on the backs of manatees. Don Johnson, just down the road, would drop by to seek their advice on the next episode of *Miami Vice*. And they were blessed with children! He and Amelia had a dozen of them. He worried, true, that they were all headless monkeys who would stump around without hands or feet, bumping into doors and walls while they frolicked. But he couldn't help laughing. Amelia assured him it was "just a stage" and they would grow up to be fine young primates who would pick the nits out of their heads when they were old. That's what she said to him, "We shall grow old together."

The only thorn in paradise was the Night Rider who came in the dark, crying, "Bring out your head! Bring out your head!" and shooting pyrotechnics into the sky, rockets whooshing great tails of flame. How he dreaded that. Each time he felt the pull of that siren voice, wanted just once to see him—that gore-spattered phantom. They would all—Amelia, the children, the jaguar—pile into bed and their weight would hold him down. Keep him safely in the afterlife. His life.

But each night the ghost stayed longer, drew closer as the fear grew in their house. Until that one horrible moment when the Night Rider galloped in—his rockets set the drying poetry aflame, burned the bone racks to ash and the poetry trees to hard steel. Their house caught fire and a great hole opened in the roof, the sky. One by one they were sucked out of his arms into that void—the jaguar, the headless children, and finally Amelia. He tried to hold on, had her hand in an iron grip. *Don't let go,* she cried. But he felt her slipping away. He couldn't hold on. *"Ajax don't let go. Don't let go!"*

"Let go, Ajax! Damn it let go!"

Ajax snapped open his eyes and shot up in his hammock. The pain in his chest seared his brain and he fell back. He saw Gladys and shut his eyes to the world.

"No! No, no, no, no, no, no! Let me go! Let me go!"

"Ajax, you're breaking my hand."

"No! NOOOOOO! LET ME GO!" He threw his head from side to side, trying to fling himself back to his life in death, the life he wanted. "Let me go!!" He kept his eyes screwed shut but hot tears flooded his face. *One more moment, please!* A lifetime's worth of grief released like the great flood, but it could not drown this world of flesh and blood.

"Let me go, let me go, let me go."

Not for the first time Gladys watched as Ajax had awoken with a start and cried himself back to sleep, or coma. Gladys looked at the young guerrilla doctor, who shrugged her shoulders—*He'll wake or not.* Gladys freed her crushed hand from his and stroked the thick stubble on his face. She sat down and opened a book of poems by Roque Dalton to read to him again, as she had every day for the last seventy-three days.

"You'll like this one: 'The captain in his hammock . . .'"

39

Ajax awoke into this life long after dark. Gladys's sleeping head was on his stomach, her hand on his chest like she was clocking his heartbeat. His throat was parched, his voice box caked. He had a look around. He was in a hammock, in a tent. Twenty or so other hammocks hung around him, their occupants making weird shadows cast by Coleman lanterns. From somewhere he heard a guitar play, three or four voices singing sweetly to a song he thought was by Silvio Rodriguez, the Cuban *cantante*. FMLN camp, he thought, had to be. If he was where he remembered and what had happened, happened, then no death squad Charlies would be singing revolutionary love songs.

He lay there for a moment, feeling his chest rise and fall, feeling air fill his lungs, his heart beating, his life being lived. It had all been a dream. He chuckled at the memory of the monkey-children stumbling around. But the laugh stuck in his throat as he recalled the feeling of Amelia's hand slipping from his. *Just a dream.*

He put his hand on Gladys's head, rubbed a strand of hair between his fingers, just to make sure, one last time. He *was* alive. His wound was healing. He could feel it, a tightness where the bullet hole puckered as it closed. Her wound would take more salve than his.

"Gladys."

A little snore escaped her. He tickled her nose. She sat up.

"Fuck!"

"That an adjective or a noun?" he croaked.

"Ajax! Thank God, thank God, thank God!"

"Water."

She fumbled for a canteen with a bamboo straw and he took a long, slow pull on it. It took a moment for his throat to open and he let it go down slowly so as not to choke himself.

He took another drink and held the water in his mouth, let it sit there a moment. The delightful feel of the liquid set off a chain reaction of nerves zinging through his body, like revelry awaking a camp of dead-tired soldiers. He swallowed.

Life. It felt good.

He looked into Gladys's eyes, her face held an expression that seemed a little broken.

"Situation report, Lieutenant."

She smiled at that.

"We're in Usulután. On the volcano. About a hundred miles southeast of San Salvador. We're with a unit from the ERP," the People's Revolutionary Army, a faction of the FMLN. "Been here five weeks."

"Five *weeks*?"

"We spent four on Guazapa."

"How long?"

"Seventy-three days."

"Jesus fucked a goat." He held up his hands. "How do I look?"

"Like a skeleton. We'll fatten you up now."

Ajax tried to remember. "Monkey Man?"

"You got them all. I set his place on fire. Burned real good."

"The generator gas."

"Yep."

"Krill?"

She nodded her head a few moments, as if replaying that night. "Dead."

"Good. The girls? Claribel?"

"They got home safe. Claribel's here. She took the pledge."

"She did?"

"She spent so long taking care of your ass they made her a nurse. She's a full-fledged compañera now."

"Good. Good for her." He rubbed his wound. "How did you . . ."

"I found Jasmine and Estela in Krill's trunk. Estela did it all."

He thought a moment. It was all coming back to him. "She was a doctor."

"Hell of a doctor. Jasmine got us to a rebel aid station, the Gs took us to Guazapa and then here."

"Jasmine. She's a Farabunda."

"Yep."

"Makes sense."

They fell into an awkward silence, each seeming to study some other part of the tent than the one they were in.

"Ajax, I . . ."

"Gladys, I don't need to discuss anything else right now. Do you?"

She nodded, yes. "No."

"Good. Me neither."

Another silence.

"You fucking shot me."

"I fucking shot you. I am so sorry, Ajax I . . . I . . ."

"It's alright." He waved a hand. "Okay. Don't go on about it now."

"Okay."

Another silence.

"You must be hungry."

"You fucking *shot* me!"

"I fucking *shot* you! I still can't believe it, Ajax. Ajax. I . . . I . . . I don't know how to explain, what to say."

"*Amoooooorrrrrrrrrrrrrrciiiiiiiita!*"

Claribel saved them from the awkward bent of the conversation, gliding in, trilling her *R*s, still sexy even in an olive-drab T-shirt and

ill-fitting fatigue pants with an old .38 clipped onto her belt. She kissed
Ajax on the mouth. Long and deep, did that thing with her tongue
under his lip.

"You fantastic man! You're alive! I told Gladys so, but she's been
hanging on to you like a *puta* on a lamppost! Haven't you, *amor*?" She
gave Gladys's nipple a pinch and blew her a kiss. "You must be hungry." She gave his balls a good shake. "What do you want? *Anything* at
all, Claribel is here."

Ajax laughed so hard he fell into a coughing fit and hacked up
seventy-three days' worth of phlegm. When he was done spitting it
out he felt good, back in his body, but weak as a baby. Or a headless
monkey.

"I am hungry. For food, at the moment, not wanting to limit
future options."

"Dessert when you want it." Claribel gave his ball sack another
shake. "I'll feed you now. But first—you two have already gotten
through the part where you've forgiven her for shooting you, yes?"

Ajax smiled. "Yes."

"Good!" Claribel kissed him again. "Because this one! With the
moping and the crying I might as well have become a nun as a revolutionary! Can you walk, *varón*?"

"Let's try."

He couldn't. It would be a few days before he fully got his legs back.
In that time he had a stream of visitors: once again his reputation had
preceded him. Monkey Man, he learned, either did or did not actually kill the padres. But he was a known and much despised *hijo de
puta,* and his killer was a welcomed guest. The camp commander,
known simply as El Ocho—his seven predecessors having perished in
the final offensive—was an old man of twenty-seven. He knew of Ajax
and made him feel welcome. He showed Ajax on a map the setup of
the camp: he was in the main hub, which was connected by jungle trails
to six satellite camps. Father Ellacuría, it turned out, had been right:

within days of the rebel offensive ending, both sides had negotiators in Caracas and a cease-fire at home.

Life was good in a rebel camp, so long as that truce held. They lacked for nothing, but then really didn't have anything either, a rather genteel poverty. January was cool and dry in El Salvador and he re-called from his own days that as long as you weren't up to your ass in mud or down with dysentery, rebel life could be like camping—but with machine guns and mortar fire. They had plenty of food, but it was only rice, beans, and tortillas, laced with whatever meat your unit could beg, borrow, or butcher. Ajax was counted amongst the wounded so got a goodly portion of a humble whole, topped off with extra rations from Claribel of actual beef.

"Get your strength back, *amor*," she'd tell him.

He wanted to ask where she got it from, fearing she was running some secret black-market of hand jobs for beef, but he did feel like he was coming back alive. Not waking up, but turning back on. He could feel parts of his brain kick back in, and each day that first week after the dream, the dream faded and faded until the moment and the meaning and the feelings became too disjointed to make sense anymore.

Claribel had come to fetch him the second morning with a wheel-barrow souped-up with bicycle tires and handlebars. The camp seemed divided into two: those who played baseball and those who played *fútbol*. There were big communal kitchens, open-air schools, and parade grounds full of new recruits learning to march or field strip an M16 blindfolded. It would have seemed a socialist outing if Ajax had been the only one in a wheelbarrow. But the field hospitals took up the most room and the dozens of injured, maimed, and the still dying to judge from the burial details, reminded the Farabundos of the cost of their "successful" offensive.

It was a few more days until he could walk without dizziness. He spent that time listening to the radio, catching up on the outside world. And what a world! Every single country of the Eastern Bloc had overthrown their communist masters—most without bloodshed—and half a century of Cold War was over. Even the Soviet Union, that other great colossus to the north, was falling apart. The world as he knew it, hell, as everyone knew it, was toppling into an undefined future. Much like himself.

And closer to home the news was just as galvanizing.

The Sandinista Front was in a fight for its life, not at war, but in an election! As part of the deal to end the Contra War, Krill's war, the government had agreed to an early election and was facing a united opposition bloc heavily subsidized by the Americans. He listened to revolutionaries, titans in their own time, make radio ads like the politicians they had become. He guessed it was a good thing. The era of the pistol-packing, fatigue-clad, bearded revolutionary was over.

There were going to be a lot of hangovers.

But in camp, life went on in the old way. Everyone had a job. Claribel left him to attend to her nursing duties, which, if he guessed correctly from the location of the tent on the far edge of the camp, meant hers was the last face many of them would see. Even Gladys, now that the death watch was over, was put to use. Ajax watched her on a pistol range giving instruction to new recruits. She'd always been a dead-eye shot, it's what'd first drawn his admiration. How many years ago was that?

"You wanna give it a try?"

Gladys held out a .357 to him, might have been the one they had in San Salvador. He put his hands up, *Don't shoot! Don't shoot!*

"The *compa* is reputed to be the best shot in Nicaragua," she told the recruits, who, from what Ajax could see, were all under fifteen or over fifty.

"How do you work this thing?" He turned the pistol over like a yokel looking over one of them new cellular phones. Gladys pretended to show him the two-handed grip. It took him two shots to get his eye back. The other four he was just showing off.

A few days after that the headaches stopped and he even felt he'd put back a few of the thirty-odd pounds he'd lost. He'd even thought to take Claribel up on dessert, but she and Gladys seemed pretty tight. Still, Ajax realized he was actually enjoying himself—for the first time in literally years he was content.

It was at the end of his second week back amongst the living that young Peck arrived in the camp.

40

It was the boy with the long eyelashes who alerted him. Gladys had returned the Needle to him, but he'd hardly touched it, tried not to think about it—him, them. The day had started well. Ajax had woken and decided it was time to pay his own way too. He'd found the armorer, knowing that after a big battle the first job was to repair broken weapons, as those captured from the enemy rarely outnumbered those lost in combat, damaged, jammed, or otherwise fouled. It was like doing a jigsaw—a spring from this one, a bolt from that one, even a single screw from another and you'd piece together a serviceable weapon. It was slow, steady work, done mostly in silence and he'd been at it a few hours when a familiar feeling made him look up.

And there he was. Ajax checked left and right to make sure no one else could see him. But it was different this time. Not the boy— he was the same. The staring eyes that did not see, the evil gash across his throat, the wet gore covering his fatigue jumper. The wound and the violence as fresh as the day Ajax had made them—perpetually fresh, like the boy lived in the moment of his death.

For the first time it made Ajax a little sad.

The boy with the long eyelashes had been a specter haunting Ajax, true. But then he'd become an ally, saving Ajax's life on more than one occasion. But Ajax wasn't sure if he could ever look on the boy again without seeing the terror in Gladys's face the night she'd shot him. She had been in fear of her life, he'd seen it and remembered it.

It had changed how he saw himself. All his adult life he'd been feted by men for his daring in battle, celebrated for his exploits as a common soldier and *comandante*. But he'd never thought of himself as a killer until he saw the fright in Gladys's face. Now he wondered if he was just another man scaring women.

So he'd tried to ignore the ghost of the boy with the long eyelashes.

A column of Farabundos arrived from another camp. Ajax looked up from an AK-47 he was repairing and saw Nora talking with El Ocho. She saw him, smiled, and joined him at the armory.

"*Comandante* Nora."

"Captain Montoya."

He shrugged.

"Then compañero Ajax."

"Better."

"Heard you got shot."

"But not killed, thanks to your people."

"So, it's good I didn't kill you in San Salvador."

"I think so."

She smiled. "Me too." She ran her hand over his stubbled cheek. "You looked better clean-shaven."

"I'll find a razor."

"I hear you got a knife would do as well."

He looked away, shook his head. "Not anymore."

She smiled again, but this time ruefully. She understood. There was an awkward pause. Nora broke it.

"So, you've heard the news from home?"

For a moment Ajax was uncertain, and then realized she meant Nicaragua.

"Yes. Seems the *comandantes* are trading fatigues and pistol for suits and slogans. Think you'll do the same here?"

She shook her head a long time. "Who knows? They say it's a new world. Cold War is over, communism dead . . . We wanted a revolution.

Like you. Now your revolution will be put to a plebiscite and we'll have to settle for peace. We lost a lot of people. Some of our best fighters."

"Whatever happened to that shoe-shine boy?"

"Ernesto? Still shining shoes, collecting intel. If the war had gone on he'd've been a *comandante* someday. Now, he might shine shoes forever."

"You never know. He might wind up running a battalion of them. He'd make a good capitalist."

She laughed. It was a nice, throaty woman's laugh and Ajax got immeasurable pleasure from having made her laugh. She looked over her shoulder and grew somber.

"I've brought someone who wants to meet you. He's a friend. Not like you, but a friend. Do you understand?"

He didn't. But then Nora signaled El Ocho and Ajax saw the crop of orange hair atop a gangly body clad in fatigues striding toward him. She'd meant: he's mine, don't hurt him.

Young Peck sat opposite Ajax and Gladys. Ajax wasn't sure what he'd expected. Maybe some arrogant gringo who'd finally made it to the big time—*Look, Ma! A gun-toting revolutionary!* But Peck seemed not that, maybe somehow chastened by the lifestyle. Or the combat.

"I hear you're looking for me."

Ajax smiled, the *Dr. Livingstone, I presume* moment. He slowly unbuttoned young Peck's shirt. Jimmy smiled but was clearly discombobulated by the intimate act. When Ajax had revealed young Peck's chest, he looked at Gladys. *See?* Peck's chest and shoulders were covered in freckles.

"No."

"No?" Peck seemed uncertain as to the turn of the conversation.

Ajax slowly re-did the buttons. "I haven't been looking for you for a while."

"Really, because . . ."

"What was the plan, Jimmy?"

He took a deep breath. "Have me kidnapped just before the offensive began. Put the government back on its heels, looking for me. And denying they'd killed me. Make sure the American press played it up big. I mean with the Berlin Wall coming down and everything, make sure they covered it, and with an American missing, presumed murdered by the government, it was an ace in the hole. Then the FMLN would rescue me . . . and . . . and . . ."

He sounded regretful. Remorseful. And rehearsed. Ajax looked at Gladys, who squinted her eyes in doubt.

"Bullshit." Ajax finished re-buttoning. Gave Peck's chest a little pat. "That's American thinking."

"What?"

"The FMLN was launching their biggest offensive of the war. That means they're going to lose their best, they wouldn't waste their time on a PR stunt like . . ." Then the clouds parted. "You did it. It was *your* idea. You were freelancing!"

"I wanted to help the Revo! I had been! You *know* I was undercover, infiltrating the death squads. This was the next step." Peck threw himself to his feet. "After all America has done, yes, I thought why not help, with the only thing America cares about: an American life!"

"Sit down! You couldn't have pulled this off without help . . ."

"Jasmine." Gladys almost whispered it.

Peck nodded. "Yes. She thinks like me, internationally. She saw the benefit and we had the resources. Me, it was just a matter of disappearing."

Ajax closed his eyes. Yes, now it all made sense. "But that wasn't enough, was it? Once you got to thinking about it. *Just disappearing.*"

"It was a start."

"Did you kill him, Jimmy?"

Peck held his hands up, like *Who me?*

Ajax felt the first twinge of anger since Gladys'd shot him. "The morgue pictures showed a body beaten to death. Red hair, pale skin, but no freckles. Did you kill him?"

Now Ajax saw the boy he'd come looking for. The good kid, the gringo who wanted to help save the world.

"No, I didn't! I swear to God! Max said he'd seen my doppelganger at the Artisans' Market. Had actually called out to him thinking it was me. He was just a tourist . . ."

Ajax shot to his feet. "Say his name!"

"Liam. Liam Donaldson."

"So you thought."

"If Jasmine and I staged my kidnapping the government would blame the Farabundos and the FMLN would blame the *escuadrones*. A checkmate. But if I could use this guy . . ."

"Say his fucking name!"

Peck recoiled from the fury. Ajax could tell he'd expected to meet a compañero, not a cop.

"Liam. If I could get Liam arrested for real, there'd be real witnesses. Then when the army figured out he was just a tourist they'd let him go! We'd claim it was me and I was still in custody. And during the offensive I'd be rescued by the Farabundos."

"How'd you work it? Liam's arrest?"

Peck rubbed his fingers through his hair, massaged his scalp like he might rearrange the recent past.

"Me and Jasmine . . ."

"You told Max. What?"

"That the guy, Liam, was an FMLN courier. He *was* a backpacker, had visa stamps in his passport from all over. Central America . . ."

"And you thought Max would turn him over to the army?"

"I . . ." He shook his head. "He said he would. Jasmine was sure he would! I just wanted to make it believable."

"Oh, you made it believable. I wish I had the morgue photos to show you. Liam Donaldson died screaming."

"I'd make him eat them." Gladys was on her feet and in front of Peck. "I'd make you fucking eat them."

"You're missing the big picture. It wasn't a huge advantage, but it was a tactical advantage. And we used it. I'm sorry he's dead, but to make omelets you have to break . . ."

Gladys snatched his skinny ass up by his shirt. "You finish that sentence and I'll break your fucking face."

Ajax took ahold of one of her bony fists. "Easy, Lieutenant."

"Fuck him, Ajax! Look what we did, what we had to do trying to find his sorry ass." She turned on Peck. "And you just playing soldier. You're a dead man."

Peck got to his feet. "Don't threaten me in my own camp."

"It's not your camp!" Gladys was nose to nose with him. "It's *their* camp. And what happens when we get back and tell Donaldson's family you got their boy killed? Huh? The FMLN's gonna have to either admit what they did, *they* got an American killed. Or they make sure you never reappear alive."

"My compañeros would never harm . . ."

"Roque Dalton." Gladys was right back in his face. "Know him?"

"Of course I do . . ."

"The greatest Salvadoran poet of the twentieth century and your compañeros killed him. This very group, the ERP. Killed him for 'ideological deviation.' You think they'd hesitate to kill your sorry orange ass? They just lost hundreds of their best and for what? To get the gringos to back off and accept a peace deal. And now *you* are gonna put American blood on *their* hands. When all they have to do is make sure you never leave this jungle."

Despite himself, Peck looked around the camp. The logic of Gladys's death sentence was overwhelming, and it was clear Peck had never thought of it before.

"Now, make an omelet with those eggs, asshole."

Ajax didn't smile, at least not on the outside. But he was admiring Gladys's thinking. Seems a lot had changed in the last ten weeks.

Peck looked lost. His swagger deflated. "Ajax, surely you understand."

"We talked about you."

Peck looked from Ajax to Gladys and back again.

"Father Ellacuría. We saw him the day they were killed."

"I know."

"We talked about you. Did you know his family, Liam's family, had called them? Asking for their help? He went to Notre Dame, and they'd called, his parents, hoping the priests might help."

"I didn't know that."

"And we talked about you. They said they thought you were naïve. Good, but naïve."

"I didn't know that."

"So that means about one of the last things they did, the padres, before they died, was to parse your lies."

He stood up, almost nose to nose with Peck.

"It just seems they should've had something more important to do. Don't you think?"

"I . . . I was trying to help."

"They always are. Go away."

Whatever bluster was left in young Peck went out of him and he limped away on luffing sails. Gladys was not mollified.

"Dead man walking."

"No. He's not. And don't say it like that, like you'd like him to be. There's a family in Indiana gonna bury their boy in an empty casket. You really want two? You spent more time with Big Jim and Margaret Mary than me. You really want them to bury their only surviving child?"

Gladys's answer did not matter. Ajax would not see harm come to Amelia's brother.

"But what he did, Ajax! All this was a waste!"

Ajax sighed. She had a point there. Even if she was talking more about shooting him than Peck's perfidy. Stupidity.

"Ajax . . ."

"It's time to go, Gladys."

"Go?"

"Home."

"Where's that?"

"I really don't know."

41

But it was time to go.

It took another week to set it up. Despite the truce in the countryside, the death squads took no holiday, respected no paper. So it was decided that Gladys and Ajax would try to travel on their expired American passports through Nicaragua where, while less than welcome, they had a better chance of not being murdered than trying to leave through the airport in San Salvador. Usulután was about forty miles from the sea, mostly by navigable rivers. They'd get a boat from there.

It was harder to leave than he'd thought.

His weeks with the Farabundos, or at least the two he'd been awake for, had assembled in him a feeling that he'd not known in years. Almost like being a child again. It wasn't *happiness*, Ajax Montoya wouldn't know happiness if it walked up and sat on his face. It was more of a situational contentment, really. They had little but everything they needed. There was always a rifle that needed repairing, a slit trench that needed digging, or some poor animal that needed skinning. There were deep and long talks about peace and politics, which he and Gladys stayed away from—they had no place in the debate over peace versus the cost of their savage war. Yet as a former *comandante guerrillero,* and one many of them had heard of, his opinion had often been sought.

But his life, whatever it was, was still out there. The boy with the long eyelashes reminded him of that each time he'd appear. Ajax no longer looked around to see if anyone else saw. It didn't matter. One family needed to know that their son would be home, the other not.

On their last day in camp, El Ocho told Ajax that Nora was walking in a cow for the party. He said it with a bit of a leer, as if the thought of fresh beef was sexy.

She arrived with a large escort, and faster than they could lay an ambush they'd strung some colored lanterns, lit the candles, and every bottle of hidden beer or rum appeared from deep inside rucksacks. The camp commanders huddled for a while, but their troops lost no time cutting up whatever fruit was to hand and pouring all the liquor over it into an enormous punch bowl made out of a crate for mortar rounds.

Ajax had just about convinced himself to end six years of sobriety when he caught Nora's eye as she came out of the tent. A great cheer went up when she appeared with El Ocho. Someone handed her a gourd filled with punch and she downed all that was in it in one go.

Another cheer went up.

She made a beeline for him.

"*Comandante.*"

"You'll go home now."

"To Nicaragua, anyways."

"There'll be no welcome for you there."

He smiled. She was teasing him about the news from Nicaragua. The Sandinista Front had lost their election. Not only for president, but the plebiscite on the Revo. For the first time in history a revolution had been voted out of office. And went.

"They say it's a new world, *comandante.*"

"Nora." She rubbed a hand over his smooth cheek. "You shaved for me."

"The least I could do."

"Yes, it was. What a pain in the ass you are. You come down here, messing with *my* operations, using our aid stations, our medicines, taking up space, eating our food, drinking our water, but not our punch, I see. Do you know how much you owe us?"

"I do, Nora."

"Good." She lifted what Ajax had mistaken as a bandolier off her chest and tossed it to him. "Carry this."

"What is it?"

"A hammock. Come with me."

Nora strode off. Ajax was a bit confused. He looked around and saw Claribel, one arm around Gladys, smiling and waving, *Go, idiota. Go!* Then she reached around Gladys and pounded her fist into her palm. *Go!*

The rest of the camp withheld comment until Ajax had followed Nora into the bush. Then an enormous cheer went up.

That was life in a rebel camp at peace.

Ajax strung the hammock down by the river where the rushing water gave them some privacy. He watched Nora step into the river. It was a cool night and he heard her shiver as she slowly submerged herself, like a baptism, he thought. When she came back to him her nipples stood at attention in the night air. She stripped Ajax of his shirt and used it to dry herself while he undressed. When she straddled him her cold skin sent a shiver through his body.

She poked his wound with professional curiosity.

"Nice job. One of ours?" She put his hands on her breasts. His breath came quick and shallow.

"No, an old woman, a doctor."

"You're lucky. Gladys your woman?" She moved her hands from the pink scar over his chest and arms.

"She's no man's woman."

"Too bad."

But he never got to ask why. Nora was a woman who knew what she wanted, knew what she needed, and how to get both. Nora made love to him like it was a military operation—carefully planned but the execution always gets sloppy once combat commences. Their combat got sloppy, but it didn't matter so long as it all came out well.

It all came out very well, indeed.

In the morning he awoke in the hammock, alone, but feeling utterly alive. He had himself a wash in the river, his own baptism, and made his way back to camp. There were no catcalls, nor knowing winks. It was another day and the camp was busy with its chores, hewing life out of the jungle.

He found Gladys with a weeping Claribel in her arms.

"What will I do? What will I do?"

She threw herself into Ajax's arms. He hugged her but shot Gladys a look, *What?* She pointed her index finger into her palm, and then drew the back of her hand over the palm: *Today. We leave.*

"It's okay, Claribel." He patted her head, but he'd never been very good at comforting others, nor himself. "Tend to your wounded. You're a good nurse. The war is over, your country's gonna need nursing. You'll be okay. Everything's going to be okay."

It was a cold-blooded lie. Their war *was* over, but Ajax knew that no matter the nobility of the fight—and few wars were ever as justified as the FMLN's battle against the oligarchs and the death squads—war in a poor country was an industry, like a town with one factory. And when this was over—when the factory shut down—the foot soldiers would become unemployed workers. Some would make the transition to the new economy, but most would be left only with the sound of vanished machines in their heads.

It had been different in Nicaragua, with his war. They had won, complete military victory. And when the Ogre's regime crumpled, there were plenty of jobs to go around. The revolution became the new factory. But that wouldn't happen here.

Two canoes were packed for their journey downstream to the coast, where a fishing boat would take them across the Gulf of Fonseca to

Nicaragua. They'd make landfall near the port of Corinto on the north coast. Ajax was excited, not about going home, but just to be going. There was little for either of them to pack. They were given civilian clothes, a sack of food, and two pistols. Ajax strapped the Needle to his belt. Not for the first time he was certain he'd never need it again, but he would not abandon it, or the boy who came with it.

"You ready?" Gladys slung a pack over her shoulder and clipped a holster to her belt.

"Yep. You? I mean, Gladys, you can stay if you want."

Gladys looked over the camp, over to the aid station on the far side. She shook her head. "It's time to go home."

"Home? Where's that?"

She smiled. "I really don't know. But what do we do when we get to Corinto?"

He shook his head. "I don't know, yet. We certainly don't have any money." He stuck his hands in his pockets and felt something. He pulled out a ten-dollar bill. The one young Peck had given to Ernesto.

"Where'd you get that?"

Ajax smiled. "Nora."

"She *paid* you?"

He shrugged. "I gave her a discount."

A platoon of well-wishers came to see them off. But not Claribel, she was back in the aid tent. El Ocho arrived and handed Ajax a wallet— Salvadoran *colones*, Nicaraguan *cordobas*, and about two hundred American. Ajax gave it to Gladys.

El Ocho shook their hands, wished them well, and returned to his camp and his new world. The canoes set off and in seconds, it seemed to Ajax, the camp was lost in the jungle.

42

The current took them downstream. Ajax did the steering, taking them past downed trees, over sand bars, and through a series of small rapids. It was nearly night when he smelled the sea.

As planned they pulled over until well past dark, then paddled their way into the port. They were looking for a fishing boat, *El Caballero,* the gentleman. They were on it just after midnight, and by the time dawn came they were in the open sea. The endless horizon got Ajax thinking. Brave new world? Maybe not even a new one. But his old one was long gone.

"What are you thinking?"

Gladys was a little green from the voyage.

"You know Krill traveled this same route, in reverse. Ten years ago he hijacked a boat, came across the gulf." Ajax indicated the water. "Landed in El Salvador. He was the only one to survive the trip."

"Well, he's dead now."

"I didn't want to ask before . . ."

"I don't want to talk about him."

"I'm talking about you." He turned to her. "You've never killed before."

"I'm good with it."

"When you kill up close like that, it's different than a firefight. You see the last thought in their mind. It stays with you, over the years. A piece of them stays with you."

"You mean like a ghost?"

Ajax looked at the boy sitting in the bow, looking toward home. "Exactly like a ghost. Mine is sitting up there in the bow, looking toward home."

Gladys turned her head and scanned the deck. They were alone.

Ajax shrugged. "Or not. He was a boy, I looked right into his eyes as he bled out."

"*Guardia?*"

He shrugged again. "He had a uniform on. Don't know if that's why I killed him. It was late in the war. But I watched him as he died. He had these beautiful eyes, long eyelashes. And he just looked sad. Not scared, not angry. He was just . . . sad."

"Krill looked confused." She spoke very rapidly. "Like, like he didn't understand why I was killing him. Like he wanted to ask, *Why? Why!* Like there was a reason? Or an explanation?"

"He needed killing."

"Yes he did. But . . ."

The "but" came out like a burp.

"But somehow you wish you hadn't."

"I do. God help me, I do."

"Well," he put his hand on her back, "you're a soldier now. All soldiers know only two things: the killing's got to be done, and they'll regret it for the rest of their lives."

They stood there by the gunwale for a long time. Gladys puked once, and Ajax patted her back and fed her water as the *Gentleman* carried them across the sea.

It was well after dark when they approached the Nicaraguan coast. Don Cholo, the skipper, held them about a mile out as Ajax had asked while he scanned the port with binoculars. The docks were lit up. Boats were tied up. He counted four lights he could not account for and kept the field glass trained on them. They blinked off and on at erratic moments—men walking in front of car headlights.

"*Capitán*, how far out are we?"

"About a mile."

"The tides?"

"Going in. I'm fighting them to stay out here and we're low on gas."

"Give me one second."

Ajax dashed belowdecks where Gladys was still queasy.

"Gladys! Gladys! Get up, get up, we gotta go!"

"What?"

"Come on! We'll have to swim it."

He dragged her topside and fitted a life jacket over her head, snapped it around her waist. Pulled one over his own head.

"There's men on the docks waiting. We gotta get in the water. Tide's going in so it won't be hard to get to the beach, but you've got to paddle in."

"What are you talking about?"

He slung a rectangular pack over her head.

"This is a little life raft, when you hit the water, pull this string." He put her hand on the string. "Got it?"

"Okay, okay, let's go."

"Wait." Ajax went to his belt and slid the Needle off. Weighed it for a moment, and then hooked it onto Gladys's belt.

"What're you doing?"

Ajax took her face in his hands, held her for a moment, looked into her eyes, and lightly kissed her on the mouth. "You're a good man, sister." Then he shoved her over the side.

She came up coughing and spluttering and immediately began to drift away from the boat toward the beach. Ajax took off his life jacket and dropped it on the deck.

"*Capitán!* Hit it!"

The engines roared and Ajax swayed as the boat moved forward.

"Ajax! Ajax! What're you doing?"

Gladys sounded pissed. He turned back to her.

"Pull the string, Gladys! Pull the string!"

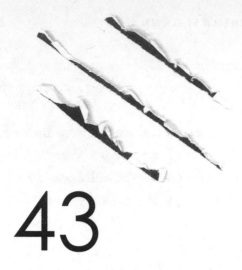

43

Managua, Nicaragua, February 1990

El Chipote prison had held many guests over the years. The Ogre had filled it with Sandinistas during his dictatorship. The current president had spent several years here. Even before the Sandinistas in the sixties and seventies the Ogre had filled it with troublemakers. One of its most prestigious prisoners had been a famed newspaper editor whose widow would now be the next president of the republic.

Ajax had dropped off his fair share of men and women back when he'd worked State Security in the early days of the Revo. As he himself had been dropped off almost a week ago, which somehow seemed only fair. The policemen on the dock in Corinto had seemed to be waiting for him, but he wasn't sure. And no one had spoken to him since. A slot slid open twice a day, and food was pushed in. He'd had worse, but he sure did miss the fare in El Ocho's camp.

He worried about Gladys. He was pretty sure he'd seen the life raft inflate, and so long as she'd gotten to rowing the tide would've carried her in. He'd heard nothing about her and that should be good news. He'd heard very little at all, in fact, but the radio. After the second day he'd figured out that if he lay on his belly near the food slot, he could just pick out a radio playing somewhere, and a draft or something would occasionally carry bits of news to him.

The revolution was over! For the first time in recorded history a revolution won by force of arms had let itself be voted out; and for the first time in Nicaraguan history the party in power had accepted an electoral defeat and agreed to go.

Well, that was *something*, wasn't it? Something for the history books? Some comfort? He wasn't sure if the dead would agree, though. All those who'd died to bring the Revo about, or died to prevent it, who'd died to overthrow or to defend it. The new order would go hard on Horacio, his ex Gio. They had thought the Revo would last forever.

They were wrong.

As for himself, he'd arrived in Nicaragua twenty years ago, driving a motor home stuffed with smuggled weapons that Horacio had packed for him in Mexico City. A young gringo with his gringo passport, passing through on his way to Panama, had been waved across the border for only a ten-dollar bribe. They'd only wanted five, but he'd told them to keep the change. Horacio had chewed his ass for that.

Twenty years. He'd been a frightened recruit, the great hero, disgraced drunk, loose cannon, international embarrassment. And now, if he calculated right, he'd serve twenty-five years for murdering a serial killer. Would the ironies never cease?

It seemed not.

That night a key went into his door. He stood, expecting the worst and accepting it.

It'd be a cop, a prosecutor, maybe that young Spanish doctor to ID him.

Instead, when the iron door swung open, in stepped Horacio de la Vega Cárdenas—mentor, teacher, father figure, master manipulator, fiend. And friend.

"Hello, Ajax."

"You come to skin me or pluck me?"

"Neither, *mijo*."

Ajax unrolled the thin mattress on the other bed. "Coffee tray will be around soon. Stay a while."

Horacio held up his gnarled hands—they were manacled.

"I will be."

Then the devil stepped into view.

Vladimir Malhora.

Now here was a ghost for you. A demon. A vengeful spirit back from the dead. Malhora was the former head of State Security, murderer of Amelia Peck and so many others. At first Ajax almost didn't recognize him—instead of a uniform Malhora wore a gray business suit with a blue tie, he'd shaved his Stalin mustache, and shed at least thirty pounds of portly.

Worst of all, he was smiling. He was real!

Ajax would curse himself later for telegraphing both his astonishment and his intentions. Before he moved a muscle Malhora tripped Horacio and shoved him into the cell. The old man fell forward and Ajax instinctively reached to catch him and break his fall. He'd curse himself for that too.

The door slammed shut and clanged like a death knell. But Ajax had seen the fear on Malhora's face—fleeting, but there. The peephole slid open.

"Now, my dear friends, look at us, all together. At last."

Horacio grabbed Ajax's shirt. "Don't let him see," he whispered.

Ajax went to the peephole, as big as a saucer, where Malhora's beaming face was framed like a cheap porn star in the money shot. Ajax kicked the door—Malhora recoiled and his triumphalist smirk slipped.

"You're still a chicken-shit, look at you!"

"And you're still an animal. But now I have caged you, so yes, look at me. Here I am on the *right* side of this door, the free side, the new regime side. Back. Back in Casa Cincuenta." House Fifty, the headquarters of State Security where Malhora had reigned for years. "Not yet back in my old office, true. But only two doors away. And once I've made myself indispensable to the new president? Well, it's a brave new world, isn't it?"

His confidence stoked Ajax's rage until he was mad enough to spit. So he did. Gobbed a good one right on the motherfucker's face. Malhora recoiled and drew a pistol, a .38 Smith and Wesson, no more Soviet Makarovs.

"Do it! Kill me now, cocksucker, or die by my hand! Do it!"

Malhora's hand shook with the desire to do it, but Ajax knew he hadn't the balls. Not now, not ever. Not himself.

Malhora wiped the spittle off. Reapplied his smile. "I don't love you enough to kill you. But I hate you enough to come visit you, the two of you, right here, every week for the next twenty-five years. I'm going to convict you both of murder. Yes, you see I found the secret files, or will find them as soon as I manufacture them, proving you and that degenerate old man killed three Americans. Yes! Can you guess who? Amelia Peck, the journalist Matthew Connelly, and Father Jerome Westerly."

He shut the peephole. Ajax pounded and kicked on the steel door. "Motherfucker! Motherfucker! MOTHERFUCKER!"

"Ajax, control yourself, please."

Ajax turned on him. "You!" The blood rage had to be loosed on someone. He took a step, murder in his heart.

"Ajax, you're not going to hurt me."

"Really? Because after him I hate you the most."

Horacio held up his manacled hands. "If that were true you wouldn't have caught me when he tripped me."

Ajax hesitated a step, and his rage, like a balloon, popped, to be replaced by despair. He sat heavily on his cot. The wound ached and he rubbed the scar under his shirt. "Gladys shot me."

"I heard."

"She killed me."

"Yet here you are."

Ajax looked around the cell. "Malhora's my jailer and you're my cell mate. Gladys killed me. And this is Hell."

Horacio hid a sly smile.

"And what are you doing here? What the fuck is *he* doing here?"

"Ajax, we have much to discuss. But you have been here a week and surely you've got something to get these off with." He held up the cuffs.

He did. The shit mattresses were made to be rolled up like dough for storage and they held their shape because of a thin wire running down the side. He pulled out about a foot, bent it until it broke, doubled it over, twisted it for strength, and then fashioned a small hook at the end. He knelt in front of Horacio and began working the lock. Horacio smiled down at him.

"I am very glad to see you."

"Fuck you."

Ajax tricked one of the cuffs open. He noticed Horacio's knotted knuckles.

"What happened to your hands?"

"It's how I bear my sins."

"Bullshit. If it were your sins you'd be covered with sores and tumors like the Elephant Man."

"Do you really think me so evil?"

Ajax looked into the old bastard's eyes and flipped his anger to full auto. But he couldn't pull the trigger. He just couldn't.

"Answer my question: you, him, how?"

Ajax popped the other cuff off. Horacio rubbed his hands, the pain visible under his white goatee. Then he took a deep breath and submerged the pain.

"You will recall, my son, that the world is divided into . . ."

"The civilized and the barbarian!" He'd heard this worldview before, the last time Horacio had justified his schemes that had left nearly everyone dead—except Malhora. "We back to that again?"

"Why don't you ask, 'Gravity? Are we back to that again?' A universal law is a universal law. Even the opposition, which is now the new government, has its civilized and its barbarians. You are not surprised to learn *their* barbarians feel *our* barbarians mistreated them when we were in power. They seek retribution against the Sandinista Front. Who better than a disgraced former Sandinista to persecute Sandinistas?"

"The Revo is over."

"Not just our revolution, Ajax. The *age* of revolution is over. Cuba is a police state. The Soviet empire is gone as will be the Soviet Union itself soon enough. China is a capitalist economy run by a communist party. It is our tragedy, Ajax, that we were both the last successful revolution of the Age of Revolution *and* the last battle of the Cold War. We are the nation of Sisyphus, and the world belongs," he indicated the steel door, "to men in blue suits."

"Were you always so pedantic?"

"Very well, ignore the big picture: the Sandinista Front has been defeated. It will take years for the revolution to be so. In the meantime the new government cannot replace every policeman, soldier, and bureaucrat. They need someone to root out the diehards and administer the loyalty oath."

"Malhora the dog."

"Precisely. He knows our secrets, our dirty laundry. Soiled most of it himself."

"Damn, almost makes you wish someone had killed him, doesn't it?"

Horacio shook his head. Their last conversation had been about precisely that: why he would not let Ajax murder the bastard.

"Political expediency at the time forbade it. I did not spare him out of kindness."

"Where's he been, Horacio?"

"You tell me."

"Well, the formerly roly-poly piece of shit looks like he's finally lost his baby fat, so I'd say prison. You couldn't've kept him here, so . . . Cuba. Isle of Pines?" Fidel's most infamous gulag.

Horacio smiled. Ajax frowned.

"Can he do it? Lay Amelia's death on us?"

"No. He is feeling triumphant, in a revengeful way, that's why I'm here. He has far less power than he thinks, and is widely despised by the . . ."

"The civilized in the new government."

"Precisely."

But Ajax had another worry. He went to the cell door and gave a listen. Then whispered his one real concern, "What about El Gordo?"

Horacio smiled. "Chepe Huembes hanged himself in his room when he found out he was going back to prison. That young Spanish doctor swore a statement to it before she returned to Barcelona." He held his hands up. "You see? Things are not *that* bad."

"Said the man in the jail cell."

Horacio pulled up his right pant leg, long red scars ran down it where a mortar had almost chewed it off years ago in the mountains. It was after he'd taken that wound that Ajax had taken command of the Northern Front and become, well, whatever he had become.

Horacio slid his sock down, revealing a cigar, a Montecristo. From his other sock he produced a match.

"I've already done the new government a good turn. I suspect we will not be here overly long."

"Said the man in the jail cell."

Horacio smiled.

"You're wearing your enigmatic smile. I'd ask you to explain, but you are bursting to tell me. You think you're Machiavelli, but you're just a show-off."

Horacio struck the match on the floor, but it failed to ignite. He rubbed a liver-spotted hand over his contorted knuckles.

"Give me that." Ajax struck it and lit the cigar.

Horacio smoked a while. "The Frente is defeated. The revolution has failed. The country must not. Especially now. The Cold War is over, the Americans will take their chess pieces and abandon Central America to clean up *their* mess. You were just in El Salvador, the savagery of that *civil* war makes our Contra war look like children in a schoolyard. Do you dispute it?"

"No. No."

"We cannot allow ourselves to fall into civil war. The Contra are on the verge of disbanding. But four months ago the rejectionists, the barbarians in the gringo Congress, wanted to give them a final ten million dollars. 'Resettlement funds' they called it. But it was meant to allow the Contras to return as an *army*. The new government was as terrified of that as we were."

Horacio puffed on the cigar, offered it to Ajax.

"I only brought the one."

Ajax studied it a moment—it was the only pleasure they were likely to have. He drew deeply on it, held the smoke in his lungs until he felt the rush of nicotine in his blood. Then he blew a smoke ring at Horacio. "Okay, ten million dollars sends the Contras home as an army. You needed them to face a different choice: stay in Honduras and starve or come home as citizens. Individual citizens."

Horacio beamed. "Precisely! Peace was still the prize. But not just for me. You too. The opposition. All the civilized. We were united on that one point: the drip bag of money from Washington had to be cut, and the needle ripped out of the Contras' arm. But the vote was going to be close. We needed a few Republicans to defect to our side." He raised his hands like Moses parting the waters. "So I offered our services."

Ajax felt another dizzy spell. But it was more than the nicotine, and worse than when he'd woken from his coma. The firmament of his life realigned so quickly he could not even rise to anger. So he lay down.

"You did it again. You did it again!"

"We did it again." He slipped the cigar from Ajax's fingers. "But what did we do?"

"You needed Republicans to defect. Senator Teal is a Republican.

You traded on his guilt over Amelia's death. In exchange for me rescuing young Peck, he'd give you his vote."

"His and four or five colleagues. He's quite the rising star."

"So that's why you sprung me from the nuthouse, where *you* put me."

"I 'put' you there because I could no longer protect you in Honduras. The cost of your life, the cost of your freedom here, at home, was too high. The hospital was the best I could do."

Home. Horacio had said the word. But where was he? Where *was* home?

Horacio studied the cigar in his hand. "What happened to young Peck?"

"He turned out to be a bit of a prick. Maybe he knew 'the Age of Revolution was over' and wanted one last ride before the carousel stopped." Ajax sat up. "He got a kid killed. Wanted to soup up his 'kidnapping' and got some college student who looked like him arrested in his place. That boy died badly, Horacio. His last hours were an agony. Then he got dumped in an unmarked grave with who knows how many others. And all so Peck could play at revolution."

Horacio blew a long stream of burned Montecristo up at the ceiling. "Yes, idealists are always the worst."

Ajax shot up off his cot. Snatched the cigar from Horacio's twisted hand. A hand as twisted as his soul. Ajax hauled him up by his shirt and blew the cigar ember to a blistering red.

"What are you doing?"

"I'm going to burn your eyes out." Ajax held the hot ember an inch from those watery windows. "'Idealistic'? You knew him? Peck? You *recruited* him! The whole fucking thing was your operation!"

Horacio held up his hands and held his breath. "I did not coerce him. He volunteered. I met him in Mexico, at the airport. He was frustrated by his work in El Salvador. Nothing he did had any effect on the war, nor America's role in feeding the slaughter. I showed him he had one asset he could use. He could affect the outcome of a war, just the one here, instead of there."

Ajax stuck the cigar in the old man's mouth and set him back on his bed. "Jasmine too."

"She is a great compañera. She has served the Frente and the Farabundos well."

"That's why we couldn't find Peck. Why no one knew where he was. He wasn't working for the death squad Charlies or the Farabundos. He was working for *you*."

"For us, for Nicaragua, for *peace*."

"Piss on your peace. How many have died for your grand Central American peace plan?"

"Don't be ridiculous. Everyone who's died in every war died for peace. And yes, we have won, again and you have helped to achieve that victory! How fucking dare you!" Horacio was off the cot in a flash, pointing the red-hot coal at Ajax. "We are a piss-poor nation, most of the world is, and you know that in our countries war is a form of employment. Pay a campesino more to pick up a gun than he earns from the plow and he will! Take away that employment and he will pick up the plowshare and the pruning hook. And it has come to pass."

"Stop sounding so biblical." Ajax paced the length of his cell, four steps. "Did it at least work? Your little scam? Did Teal deliver?"

He turned his palms up. "The ten million was defeated. But it seems the vote was not as close as we expected. But had it been, we had our ace in the hole."

"What if Teal finds out?"

"Not Teal! You. And Gladys."

Ajax sat down. "I'm assuming if she wasn't safe you'd have told me by now."

"She is quite safe. I could've had her out a week ago, but she has an absurd loyalty to you."

"Well, she shot me. More like guilt."

"I think not, she said something about 'the obsessive-compulsive and the catatonic'?"

Ajax chuckled. It was a good feeling, made him less inclined to strangle Horacio.

"You're very valuable operatives, you know. You two. You've got a skill set that could be of great use in this new world."

Ajax sat down. "Said the man in the jail cell."

But Horacio seemed excited by the idea. "Ajax, you know the old saw, when a door closes, another opens. The Americans are riding high now. They think they won the Cold War with fortitude and budget deficits. But they have been wrong on most things for most of this century. Get into the First World War? A mistake. Staying out of the Second World War? A mistake. Squandering their wealth in Vietnam? A mistake. Arming these mujahideen to bleed the Soviets in Afghanistan? Wait to see that mistake blossom. No, if you want to know which way the wind is blowing, look where the Americans point and turn in the other direction. They think we are at the end of history, that everywhere will become America . . ."

"A McDonald's in every capital."

"More likely a Starbucks nowadays."

"A who?"

"Didn't you get out in Miami at all? Starbucks is the new Mc-Donald's as the icon of the Americanization of the world. It's a European café, but without the *je ne sais quoi*. They call it a 'coffee shop.'"

"Why?"

"The Americans are fetishizing coffee, the way they once did burgers and fries. I personally think it is a sign of their cultural collapse, but that's been predicted before. Still, it might do wonders for our coffee prices."

By this point Ajax had laid his head over, like a quizzical dog. "How the fuck do you know all this?"

"Because I pay attention to the big picture you so despise, and to all its smallest components. Because the world *is* like a jigsaw puzzle.

Because you must *have* the larger picture in your mind to put it together. Because individual pieces will pop out, come loose, and they must be put back or the entire jigsaw is in danger of collapse."

He reached over and tapped Ajax's chest. "You know this in your heart, my son. There will be a respite after the collapse of communism while the stars realign, but this 'brave new world' will be neither. Nevertheless it is *our* world, and it must be protected by people who are brave, and sometimes bloody-minded."

Ajax took the cigar back. "Said the man in the jail cell."

"I maintain not for long. And if I am right will you consider my offer?"

"I didn't hear an offer."

"Will you at least consider my reasoning as to the value of you and Gladys as operatives?"

"I don't even have a passport."

"Oh, I'm sure Senator Teal will help with that. After all, you and Gladys did save Jimmy."

"No, we didn't."

"Really? Because James Peck returned to the bosom of his family a week ago with an amazing tale about being rescued by the dashing Ajax Montoya and the daring Gladys Darío with much added praise for his home-state senator. And as young Peck will stick to that tale, Senator Teal will doubtless help both of you with your nebulous immigration status."

Horacio held out his hand for the cigar, like a magician finishing his last trick—the big finale. But Ajax refused to applaud and put it in his mouth. "Did you run all this by Gladys?"

"Certainly not!" He rubbed his throat as if at some memory. "That woman thinks I'm her enemy."

"Yeah, she's funny that way." He took a long drag on the cigar, it was down to a stub, but somehow Ajax thought he *wouldn't* be here very long. "You guarantee me she'll get out of Nicaragua safely, I'll consider the offer you didn't really make."

Horacio looked at his watch.

"She should be in Miami soon."

Ajax let him have the cigar.

"And as I didn't tell you about Gladys until you asked, you haven't told me about Krill. So I ask: is he dead?"

Ajax nodded.

"And you didn't kill him?"

Ajax shook his head.

"Good. Gladys will no longer need her moist towelettes."

44

Gladys Darío looked out the window of the 727 as it left Nicaraguan territory for the Caribbean Sea. She was painfully aware that the last time she'd seen that sight she'd had Ajax by her side and a bag full of money and the Needle at her feet. Now she was alone, was leaving Ajax behind, again. But at least she had the Needle, it was her talisman now—if she brought it to Miami, Ajax was bound to follow.

She'd known almost before she'd hit the water what he was doing. Again. She'd hitchhiked to Managua and spent three days staking out Horacio's house before slipping over the back wall and into his bedroom. She'd awoken him with the Needle to his Adam's apple and the promise he'd help Ajax or die where he was.

"I already have. He's in a safe house."

That had thrown her. More so the news that it was Jasmine who'd told him when and where to pick them up.

She'd dragged him out of bed. "Take me to him, now!" But he'd insisted Ajax had to remain hidden because he was wanted for killing El Gordo Sangroso and had to be smuggled out of the country.

"Gladys, he said nothing would be worse than for you to be implicated in the murder, you *were* there that night. He said you would know to trust me if I gave you this message: 'You have one more mission: to deliver bad news to Indiana. Get it done.'"

•   •   •

"Is Miami your final destination?" A pretty blond flight attendant whose legs Gladys had already admired leaned over, a sheaf of immigration papers in her hand.

"Indiana."

"It's cold up there. Are you connecting through Miami?"

"Yes."

"Are you an American citizen?"

Gladys wasn't sure anymore. "I have an American passport."

"Then you'll need one of these."

Gladys politely accepted the card, and turned her gaze back out the window. The leggy stewardess did not offer an immigration card to the passenger next to Gladys. And Gladys did not speak to the handsome young man with the beautiful eyes.

But there he sat, in his gore-spattered uniform. The boy with the long eyelashes sat very still, looking straight ahead, waiting patiently.